McNally's Dare

Also by Lawrence Sanders
in Large Print:

Capital Crimes
McNally's Caper
McNally's Dilemma
McNally's Luck
McNally's Puzzle
McNally's Secret

Also by Vincent Lardo
in Large Print:

Lawrence Sanders' McNally's Folly
Lawrence Sanders' McNally's Chance
Lawrence Sanders' McNally's Alibi

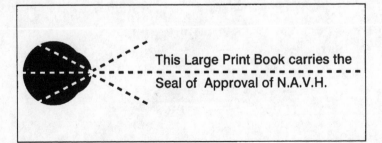

This Large Print Book carries the
Seal of Approval of N.A.V.H.

LAWRENCE SANDERS

McNally's Dare

An Archy McNally Novel
by Vincent Lardo

LARGE
PRINT
PRESS

Waterville, Maine

Published in 2004 by arrangement with G. P. Putnam's Sons, a member of Penguin Group, (USA) Inc.

The text of this Large Print edition is unabridged. Other aspects of the book may vary from the original edition.

Set in 16 pt. Plantin by Minnie B. Raven.

Printed in the United States on permanent paper.

The Library of Congress has cataloged the Thorndike Press® edition as follows:

Lardo, Vincent.
    McNally's dare / [based on the character created by] Lawrence Sanders ; an Archy McNally novel by Vincent Lardo.
      p. cm.
    ISBN 0-7862-5880-2 (lg. print : hc : alk. paper)
    ISBN 1-59413-039-6 (lg. print : sc : alk. paper)
    1. McNally, Archy (Fictitious character) — Fiction.
2. Private investigators — Florida — Palm Beach — Fiction.   3. Palm Beach (Fla.) — Fiction.
4. Large type books.   I. Title.
PS3562.A7213M36 2003b
    813'.54—dc22   2003058142

McNally's Dare

As the Founder/CEO of NAVH, the only national health agency solely devoted to those who, although not totally blind, have an eye disease which could lead to serious visual impairment, I am pleased to recognize Thorndike Press★ as one of the leading publishers in the large print field.

Founded in 1954 in San Francisco to prepare large print textbooks for partially seeing children, NAVH became the pioneer and standard setting agency in the preparation of large type.

Today, those publishers who meet our standards carry the prestigious "Seal of Approval" indicating high quality large print. We are delighted that Thorndike Press is one of the publishers whose titles meet these standards. We are also pleased to recognize the significant contribution Thorndike Press is making in this important and growing field.

Lorraine H. Marchi, L.H.D.
Founder/CEO
NAVH

★ Thorndike Press encompasses the following imprints: Thorndike, Wheeler, Walker and Large Print Press.

ONE

I am lying facedown on the leather-padded massage table clad immodestly in my heather-gray briefs while a curvaceous masseuse in a rather abbreviated nurse's uniform strokes my left hand, one finger at a time. Seductive music — Ravel's *Bolero*, I believe — floats on the jasmine-scented air.

Lest you think you walked in on an opiate-induced pipe dream, let me state that I am in the offices of Touch Therapy — A New-Age Approach to Subliminal Relaxation and Human Bonding. This enterprising establishment is located on a pricey stretch of Via Bethesda in pricey Palm Beach, Florida. My auburn-tressed bonding therapist is called Bunny. Probably no relation to Mr. Hefner's crew, but in her Florence Nightingale attire she looks ready to join the warren.

We are in the converted family room of a former dwelling that has been stripped of all amenities except for a plush rug, the table, a couch that becomes a bed at the flip of a lever, and the type of screen one finds in doctors' offices. Bunny instructs me to undress behind the screen, stretch out on the table and concentrate on my navel. Well, I think she said navel. With that she leaves the room.

I note the room has another door behind the screen, and it is from this door Bunny emerges, materializing from behind the screen like a benevolent specter. She takes hold of my hand, raises my arm, then releases her grip. My arm remains rigid.

"Tense, tense, tense, Mr. Davis. That will never do. Go limp, go limp," she implores.

Again she raises my arm and lets go. This time I allow it to sag somewhat.

"Better," she sighs, "but not much. We have a long way to go, Mr. Davis."

She fiddles with my fingers then runs a cool hand down my spine, vertebra by vertebra; when she reaches the bottom she giggles. "Oh, Mr. Davis, you naughty man."

I assume she has just noticed the elastic waistband of my shorts, which are embroidered with the famed biblical scene of Eve being tempted by the serpent. Quite adorable, actually.

I sense the moment has come. If Bunny is a licensed masseuse, I am Linus Pauling. "Your lovely receptionist told me you offered three human bonding techniques to achieve total subliminal relaxation," I tell her.

"That's correct, Mr. Davis. Her name, by the way, is Honey. For three hundred dollars we perform the standard hands-on bonding. For double that sum, we offer a more intense approach wherein the therapist interacts with the client in the buff, so to speak."

"In the buff? You or the client?"

"For a thousand dollars, Mr. Davis, I open the specially designed therapy couch and it's your call. Honey, by the way, is also a skilled therapist. For two thousand dollars we work as a team. Now if you'll roll over . . ."

"Oh, I couldn't do that, Bunny."

"Come, come, Mr. Davis. No need to be shy. I'm here to relieve the tension. We'll begin with a simple hands-on and work up from there."

"Well, if you insist, Bunny." I roll over, she gawks, then screams. "There, there, Bunny, nothing to be afraid of." I reach into my shorts and pull out the transmitter. "Welcome to Candid Radio. We're on the air to several witnesses in my office and being recorded as well. Would you like to give us a few choruses of *Love For Sale*?"

"Why, you . . ."

"Easy, Bunny. The technicians must bleep all expletives."

"What the hell do you want from me?"

"Glad you asked," I say. "For starters, I want the snaps you took of Mr. Randolph Seymour as the two of you bonded on the Castro convertible. You remember, Bunny, the ones you wanted to sell to Mr. Seymour for ten thousand bucks or, should he refuse, give to his wife for free. I would strongly advise you and Honey to fold up your massage table and move on. I intend to give your radio performance, which includes the Touch Therapy menu, to the police in twenty-four hours."

Looking around, I added, "By the way, where is your photographer? I'm guessing behind the screen. Hi, Honey, come out, come out, wherever you are."

"Who the hell are you?" Bunny cries, still slightly dazed. A transmitter is the last thing she expects to see popping out of my shorts.

Honey comes flying out from behind the screen waving the business card she had no doubt taken from the wallet I had foolishly left in the inside pocket of my jacket.

"His name isn't Davis," Honey bellows, "it's McNally. Archy McNally, Discreet Inquirer."

TWO

(From the *Palm Beach Daily News*)
JACKET REQUIRED
Interview and Photography
by Michael Price

Editor's Note: This is a weekly series of question-and-answer portraits of Palm Beach notables by freelance photographer Michael Price. The subjects will all be photographed wearing the vintage Lilly Pulitzer blazer Price rescued from a thrift shop 10 years ago.

Archy McNally is one of Palm Beach's most eligible bachelors. He is employed by the prestigious law firm McNally & Son, located in the McNally Building on Royal Palm Way. Archy attended Yale University, swims two miles every day (weather permitting), considers himself an avant-garde Beau Brummell and a connoisseur of wine, women and song, not necessarily in that order. His clubs include the Pelican and he was once invited for a drink at the Everglades.

What is the best thing that has ever happened to you?
Being interviewed for JACKET REQUIRED.

What is the worst thing that has ever happened to you?
Being photographed in a Lilly Pulitzer blazer my father donated to a thrift shop forty years ago.

Who is your favorite screen actress?
Lila Lee.

Who is your favorite living screen actress?
Living screen actress is an oxymoron.

What do you like best about Palm Beach?
Thong bikinis.

What do you like least about Palm Beach?
People in thong bikinis who should know better.

What do you do at McNally & Son?
Everything but windows.

What is your favorite sport?
Watching other people play.

Do you have a pet?
Yes.

Name?
Georgia.

Cat or dog?

12

Oh, that pet? Sorry. His name is Hobo and he's a canine of blended heritage.

Who is Georgia?

None of your business.

Thank you, Archy McNally.

My pleasure.

THREE

Tennis Everyone!

It was the height of the season in Palm Beach, where anyone knows a benefit a day keeps ennui away. After the previous night's encounter with Bunny and Honey and their traveling circus, a bit of good clean fund-raising was just what I needed to restore my faith in humankind.

Malcolm MacNiff's *Tennis Everyone!* has long been the town's premier fund raiser for those who can afford to fork over five thousand bucks for the privilege of donning their tennis togs (white only on the court, please) to strut their stuff across MacNiff's courts — one clay, one grass.

Nifty, as he was called at St. Paul's and still is because boys who prep together stick together, opens his courts once a year for his private scholarship fund benefiting deserving high school graduates who would otherwise never see the inside of a college lecture hall. Nifty's backyard courts cover five prime acres on the west side of S. Ocean Boulevard.

The downside of being on the west side of the Boulevard is that you have to cross it to get to the beach. The upside is that were you wise as well as rich, you tunneled under the highway, thereby proving the mathematical axiom about a straight line being the shortest distance between two points. The gates to the tunnel were invitingly open on this tropical winter day, but no one seemed eager to leave the party for a stroll on the beach.

Tennis Everyone! redefines "exclusive." Only one hundred check writers in white can indulge in an afternoon of doubles involving both mixed couples, and ladies only and gentlemen only, all drawn by lots. I would like to report that those chosen to participate in Nifty's tennis marathon are summoned by a higher power but, alas, this being Palm Beach they are summoned by a coveted invitation from Mr. and Mrs. Malcolm MacNiff.

That's correct. By invitation. So popular is Nifty's fund-raiser that only those carefully selected by the MacNiffs can give them five grand for the privilege of whacking the hell out of a Spaulding wrapped in fuzzy wool. The uninvited don't dare show their faces in town on the day of Nifty's event. The boutiques on

Worth Avenue are empty of shoppers and the ladies who lunch are stricken with the vapors or suddenly remember pressing engagements in Nepal and Zimbabwe.

The event's main attraction is usually a tennis superstar, and today's chosen was none other than the *enfant terrible* of the pro circuit, Jackson (Jackie) Barnett. The six-foot-two blond with the looks of a comic strip hero and the temper of a two-year-old was garnering all the attention of the stargazers this afternoon and basking in the adulation.

At Wimbledon he had been cheered, then chased all over London by a titled lady who did or did not catch him, depending on the tabloid you read. He had been offered a million dollars for a five-minute cameo in the film version of this year's best-selling novel and, most notably, he was applauded by spectators when he flung to the ground the racket that bore his name when it, not the player, failed to answer an opponent's volley.

Jackie's name was tossed into the hopper, just like the common folks, so his partners or opponents were strictly the luck of the draw and, to be sure, it was a great party booster each time Nifty pulled the names out of the hat to arrange the foursomes. Ladies who teamed with Jackie screamed when their names were called; the gentlemen, similarly honored, were obliged to square their shoulders and stiffen their upper lips. Losers could look forward to the next lottery, keeping all in a state of happy expectation.

Me? I'm Archy McNally, the only person here by the grace of a higher power, namely, my father, the CEO of McNally & Son, Attorney-at-Law. As representatives of the MacNiff interests we are always on the invited list. Like most firms doing business in Palm Beach, we are forced to subscribe to several charity events each season, though *Tennis Everyone!* is one of the few I would be sorry to miss. Although my serve leaves something to be desired and my backhand has been referred to as weak, I have a great pair of legs — and in Palm Beach it's the visuals that matter.

When not at play, guests are invited to nosh at the enormous catered smorgasbord featuring the alpha and omega of party food: grilled filet mignon, sliced by a master carver before your very eyes; poached salmon; pheasant; fried chicken; foie gras; caviar; deviled eggs; every garnish, dip and crudité known to man, including ketchup and mustard for the burgers and hot dogs. Who said the rich aren't catholic in their tastes?

There were, of course, several portable bars strategically positioned on the property so that one was never out of sight of a gin and tonic or the young lads and lassies who serve, bus and look so splendid in their black pants, white shirts and black bow ties. Among them I spotted Todd, who waits tables at the Pelican Club on busy Saturday nights. Todd was christened Edward but redubbed himself in anticipation of a career on the silver screen. I don't think Todd is any improvement over Edward, but it beats Jeb, Rock or Rip. Like many young folks in the surrounding communities, namely Lake Worth and West Palm Beach, Todd survives by toiling for the caterers and restaurants that abound in our upscale resort.

While I hadn't yet been paired with or against Jackie Barnett, I did get called for the mixed doubles and found myself with a very attractive lady introduced as Holga von Brecht. The von made me wonder if she was a titled lady of German descent, though her accent was strictly New England Yankee. I guessed her age at forty, give or take, but these days she could have been a decade older and either well preserved or well connected to a surgeon with hands of gold.

We were opposite a young man named Joe Gallo and his partner, Vivian Emerson, who was a good deal older than Joe but, like Holga, a looker with a figure to match. Why the name Joe Gallo struck a chord I had no idea and, chosen to serve, didn't have time to ponder the mystery. We played the allotted three sets and Holga and I took two of them. When we shook hands across the net I believe Vivian shot daggers at Holga. This being Palm Beach I immediately jumped to the conclusion that Joey belonged to Vivian and Holga was trying to make some points that had nothing to do with tennis. Ho-hum and pardon my lack of interest.

Later I drew an all-male foursome and was paired with Lance Talbot, a young man of sudden great wealth, due to his maternal grandmother's demise. Grandmama was the daughter of a Detroit pioneer who had been on a first-name basis with the Fords, Chryslers, Dodges and Fishers. I recalled that Lance and his grandmother were estranged for years but it seems they kissed and made up just in time to keep Lance a member in good standing of the jet set. Palm Beach is chock-full of such heartwrenching tales.

We were opposite Nifty himself and, if I had heard correctly, a man Nifty introduced as Darling. This I believe was the gentleman's surname unless, of course, Nifty was taking liberties with the guy, which I doubted. Nifty and Darling took all three sets.

"I liked your interview in 'Jacket Required,'" Lance complimented me when we parted company.

Dark crew cut, blue eyes and a physique that bespoke a personal trainer, Lance Talbot was the answer to a working maiden's prayer. I was also amazed that he took notice of the likes of me. "Thanks. I assume you'll be tapped for the honor in the near future," I told him.

"I would refuse," he said. "I'm not as clever as you, Mr. McNally."

With that he pulled a cell phone out of the pocket of his tennis shorts and proceeded to make a call. Really!

Not sure if I had been praised or panned by young Talbot I beckoned to Todd, who proffered his tray of goodies. "Juice?" he asked.

"No, thanks, I hear it can rust your pipes," I answered, reaching for a gin and tonic. "How goes it, Todd?"

"Working my tail off, Mr. McNally. Jeff is supposed to be bussing this station with me but he went for a smoke a half hour ago and I haven't seen him since."

An ex-smoker myself, I imagined Jeff had most likely escaped via the tunnel and was now on the beach, happily puffing away. "When he gets back, take a break," I advised the aspiring thespian. "You certainly deserve it."

I saw a familiar figure at the dessert table and ambled over to Lolly Spindrift to hear all the news that's not fit to print. Our resident gossip columnist is a small guy with the appetite of a giant. Today Lol was clad in his trademark white suit, hand-painted silk tie and Panama hat, resembling a guy who had just caught the last train out of a banana republic in a state of flux. Lol's column is titled "Hither and Yon" which the locals call, affectionately I'm sure, "Dither and Yawn."

"Good afternoon, Lol," I opened.

Without taking his eyes off the array of sweets he declaimed, with attitude, "Saw your interview."

My, my. That bit of fluff was certainly proving to be provocative. "What did you think?"

Still paying more attention to the stuffed

pastries, chocolate delights and puffed creams than to his visitor, he recited, "Fools' names, like fools' faces, often appear in public places." This told me Lolly had not been asked to don the Lilly Pulitzer blazer and was miffed over the slight.

"I could say the same about most of the people whose names fill your column, Lol."

He reached for something wrapped in a mocha colored shell and topped with a cherry but withdrew before his hand made contact with the item. "You'll get no argument from me on that score," he said, "but at least I provide a service for my foolish readers."

"Really? Pray tell, Lol."

"They read me to learn where they were last night and where they might be headed this evening. Without me they wouldn't know how much fun they were having. You might say I am as indispensable to the community as sun and surf." Now he went for a strawberry mousse, hesitated, then once again aborted the mission.

"Why are you so cryptic about your job at McNally and Son?" he probed, still dishing my little interview. "Everyone in this town that matters knows you're a PI despite the fancy Discreet Inquirer label printed on your card."

"What about the people in this town that don't matter?" I quickly responded.

"Well," he laughed, "obviously it doesn't matter what they think, does it?"

He continued to scrutinize the goodies like a health inspector at a salad bar with a faulty sneeze guard, still unable to make up his mind. Poor Lolly. I was certain he had gone through the other tables with all the restraint of swarming locusts but had thoughtfully left room in his seemingly bottomless pit for just one *dolce;* hence it had to be the most exquisite of all bonbons.

Examining the *petits fours* he rambled on, "I get invited to these benefits so I can tell those who didn't attend what they missed, thereby raising the attendance and the ante for next year's clambake." Again he reached and retreated.

"What do you think of Jackson Barnett?" I teased.

"I hear he swings both ways," Lolly answered. Knowing Lolly's propensities I knew he didn't mean fore- and backhand.

"Wishful thinking, Lolly," I said. "How is your bartender pal, Ramón?"

"He's gone to work on Phil Meecham's yacht."

"That's nice. What's he doing for Meecham?"

Finished counting the *petits fours*, he sighed, "Trust me, Archy, you don't want to know."

Well, Ramón was no longer a mixologist, that's for sure. Whether he had traded up was questionable.

"I saw you on the court with the latest addition to Palm Beach's most eligible bachelor list," Lolly was saying. "Anything to report?"

"You mean the Talbot kid? I think he sassed me."

"Poor Archy. I'm sure he meant no offense. Do you think he'll hire you to find his father?"

I shrugged. "I didn't know he had lost him."

"Surely you know he bears the same name as his late grandmother, Mrs. Ronald Talbot. His maternal grandmother, that is."

"You mean . . ."

Lolly gave up his quest for a sweet and indulged himself in his next favorite pastime — rumormongering. "Twenty years ago, Mrs. Talbot's daughter, Jessica, had Lance but refused to tell her mama where he came from. The two fought for a decade over the matter until Jessie packed herself and young Lance off to Switzerland and stayed there until poor Jessie was hit by a humongous snowball, leaving Lance an orphan. Grandma, who was on her deathbed, immediately sent for the boy and presto, we have a new rich kid on the block and you get sassed on the tennis court."

"Do you mean Jessica Talbot was killed in an avalanche?"

"That's what I said, didn't I? I believe it was on the slopes at Winterthur."

Looking across the crowded lawn I could see Lance and Holga in conversation with our tennis pro. "Is he a friend of the von Brecht woman?" I asked Lolly.

"Friend? I wouldn't hire you to find a starlet in Jollywood. Lance and Holga are an item, dear boy."

Amazed, I foolishly blurted, "But she's old enough to be his mother."

"She's even older than that, or so it's rumored. She followed the boy here from Switzerland, where she was a friend of his mother's, or so they say, and please don't ask me who *they* are. I don't make up the hearsay, I just repeat it. *They* also say she's the finished product of a Swiss doctor who runs an Alpine rejuvenation clinic where he injects his rich patrons with a serum derived from — well, I won't spoil your appetite.

"Of course, all our lovely Palm Beach ladies, including your pal, Lady Cynthia Horowitz, are dying to know the name of the clinic and who they have to bribe to get in. Holga is the season's most sought-after enigma."

Ask Lolly a question and get someone's biography in return. "I think the boy could do better," I offered.

"Mine not to reason why," he said. "Mine but to do and spy. Speaking of which, I see you also met Dennis Darling, the predator in our midst. I hope you kept your mouth shut."

"I didn't have a chance to open it. Should I know who he is?"

"My dear boy, what you don't know could fill volumes. How do you survive a day in this sun-drenched abyss of egocentric consumption? Promise me you'll never wander out alone at night without Lolly by your side." He paused, briefly, to breathe. "Dennis Darling is the so-called investigative reporter for *Bare Facts* magazine and is here researching his next exposé, which is said to be called *The Palm Beach Story*."

If true, the title wasn't original. The late,

great Preston Sturges wrote and directed *The Palm Beach Story*, which had Rudy Vallee, of all people, playing a Palm Beach playboy with all the panache of a department store mannequin.

"How did he get invited to Nifty's?" I wondered aloud.

"No doubt a donation by his employers that Nifty couldn't refuse in good conscience. Money not only talks, Archy, it shouts, intimidates and coerces, never failing to get its way." Evoking the royal *we*, Lolly expounded, "*We* have decided to give Mr. Darling the PBCS. And remember, you heard it here first."

For the uninitiated, the PBCS translates to the Palm Beach Cold Shoulder, which is the kiss of death to anyone in this town with social aspirations. "Why such drastic measures, Lol?"

"Remember what Edna Ferber did to Texans? They took her into their confidence and she repaid them with *Giant*."

Not a bad opus, I thought, and Palm Beach should be so lucky, but I kept it to myself. If I were earmarked for the PBCS, I would be out of business and possibly a home. "Is everyone with a skeleton in their closet fleeing Palm Beach?"

"If so, dear boy, you and I will be the

only people left in town, and I'm not so sure about you. Which reminds me, I hear Connie Garcia is practically engaged to that gorgeous Alejandro Gomez y Zapata. I assume you and Connie are history."

"Assume nothing," I told him.

"Can I quote you?"

"Be my guest."

Undaunted, he asked, "Are you still dating the policeman?"

That was too much. "Officer O'Hara is a policewoman. There's a difference."

With a sly wink, he posed, "Does Archy protest too much?" Then he swooped down on a seven-layer extravaganza topped with mocha buttercream.

"Why did you pick that?" I wanted to know.

"Mae West," he said.

"Mae West?"

"That's right. Mae said, 'Between two evils I always choose the one I never tried before.' "

Pondering that I left Lolly Spindrift to his just desserts and went forth to mix and mingle. As I returned my empty glass to the bar I ran into Nifty. "Lolly tells me the Darling guy is a mole for *Bare Facts* magazine. Do you think he'll tell the world about our tennis match?"

"Only if he caught us cheating," Nifty surmised. "By the by, Archy, could you spare the time to lunch with me tomorrow?"

As Nifty belongs to the set more in keeping with my parents' generation than mine, I took it the invitation was more a summons than a social event. "I would be delighted, sir."

"I'm at Mar-a-Lago these days. Would noon suit you?"

"Perfectly. I . . ."

The cry was as shrill and foreboding as a bobby's whistle on a foggy London street. Everything and everyone came to a halt, like a motion picture suddenly frozen on a single frame. One of the waitresses was at the north end of the property beside the MacNiffs' pool, screaming at the top of her lungs.

Nifty and I led the stampede and were first to reach the hysterical girl who pointed to the body of a young man clad in black trousers, white shirt and black bow tie, lying still at the bottom of the pool's shallow end. He was barefoot and the butt of a cigarette floated above the body.

Young Jeff had smoked his last cigarette before dying with his boots off.

FOUR

"Poor Malcolm," Father said, snipping the end off an expensive cigar. "This unfortunate incident will cast a pall over his popular fund-raiser for years to come."

We were in the den of the McNally abode on Ocean Boulevard (west side but, alas, no tunnel), where a cardinal rule is never to discuss business of an unsavory nature at the dinner table. We do not wish to upset Mother; she suffers from hypertension and is experiencing what is politely now termed "senior moments" with a bit more frequency. Mother usually retires early, which allows my father and me to indulge in the manly pursuit of after-dinner port and tobacco.

If this sounds vaguely nineteenth-century, let me assure you that it is. If my father, Prescott McNally, had his druthers, he would have been born into the London of Charles Dickens's era, rather than Palm Beach in the twentieth century. Having arrived too late, he compensates by reading only Dickens, nightly, to keep in touch

30

with a past that had so cruelly eluded him. And though I said I had given up smoking, I must confess: I lied. However, I am down to one English Oval (the only brand I smoke) after dinner and, perhaps, one before bed. Not bad for a former two-pack-a-day addict.

The early evening television news had reported what Father had just termed "the unfortunate incident," stating only that the cause of Jeffrey Rodgers's apparent drowning was as yet undetermined, pending the medical examiner's post-mortem. The poor boy was just twenty years old. The story of Rodgers's demise quickly took a backseat to a detailed description of Nifty's spread on Ocean Boulevard and the socialites gathered therein.

Experience and close observation told me what I knew the PM would find: Jeffrey Rodgers was done in by a person or persons unknown. I said as much to my father as soon as I had poured the wine and we had each lit up our nicotine of choice.

"Are you certain, Archy?"

"Unless he had some sort of seizure or stroke, which I doubt, I don't see how a healthy, young six-footer could drown in three feet of water. Even if he fell into the pool by accident, which I also doubt, he could have picked himself up and climbed out. I think the police will discover he was rendered unconscious, dumped into the pool and left to drown."

Father stroked his bushy guardsman mustache and shook his head. "In the broad light of day before more than a hundred people? It just doesn't seem possible."

But it was possible simply because it had been done. "You know the MacNiff property, sir. Five acres, running north and south. Mr. MacNiff's beloved tennis courts are almost directly behind the house at the extreme south end of the property. The pool is at the extreme north end of the property because I believe Mr. MacNiff found it a distraction for serious players, especially when his grandchildren and their friends cavorted in the water.

"The courts and the pool are five acres apart. Everyone was congregated around the courts and buffet tables. With all the activity in that area no one was looking in the opposite direction. Rodgers's shoes and socks were found near the pool. The police soon learned that the help was using the pool area as a retreat on their breaks as a place to grab a smoke or stick their feet in the cool water.

"I think it's obvious that Rodgers was

sitting at the edge of the pool enjoying a smoke and soaking his feet. Someone most likely came up behind him, clobbered him and tossed him in the water. If the help was using the pool area as a hangout, anyone glancing in that direction would have become accustomed to seeing a few of the wait staff hanging out there. From that distance all one would see was the murderer's back, never knowing that Jeff was sitting in front of him."

Yes, Jeff Rodgers could have been clobbered and dumped into the pool in the broad light of day, and I was convinced that he had been.

The ambulance and police were on the scene in less than ten minutes after someone had the good sense to punch out 911 on their cell phone. My friend and occasional cohort, Sergeant Al Rogoff, was part of the police contingent but, as is our custom, we did not exchange more than a nod in the ensuing pandemonium. When Rodgers was taken away on a stretcher, covered from head to foot, the boys and girls who were his friends sobbed openly and clung to each other for comfort. The girl who had discovered the body was being tended to by the paramedics. The scene, as one may imagine, was eerily incongruous with the splendid weather and the palatial surroundings.

The rest of the guests wandered about aimlessly, whispering in small groups, awkwardly shifting their tennis racquets from hand to hand. The caterers busied themselves with clearing the tables. Nothing like a sudden death to spoil a party.

I stayed close to Mr. and Mrs. MacNiff and their guest of honor, Jackson Barnett, the latter looking a little pale under his tan. The pro was a publicity hound but this wasn't the kind of notoriety that would help him secure more product endorsements. Lolly Spindrift was on his cell phone, calling in the story, and Dennis Darling was here, there and everywhere all at once, chatting into a portable tape recorder. Curious. Did he consider Jeff Rodgers's death a bonus, given his mission?

Nifty assured the police lieutenant in charge that he had the names and addresses of all the guests present and the caterer stated that he had the same information for all his staff. This made it possible for all of us to leave as soon as the police had finished taking photos of the scene before and after the removal of

Rodgers's body. All present were advised that they could be called upon to give statements when and if the necessity arose.

Jackson Barnett complained that he had to be in Los Angeles tomorrow for makeup and costume tests. He was told not to leave town without first clearing his departure with headquarters. Lolly offered Jackie the comforts of Phil Meecham's yacht should he have to spend another night in PB, and I think the pro accepted. Woe be to Jackie Barnett. After a night aboard Meecham's floating Sodom and Gomorrah, Jackie would wish the police had locked him up.

I stayed to the bitter end, feeling it my duty to stand by our client and, of course, to report the situation back to my father.

"What do you make of this, Archy?" Nifty asked when we were in his drawing room, where he was taking comfort in a generous shot of Ballantine on the rocks. Mrs. MacNiff had retired to her room after ordering a cold compress and a cup of tea.

"The worst, sir. I think you should be prepared for a complete investigation based on suspicion of foul play."

Malcolm MacNiff is tall and lean with a complexion that freckles in the sun, the only reminder of the redhead he was before going gray. His blue eyes opened wide at my candid pronouncement. "But surely you don't think one of us is responsible for this accident?"

Us being the Palm Beach fraternal order whose money was a safe three generations away from the sweat and tears that made it. This group clung to one another like ivy to the brick walls of their alma maters. To protect their turf and those who rule it, this crowd has been known to see no evil, hear no evil and, foremost, speak no evil. I'm not saying they would condone murder, though they might not condemn it either.

The late Jeffrey Rodgers was not a member of *us*, therefore he was one of *them*. To ease Nifty's conscience on this dark day (it's what I get paid to do), I told him the lad's demise was probably the result of a feud between the young and reckless that got out of hand.

"But how could it happen before our very eyes?" he moaned.

I explained my theory to which he listened thoughtfully, nodding between sips of scotch. "It's possible," he said, not sounding completely convinced. "But those youngsters all seemed so upset over the boy's death."

"And the guilty party, I'm sure, cried the loudest."

"Yes. Yes," Nifty said. "I see what you mean." With a shrug he continued, "Lolly asked me for a statement. I was too upset to give him one and said I would call him before he filed his story. Any suggestions, Archy?"

I have several stock quotes for clients in thorny situations and pulled up the one best suited for today's misfortune.

"Mrs. MacNiff and I are deeply saddened by this terrible tragedy and extend our sympathies to Jeff's family and friends. We will of course assist the family in any way we can in the difficult days ahead. Until the authorities can give us a more detailed explanation of what happened to the young man I'm afraid that is all I have to say at this time. I wish also to apologize to my guests and benefactors for the abrupt termination of my *Tennis Everyone!* fete and beg their understanding."

Nifty nodded his approval, his blue eyes glassy with grief, fear or booze. "That's splendid, Archy. Will you write it out for me? I'm afraid my memory is not what it used to be."

He produced a pad and pen from the top drawer of a museum quality desk-on-frame. I wrote out the paragraph, which I was sure Lolly would recognize as having come from me and, before leaving, asked Nifty if he wanted to keep our lunch date tomorrow.

"Oh, I do, Archy. I most certainly do. That's another matter that needs clearing up."

Now, as I related this to father, he puffed on his cigar and repeated, "Another matter. How odd. So the lunch will have nothing to do with the boy's death."

"I didn't think it would," I answered. "He made the date with me before we knew Rodgers was dead, if only by a few minutes."

"Do you truly believe one of the wait staff is responsible for this, Archy?"

With regrets I stubbed out my cigarette and answered, "I said that to take the edge off Mr. MacNiff's trying day. At this juncture I believe the field is wide open. If my theory is correct, anyone there today could have done it."

"Even one of *us?*" Father said, echoing Malcolm MacNiff.

We of the McNally clan do not belong to the upper echelons of Palm Beach society, as our start came from my grandfather, Freddy McNally, a burlesque comic with the Minsky circuit who invested in Florida real estate at the low and got out at the high. Hence our house on Ocean Boulevard, though it would show flaws upon close inspection like a suspect diamond under a jeweler's loupe. Witness our leaky roof: the drip, drip, drip of the raindrops happens to be located over my third-floor digs.

Father went to Yale, where he majored in law and denial, graduating with a bright future and a dim past. I do nothing to burst his bubble as a leaky roof is preferable to no roof. 'Nuff said?

"Palm Beach has had its share of society murders, sir," I reminded the squire. As we spoke the town was agog over the exploits of a man with more money than sense who came to Palm Beach wanting desperately to join the *us* crowd but was encumbered by an inconvenient wife. Not to worry. It's believed he hired a hit man to expedite a divorce and is now in parts unknown. True, it's an extreme case of one who wanted to push his way into Palm Beach society, which is as rewarding as pushing a Sherman tank uphill.

"Do you think you'll get involved in this, Archy? You were on the scene."

"Not unless I'm asked, sir, and I don't see who would hire me to investigate the matter. Certainly not Mr. MacNiff, who just wants the whole thing to go away. Besides, until the police make a statement we won't know if we have a case of murder or misadventure."

If it was murder, as I strongly suspected, I might presently be the only person who knew when it occurred. When I took that drink from Todd's tray I glanced at my watch and both of Mickey's hands were pointing at three. Todd said Rodgers had gone on his break a half hour before, so the boy headed for the pool about a quarter to three and was found dead at a quarter to four, giving you a window for the time of death between 2:45 and 3:45.

"Let's hope for misadventure," Father offered before turning to matters closer to his heart. "So you met the Talbot boy. What did you think of him?"

"*Met* might be an exaggeration. We played the required three sets together and then exchanged a few words." I didn't mention Talbot's comment on my interview in today's paper because I didn't know if Father had seen it. Nor did I know if the pater would approve. *Never trouble trouble till trouble troubles you* is one of my favorite edicts.

"He's a handsome boy, about twenty I

would guess," I added. This had me thinking that he was about the same age as the late Jeffrey Rodgers, the two being as close in years as they were distant socially.

"I was hoping he might consider taking us on as his legal representatives," Father said. "Malcolm was a good friend of the boy's grandmother. In fact Malcolm was the executor of Mrs. Talbot's will. As we represent Malcolm I thought young Talbot would follow suit."

"I understand the boy carries his maternal grandmother's name because he was born out of wedlock and his mother never said who done her wrong."

Father tugged on his mustache. A sure sign of his displeasure. "So I've heard, but naturally that's none of our business."

Pushing the envelope, I ventured, "And they say he's involved with a lady named Holga von Brecht who's at least twenty years his senior. I met her, too, on the courts."

Father gave his whiskers another yank. "That too is not our concern. What is, is the fact that Talbot has come into a fortune conservatively estimated at five hundred million."

Half a billion. I didn't whistle because that would be uncouth. No wonder Holga followed him here all the way from Switzerland. I assume she was Mrs. von Brecht. Or, more likely, the Baroness von Brecht. So where was the Baron? Perhaps sulking in the schloss with the drawbridge raised, but for a half billion in American currency Holga would have swam the moat.

I did not ask Father if he wanted me to put in a good word for the Talbot account over lunch with Nifty, as that would be *de trop*. As I did not go all the way at Yale (no pun intended, there was a little streaking incident), my sole function at McNally & Son is to assist those who come to me with problems they would rather not read about in the shiny sheet.

In case you don't know, or don't care, the shiny sheet is the sobriquet of our local daily that chronicles the *what, where, when* and the *who, how* and *why* of the denizens of our little island. The name comes from the paper on which it's printed, which prevents madam from getting her hands soiled with printer's ink as she keeps up with the Joneses and, of course, the price of alligator pumps on the Esplanade.

During my briefing of the afternoon's events, I mentioned Dennis Darling and Father, puffing contentedly and perhaps dreaming of young Talbot's patronage, asked me what I thought of the man.

"As with Talbot, sir, it was a brief encounter on the tennis court. Lolly told me the man is here to write on Palm Beach for his magazine, *Bare Facts*." Father winced at the name and tossed back what was left of his port. I got up and refilled our glasses.

"Is he here to make trouble, Archy?"

"I hope not," I answered, thinking of the man chatting into his portable recorder following the discovery of Jeff Rodgers's body in the pool and the mayhem that followed. "He'll dig up all the old scandals and drop all the names that he'll never get to meet one-on-one. Lolly tells me the long knives are being sharpened for Mr. Darling."

Dennis Darling wouldn't be the first interloper to come to Palm Beach in search of caviar and leave with egg on his face. A few seasons back we had a television crew down here doing a documentary on the rich and famous of our resort. The only people who would go before the cameras were the new rich, who don't matter to the old rich, while those who do matter were presented from newspaper photos, shots of their homes from outside locked gates and hearsay. I will admit that Dennis's invitation to *Tennis Everyone!* was a coup but, as Lolly had said, money never fails to get its way.

"I hope he doesn't try to connect the MacNiffs with today's tragedy," Father said.

"I was thinking the same thing, sir. I'll caution Mr. MacNiff at lunch tomorrow."

Fingering a beautifully bound edition of *Hard Times*, Father exclaimed, "Quite a cast of characters the police will be obliged to sift through, should it come to that."

Leaving him to sift through Charlie's thoughts on England's economy in the mid-nineteenth century, I retired to the peace, solitude and comfort of my grace-and-favor third-floor suite.

Enjoying another English Oval while getting ready for the sandman, Father's parting words echoed in my head. *Quite a cast of characters* . . . And indeed they were. Excuse the cliché, but if hindsight were foresight I would have paid more attention to the rancor between Vivian Emerson and Holga von Brecht, Talbot's affair with Holga, Dennis Darling's mission in Palm Beach and Nifty's lunch invitation.

Connect all the dots and you get a picture of a young man lying dead in three feet of water.

FIVE

We breakfast in the family kitchen, attended to by our housekeeper and cook, Ursi Olson, who, along with her husband, Jamie, cater to the McNallys. This bit of egalitarianism is an isolated occurrence in our faux Tudor manse with its mullioned windows and faulty copper roof. Our neighbors rough it in faux Spanish haciendas with red tile overhead.

As Father and I both work there is no set lunch hour, except for Mother, who takes tea and toast before her afternoon siesta. Dinner in the formal dining room is strictly damask linen, Limoges china and the kind of stemware that explodes if put in the dishwasher. It gives new meaning to the word *pretentious* but thanks to Ursi's superb cuisine one gladly endures the pomp and circumstance for the gastronomic delights that go with it.

Father will occasionally lament the cost of maintaining such a lifestyle and I once suggested that we replace the damask with paper napkins, a move sanctioned by

Queen Elizabeth when feeling financially pinched. A member of Parliament went on record as saying that Her Majesty would fare better pound-wise if she stuck to her linen napkins and gave up her fleet of Rolls-Royces. The queen was not amused — and neither was Father.

Eating in the kitchen does not in any way prevent the Lord of the Manor from dressing as if he were arguing a case before the United States Supreme Court. Vested suit, tie and cuff links are his work clothes and, come to think of it, his play clothes. For Father, casual Friday means donning a shirt without extra starch in collar and cuffs.

Mother always looks lovely and serene in a flowery print dress and, when gardening or shopping, a wide-brimmed straw bonnet. Owing to lunch at Mar-a-Lago I dressed down this morning and looked rather clubbish in white linen trousers, pink polo shirt of Sea Island cotton and a seersucker jacket. Jeff Rodgers's drowning made all the front pages, but thanks to my interview it was yrs. truly who got all the attention this morning, saving us the trouble of awkwardly trying to avoid discussing the more disquieting news in front of mother.

"Everyone called," Ursi said, pouring herself a cuppa at the stove. "I felt like a movie star."

Ursi's "everyone" are the domestics along Ocean Boulevard for whom she acts as spokesperson, friend and advisor. Why my fifteen minutes made her feel like a celebrity I don't know and didn't dare ask.

Father, scooping up his scrambled eggs, looked somber and morose.

"How good you look in that jacket, Archy," Mother cooed. "I remember when all the men were wearing them."

Father, nibbling on a piece of dry toast, looked somber and morose.

Jamie, who never says a word unless coaxed at gunpoint, didn't say a word.

Finishing my poached eggs on an English muffin I modestly quoted Lolly Spindrift. "Fools' names, like fools' faces, often appear in public places."

Jamie nodded, as if in agreement. Ursi dismissed it with a wave of her hand and mother cried, "Nonsense, Archy. You're smarter than most of the men in this town, and far more handsome."

Father, sipping his coffee, looked somber and morose.

When breakfast with the McNallys came to a close, Father rose, looked at his watch and announced, "I want to go on record as stating that I never owned a Lilly Pulitzer blazer and therefore could not have donated such a garment to a thrift shop." With that he kissed mother's powdered cheek and headed for the garage and his Lexus LS400.

I gave Mother a wink and she giggled. Before leaving for the greenhouse to minister to her countless varieties of begonias, mother gently patted my face and said, "You're not going to get involved in that poor boy's death, Archy, are you?"

"I don't think so, mother. It appears to be a tragic accident."

"The papers say the police believe it's a suspicious death. Poor Helen MacNiff. Do you think I should call on her?"

I don't know why we try to keep these things from mother, who is an avid reader and keeps up with current events. She may be a little forgetful but she certainly doesn't forget to humor us in our attempts to cushion her from the facts of life.

"I wouldn't call on her until we have a clearer picture of what happened," I advised. "I'm having lunch with Mr. MacNiff this afternoon and I'll express your concern for him and his wife."

"Thank you, Archy. And you do look so

like John Ford in that newspaper photo."

"I hope you mean Harrison Ford, Mother."

"Is there a difference, dear?"

"One is a long-dead director, the other a handsome current film personality."

"Oh, dear. How confusing everything is these days. Well, I think you look like whomever you want to look like, Archy."

"Bless you, Mother."

As soon as the back door closed on my mother's retreating form, Ursi brought her coffee to the table and took the seat opposite me. "So," she began, "do you think the boy was murdered, Archy?" Ursi is a kind soul whose only vice is gossiping over the back fence. But, if that's a vice, no one in PB could cast the first stone.

"Still early days, Ursi. What do you hear?"

"Well, I got a call from Mrs. MacNiff's girl, Maria Sanchez, yesterday, as soon as she got the Mrs. to lie down with a cold compress, the madam was that upset, and can you blame her? Maria told me you were in conference with Mr. MacNiff."

So, as usual, the domestic grapevine had spread the news of Jeff Rodgers's death minutes after it happened. Ursi was too polite to say, but I'm sure she also knew the nature of my conference with Malcolm MacNiff if he had discussed it with his wife and she, in turn, had discussed it with Maria Sanchez. Maria would have been on the horn with Ursi at the crack of dawn.

"Maria called this morning," Ursi went on, confirming my assumption, "and said the police asked Mr. MacNiff to report to the station house at his earliest convenience."

This meant I would get an earful at lunch but, with a little bit of luck, I might just get the jump on Nifty's news and even go him one better.

"I can't see why any of the MacNiffs' guests would want to do in a lad working for the caterer," Ursi said, clearly bursting to convey the gossip that was traveling up and down the Boulevard at the speed of sound. Thanks to the invention of the cellular telephone, this crowd could now swap stories while waiting in line at the supermarket, lounging on the beach and, horror of horrors, while driving. "It must have been one of his friends who did it," she pronounced. "Most likely over a girl."

No story in Palm Beach, above and below stairs, is ever complete without a hint of romance thrown in to thicken the plot. "It was my thought, too," I told her, merely confirming what s̶ from Maria. "If it is murd̶ have the names and address̶ suspects."

Jamie, who had been lool̶ newspaper since I came down t̶ ̶ ̶ ̶akfast but had yet to turn a page, offered, "Mr. Van Fleet's man, Abe Calhoun, told me the cigarette they fished out of the pool was pure cannabis. Look for a drug connection."

Jamie doesn't say much but when he does it's a mouthful. If the boy was high he could very well have fallen into the pool and been too disoriented to pull himself out. "If that's true," I said to Jamie, "this is a whole new ball game. I don't see a drug hit over a little grass, but it could have incapacitated the boy. Where did Calhoun hear this?"

"He didn't say," Jamie confessed and went back to pretending to read his newspaper.

The rumors were already flying fast, high and wide and, par for the course, mostly unfounded. I didn't bother to tell Jamie that the cigarette I saw floating in the pool had a filter tip.

"What did you think of Holga von Brecht, Archy?" Like the media, Ursi

...rom Jeffrey Rodgers's death to so-commentary with nary a backward ...ance. "They say she's ninety years old if she's a day."

"That would be pushing it by forty years, at least," I said. "She's a beautiful woman with good skin. If she's had a little work it was done by an expert."

"It's the injections," Ursi gushed. "The doctor in Switzerland invented some concoction that works better than plastic surgery. The years fade away after each shot. It's derived from — well, I don't want to spoil your appetite."

The more I heard about this doctor's anti-aging vaccine the less I wanted to know about it. "There is no magic formula, Ursi. There are just those who age better than others but there will always be a hustler to cash in on the less fortunate. Now tell me your secret?"

That got a laugh from Ursi and a grunt from her husband. "Whatever her age, they say she's bewitched the Talbot boy."

So bewitched was Ursi with murder, rejuvenation and May/December coupling, she neglected to offer me a second cup of coffee. Very unusual for our Ursi, but this was just the first anomaly in a day rife with surprises.

★ ★ ★

In fact and fiction, the police and private investigators go together like a lit match and a short fuse. Al Rogoff and I are the exception to the rule for a variety of reasons, mainly because we don't compete. When working on the same case, which happens surprisingly often, we keep each other informed and gladly take a back seat when the other is in hot pursuit.

Also, we don't mix socially. It's no secret that I'm one of Palm Beach's most eligible bachelors, though my society connections come just as much from my last name as from my own charm. Al is also a bachelor, a big, beefy guy whose charm is, well, a bit more elusive. He may mangle the English language and prefer a Big Mac to a rack of lamb, but his appreciation and love of classical music, opera and ballet are awesome.

I have knowledge of and entrée into the Palm Beach social scene and he has all the amazing paraphernalia of a modern crime-fighting force at his disposal. In short, we are an odd couple dynamic duo *sans* the black tights and capes, but don't tell Al I said that.

Sergeant Rogoff and I have several local rendezvous, our favorite being the parking lot of the Publix market on Sunset. After yesterday's catastrophe I knew Al would be as anxious to speak to me as I was to learn the department's official stand on Jeff Rodgers's death. Playing an educated hunch I headed for the Publix after breakfast and spotted Al's police cruiser at the far end of the lot. I pulled into a space a respectable distance from Al and saw him get out of his car as soon as he spotted my red Miata.

Chewing on the butt of a stogie he got in beside me with all the poise of a linebacker easing into a toddler's Cozy Coupe. "Fancy seeing you at the MacNiffs' shindig," I greeted him. "In case you don't know it, Sergeant, you weren't properly dressed for the occasion."

"From the look of some of them dames, neither was they. You could see their unmentionables under them short skirts. But there were some fine lookers on that lawn, I'll say that for your fancy dress party."

"It's called dressing *pour le sport,* Al, and when on duty I don't think you should be looking at unmentionables while the culprit flees the scene of the crime. You are a servant of the people, remember."

"Dressing *pour le sport,*" he mimicked. "That's rich. I call it dressed to kill, pal."

A moment of silence followed, as if in

commemoration of the recently departed. Al chomped on his unlit stogie while I thought about the English Ovals safely locked away in the Miata's glove compartment. When my nicotine urgings became too acute, I broke the silence. "The boy was murdered." It was a statement, not a question.

Al turned to look directly at me, removing the cigar from between his teeth. "We don't know who did it — yet — but we got a list of suspects that reads like the Palm Beach social register."

I protested, "You don't think one of the MacNiffs' guests did the kid in? He was a waiter, for cripes' sake, Al."

"What he was, pal, was a good-looking young stud, and this is Palm Beach in season. You want I should elucidate on that theme?"

It was I who taught him that ten-buck word and now I was sorry I had. "No need to elucidate, Sergeant, but I think you're on the wrong track."

"What do you know, Archy?"

"Right now, less than you, I'm sure. I guessed that he was clobbered and shoved into the water unconscious."

"He was unconscious, all right, but not from a knock on the noggin. He was chloroformed."

That was a shocker, to say the least. I was sure Jeff didn't inhale it for kicks, so I guessed someone put a handkerchief or wad of gauze soaked in chloroform over his nose in typical Hollywood cloak-and-dagger fashion. Al told me that's just how it was done.

The PM detected traces of the chemical, often derived from ethyl alcohol, in the boy's blood. Tiny threads of cotton found in his nose and mouth also tested positive for chloroform. State-of-the-art forensic medicine is a marvel of the new millennium. We now knew how it was done. Who did it, and why, would take brains, brawn, legwork and an assist from Dame Fortune.

The murder weapon, as you might call it, was not exactly indicative of a confrontation between a couple of young punks or a *crime passionnel*. I knew that and so did Al. Reluctantly, I mumbled, "Rather sophisticated."

"Yeah, ain't it. Like dressing *pour le sport*," Al got in. "He was alive when he was shoved into the pool so the actual cause of death is drowning. His lungs were filled with water and he expired about an hour before he was fished out."

About three o'clock, just as I had pegged it. "Did they tell Nifty all this when he reported to the station house this morning?"

"If you mean Mr. MacNiff, we did, and how do you know he came in this morning?"

"Maria Sanchez, who works for Mrs. MacNiff, told our Ursi, who told me. I'm sure everyone up and down the Boulevard also knows it as our Ursi suffers from telephonitis."

"What a town," Al groused.

"I'm having lunch with Nifty this afternoon," I confessed. "Mar-a-Lago."

"Is that what you're dressed for? I thought you had a date with Phil Meecham."

"You're a scream, Al."

"I got my fans." He started to eject himself from the passenger seat. "Keep me posted."

"Also being rumored is that the victim was smoking a funny cigarette," I called after him. "True?"

"It was a Marlboro Light. Where did you hear that one?"

"Abe Calhoun."

"So who's that?" Al asked.

"He does for Mr. Van Fleet," I answered.

"Yeah? How come I ain't got nobody to do for me?"

"Get married, Sergeant."

"Get lost, pal."

SIX

Mar-a-Lago is easily the most elegant if not the most famous beach house in the world. Built by Post Toasties heiress Marjorie Merriweather Post, it was the palace at 1100 S. Ocean Boulevard from which she ruled the island with a velvet glove worn over a steel fist. Ms. Post was keen on square dancing and often had the crowd in for a hoedown. Folks were tired of do-si-do-ing around her posh digs but dared not refuse for fear of never being invited again which, back then, was on par with being unable to secure a lunch reservation at Club Colette today. Don't sneer; people around here take such things very seriously.

Stories about the cereal lady abound. My favorite has her meowing that Evalyn Walsh McLean's diamond tiara was "tinny from behind." (Evalyn owned the Hope Diamond, in case you didn't know.)

Another is the one about suspecting her husband (I don't recall which husband) of having it off with the help. She covered the area outside the servants' quarters with talc (like a policeman dusting for prints) and the next morning discovered his size eleven hoofprints going from the back door to his nocturnal tryst. A divorce followed and, we can assume, a square dance to celebrate the occasion.

So depressed was Marjorie during the Great Depression, she gathered a group of fun people aboard her yacht and sailed away from it all. Who says the rich are insensitive to the plight of the less fortunate?

The mansion's facade is fossilized stone, giving it the appearance of antiquity that its owner's lineage lacked.

Mar-a-Lago was bought by a New York real estate tycoon who has turned it into a club and spa for those who can afford a hefty six-figure entrance fee. Amusingly enough, the spa is located where the old servants' quarters once stood. One of its most prized features is a round copper tub that holds umpteen gallons of water in which one can soak and absorb the supposed benefits of the mineral.

A car jockey was on hand to help me out of my Miata and drive it off to the parking facilities. The boy reminded me of the late Jeff, as well as our Todd, and all the other boys and girls who labor in Palm Beach's thriving service industry. They deserved better than what the fates had dealt Jeffrey Rodgers.

I was told at the desk that Mr. MacNiff awaited me on the terrace and walked through the great room, which truly lives up to that oft-used name in size and decor, then out the back to the terrace where I saw Nifty at a table overlooking the pool and, beyond, a golf cart picturesquely poised at the perimeter of the pristine nine-hole course that is Mar-a-Lago's backyard.

"I hope I haven't kept you waiting, Mr. MacNiff."

"No, no, not at all, Archy. I had to go to the police station this morning and I came directly here for a late coffee." With a lethargic wave of his hand, like royalty on parade, he said, "Isn't the view stunning?"

I agreed it was, and then got down to business. "And calming, I'm sure, after your morning meeting with the police."

Looking at a pair of youngsters splashing about the pool, he said, "The boy was murdered, Archy."

"I know, sir."

"I've heard you have your contacts at headquarters. How very clever of you. It happened very much as you suggested."

He said this almost as if my guess had

precipitated the PM's verdict. I was spared from answering by the arrival of our waiter bearing a bottle of wine submerged in a bucket of ice and a tripod on which to mount it.

"I took the liberty of ordering a white wine to go with lunch. A simple pinot. Nothing pretentious."

Why do the very rich insist on simplicity when picking up the tab? But it was a Collio, a very fine pinot and among my favorites. After Nifty had his sip and declared it drinkable, I got my share and raised my glass in a silent toast.

"The police are fairly certain, and so am I, that one of the boy's friends is responsible. Trouble over a girl, I would think. I would like you to look into it, Archy, and see what you can learn."

Was this a mandate to make sure *them* and not *us* was the guilty party? I believe it was and I sincerely hoped I wouldn't have to disappoint one of our richest and most respected clients. "I will make some inquiries, sir, and report directly to you."

"That would be fine, Archy." His point made, noted and set in stone, Nifty moved on to more pressing matters. "Have you seen the menu?" he asked. "The lobster salad is top drawer."

We both ordered the top drawer and I chose the shrimp cocktail for starters while Nifty went for the escargot. Hot rolls and butter were served just as a jet roared above us close enough to clearly see its wheels being ingested into the body of the craft. One of the drawbacks of dining on Mar-a-Lago's terrace is that it is in the direct path of the airport's take-off runway in West Palm, so close that the plane hasn't had a chance to gain much altitude before soaring over the Atlantic.

When we could once again hear ourselves talk, I said, "I believe you had something else on your mind when you invited me to lunch yesterday."

"Yes, I did. It's confidential, Archy, and it concerns young Lance Talbot."

Another surprise.

"I dare say you know the story," he continued. "It was the talk of Palm Beach a few months back."

Nifty went on to tell me much of what I had already heard from Lolly Spindrift, with some embellishments only an insider could know. When the call came informing Mrs. Talbot of her daughter's death, it was assumed that the boy, Lance, was also a victim of the accident. Later it was discovered that Lance had not gone on the slopes with his mother as was assumed, but had left her to go off on his own.

"Who called Mrs. Talbot?" I asked.

"Jessica's Swiss lawyer. He learned of the tragedy from newspaper reports that stated both mother and son had died in the avalanche. A day or two later, the lawyer received a call from Lance and he immediately put in another call to Mrs. Talbot to correct the error."

When Mrs. Talbot learned that her grandson was alive she immediately summoned him to Palm Beach where she was on her deathbed and, reunited with the boy, made him her sole heir.

"I was Aunt Margaret's executor," Nifty told me. "She's not a relation but was a close friend of my parents and I've referred to her as my aunt since I was a boy. Margaret Talbot was near ninety when she died."

Thinking that Nifty wanted help in ending the affair between young Talbot and Holga von Brecht, I cut directly to the chase and asked, "And the problem, sir?"

"The problem is that I believe Aunt Margaret thought the man calling himself Lance Talbot is an imposter."

And wasn't that a kick in the kimono?

"You must remember, Archy," he quickly

went on, "that Aunt Margaret had suffered a stroke that affected her speech and she was rather addled the last days of her life. I visited often and she asked me several times, as best she could, what I thought of Lance. I told her, of course, that he was a fine lad, but now I don't think that's what she wanted to hear. In retrospect, I now believe she knew something was amiss but either didn't know what it was or couldn't articulate her suspicion. Then she said, 'He doesn't talk like a king.' I assume she meant her grandson but had no idea what she meant and still don't."

"Did you ask her, sir?"

"Oh, yes, but it was so pathetic to see her struggle to answer, actually crying in desperation until the nurse insisted I leave, and rightly so. You must see how difficult this was. Aunt Margaret was a very intelligent woman who spoke like an orator. So sad. So very sad."

I was thinking of my own mother when I told him I understood his predicament.

"The last time I saw her alive, she seemed to have surrendered to the inevitable or been given a powerful sedative on doctor's orders. Taking my hand and smiling benignly she said quite clearly, 'The king is dead, Malcolm.' After that she lost consciousness and never regained it."

"Had Lance ever been referred to as a king? Even in jest or a nickname?"

"Not that I know of," Nifty said.

"Then I think the old lady was hallucinating, sir. Between her recent stroke and the medication it wouldn't be unusual."

Nifty nodded. "That's what the doctor said, Archy, but I feel I owe Aunt Margaret the benefit of what I think was her doubt."

"Thanks to modern technology, it couldn't be simpler. A DNA test can tell you if Lance Talbot is who he says he is."

"Well, it's not so simple," Nifty lamented. "His mother was cremated in Switzerland, her ashes scattered over her beloved Alps, and Aunt Margaret was cremated here and, as per her will, her ashes sprinkled over the Atlantic. Margaret Talbot, as you know, was the daughter of the Detroit tycoon, Woodrow Reynolds. Woody's marriage was *sine prole*."

I had studied Latin at Yale and retained enough of it to know that Woodrow Reynolds and his wife were childless.

"Margaret was adopted and had no known blood relatives. Lance's claim comes via his mother and grandmother. As for Aunt Margaret's husband, Luke Talbot, he was an officer in the last big war and re-

65

called at the time of the Korean conflict where his helicopter was shot out of the sky and his remains never recovered. If he has any relatives they are not known to me or to anyone that I know. I believe Aunt Margaret married for love and poor Luke's antecedents did not live up to old man Reynolds's expectation, hence they were erased from the record, if you know what I mean.

"So none of them can supply DNA samples to compare with Lance."

Like the last czar of Russia, I was thinking, whose remains, along with his family, were found decades after their execution and DNA samples taken and compared to their cousin, Prince Philip, for positive identification. I also calculated that Lance could have had his mother's ashes consigned to the Alps, if she was his mother, but if it was in old Mrs. Talbot's will that her ashes be dropped into the ocean it surely wasn't young Talbot who made them disappear.

Our now empty appetizer plates were removed as I refilled our wineglasses and casually asked, "What do you want me to do, sir?"

"I would like you to look into the matter, Archy. You know the young set, you mix and mingle and get invited hither and yon, as Lolly might say. You are in a much better position than this old man to learn what our newest millionaire is all about."

"Did you know Lance as a child? Before his mother took him to Switzerland?"

"I saw him a few times, certainly. To tell the truth, Archy, he was a bit of an embarrassment to Aunt Margaret, not knowing who his father was, and her friends more or less looked the other way out of respect for her. I remember a boy with a dark crew cut and blue eyes. Our Lance Talbot certainly fits the bill in that respect. As for facial features, one does change from age ten to age twenty."

Our lobster salads arrived, looking top drawer as promised, and I spoke the name, "Holga von Brecht."

Nifty laughed, or snorted, and said, "I was saving her for dessert — not literally," and laughed, or snorted, again. "She was a friend of Jessica's and arrived here with Lance. They are inseparable and it's a scandal. They say she's seventy."

"Some say ninety, sir, but I'd go for fifty."

"Whatever her age, she's a beautiful woman, Archy, but I don't have to tell that to a healthy American boy. All the women want to know about this clinic she is supposed to have gone to for injections of — well, I won't spoil your appetite."

Now I had to know what was rumored to be in those injections but would defer my curiosity to a time when I wasn't at table.

"Lance is living in his grandmother's house — sorry, it's now his house — and Holga is his guest. Don't ask me if they share a bedroom because I don't know, but I'm sure you can find out."

Nifty's belief in my powers of detection was heartening, if a trifle overrated. I thought it best not to tell him I didn't have a clue as to how to go about learning who Lance Talbot was, if he wasn't Lance Talbot, and even less of an idea of how to spy into his bedroom. I thought of getting a position as his valet but dismissed that as being too much like work. But I didn't rule out having Jamie befriend Lance's valet, if Jamie didn't already know the bloke.

"How friendly are you with the boy?" I wanted to know.

"Not very. He is certainly polite and most respectful. My wife adores him, but few women can resist a lad with a crew cut."

Really? I had to remember that next time I was tonsured.

"As I'm the executor of his grandmother's estate, our meetings are usually of a business nature," Nifty said.

"Does Holga attend?"

"No. I would not countenance that and I'm sure the boy knows it."

"And your relationship with Holga von Brecht, sir?"

Nifty thought a moment before answering. "Again, polite and respectful but, unlike Lance, most seductive."

For a woman like Holga von Brecht this would be her natural approach to men, especially older men and certainly rich men. Recalling Holga's blond good looks and what I had discerned as a manner of speech acquired at one of the Seven Sisters colleges, I inquired after Holga's husband. "She's a Yankee," I said, "not a von Brecht from Switzerland."

"She was introduced to us as Mrs. von Brecht, Archy, so I believe there is a Mr. von Brecht, but I'll be damned if I know who he is or where he is or, for that matter, what he does to keep Holga in those clothes my wife tells me are all couture."

And, I added to myself, the MacNiffs are too well bred to ask. As for Holga's wardrobe, it could very well be the result of Lance's largesse.

"There was one Vivian Emerson at yesterday's event. Do you know if she's a friend of the von Brecht woman?"

Nifty shook his head as another jet threatened to join us for lunch. When it had passed he said, "Don't know. You'll have to ask Helen. She does all the inviting. I can't keep up. The old days when our crowd were all kissin' kin are long gone. The island is crawling with social climbers, con artists and Guccibaggers. Crying shame, I call it."

Glancing around the terrace, I noticed several persons I hoped had not heard Nifty trash certain members of our town's newest club. But I rather liked the play on "carpetbaggers" and filed it for future use.

The lobster salad was succulent and to express my gratitude I began talking like I had a game plan. "I would like the name and fax of Jessica's Swiss lawyer and, if possible, a picture of Lance Talbot when he was a boy."

"I can give you all the information on the lawyer, but I'll have to check with Helen to see if we have any pictures. She keeps albums of them, don't you know. Children, weddings, grandchildren, the lot."

"Which reminds me, sir, my mother

asked me to express her concern for you and Mrs. MacNiff after yesterday's tragedy."

"How very kind of Madelaine. How is she, Archy?"

"Hanging in, as they say."

"That's all we can do these days."

We finished the last of the wine and ordered coffee and the caramel custard for dessert.

"I almost forgot," Nifty said holding a spoon full of custard aloft, "Lance's foot."

"I beg your pardon?"

"His foot," Nifty repeated. "When he was a boy his foot was injured in some freak accident. I believe the chauffeur accidently slammed the car door on it when the boy was climbing in. A toe had to be amputated. I believe the small toe on his right foot."

"I take it you haven't . . ."

"Asked to see his foot? Good Lord, no. I thought you might have a go at it."

When I got back to my office, which is about the size of your handkerchief if you don't go in for bandannas, the little red light on my answering machine was blinking. Yes, I have succumbed and entered the new century, not by choice but on orders of the executive suite, which consists of Father and his secretary, Mrs. Trelawney, the bane of my existence on Royal Palm Way.

She of the gray polyester tresses has been urging me to install voice mail since declaring herself too busy to intercept my calls and take messages for the firm's most expendable employee. To this end she had Father sign a memo stating that all personnel of McNally & Son would be obliged to install such a device on their desk phones if they hadn't already done so. As I was the only personnel person who did not possess the odious thing, it was clear whom she meant. Trelawney had won the battle, but not the war.

I pressed the button and heard:

"Archy? It's Connie. Lady Cynthia is furious because Phil Meecham has snared Jackson Barnett. She wants you to get the athlete out of Phil's clutches and into hers. Pronto." Click.

"Archy? Georgy girl. I heard you played tennis with Joey Gallo. Doesn't he have great legs? What do you know about the murder? I'll be home tonight. Call me." Click.

"Mr. McNally? This is Dennis Darling. I am stopping at the GulfStream hotel just over the bridge in Lake Worth. Please call me at your earliest convenience regarding the death of Jeffrey Rodgers. Thank you." Click.

I pulled the plug on the bloody machine. How much can a healthy American boy take in one afternoon?

SEVEN

The Route 802 bridge does not separate Palm Beach Island from Lake Worth, but links Lake Worth to the Lake Worth Municipal Beach, which is on Palm Beach Island. The Pier contains several shops that cater to tourists and a coffee shop the hungry queue up in front of every morning for their bacon and eggs fix. The area is a favorite hangout for teen surfers and as I approached it to hang a right onto the bridge I thought of Jeff Rodgers and wondered, as I had been doing since listening to Darling's urgent message, if his summons would end up shedding light on Jeff's murder.

The bridge exits on Lucerne Avenue, which is one way, west, and skirts the Lake Worth Municipal Golf Club. The course is popular with Palm Beachers and boasts a new clubhouse. The par-70 spread was a favorite of baseball great Babe Ruth and is now home to the Nine Hole Club, a merry group of golfers who discourage competition with the motto, "Low handicap players need not apply."

The GulfStream Hotel is at the foot of the bridge on Lake Avenue, which is one way, east, forcing me to go up Lucerne, cross over, and come down Lake to arrive where I had just about started.

The GulfStream is a first-class hostelry that offers guests a great panorama of Lake Worth and the southern end of Palm Beach. Daniel's Lake Avenue Grill is the hotel's restaurant, situated just off the lobby and features an outdoor terrace that fronts Lake Worth. It also features an oval-shaped bar that runs almost the entire length of the big room, keeping the two lovely barmaids it engulfed on the run this cocktail hour.

My experienced eye judged the crowd to be a mix of tourists (shirts embossed with palm trees and Bermuda shorts with knee-length stockings, ugh!) and Floridians in more somber attire, making an oasis stop between work and home. Music was being piped in and those in conversation with their neighbor had to shout above it to be heard. The resulting din was more conducive to making whoopee than indulging in a tête-à-tête with the formidable Dennis Darling.

I spotted Darling at a table for two abutting the windows facing the outside terrace and was tempted to go rushing over and shout, "Darling, I hope I haven't kept you waiting long." But with a name like Darling, a good Yankee name by the way, he must have grown callous to the approach or, more likely, might respond by getting up and kissing me on the cheek. At Daniel's on a crowded evening the game was not worth the candle so I approached with caution and said instead, "Mr. Darling? Archy McNally here."

He rose and extended his hand, and we shook like civilized people. Remember, I had only seen Dennis Darling on the tennis court at Nifty's so had no idea of what he might be like when clothed and shod for company. I was not disappointed. In fact, I was impressed. The summer grays with a white open-collar dress shirt and a lightweight navy blazer bespoke New York chic and was an outfit I myself have been known to favor. Darling was about my height, six feet, with dark hair and eyes that suggested a dash of the Mediterranean in the woodpile. Had his reputation not preceded him, I knew several PB hostesses who would have made Dennis Darling's stay more welcome.

Happily, I had gone for Ermenegildo Zegna jeans and a striped polo shirt in soft greens and blues, *sans* circus animal over the left breast, so we didn't appear to be gazing in a mirror as we appraised each other.

"We meet again, Mr. McNally. You do remember we played a few sets together on MacNiff's court yesterday."

"On opposite sides of the net, Mr. Darling."

"Of course," he said. "But perhaps we can play on the same team this time around."

"I'm not much of a team player," I assured him.

"So I understand," he answered, eying me as if I were a job applicant. "Let me say how much I appreciate your coming, Mr. McNally." He pointed invitingly to the empty chair opposite his and continued, "I'm a stranger on your tropical island and about as welcome as a blizzard." Signaling a passing waitress, he asked, "What are you drinking?"

"Before you buy me a drink," I answered, easing into the chair, "I want you to know that I will discuss neither the flora nor the fauna of Palm Beach only to be misquoted in *Bare Facts* magazine."

"Relax," he said. "I didn't get you here to find out what you know about Palm

Beach society, but to tell you what I know about Jeff Rodgers. Interested?"

I looked up at the waitress and ordered a vodka martini with a twist, straight up. Darling told her to bring him another Johnnie Walker Red Label, on the rocks. I have always been wary of men who take their whiskey neat but rationalized that the added ice gave Mr. Darling the benefit of any doubts I might have about him. "I didn't think you knew anyone in these parts, Mr. Darling."

"I don't," he told me, adding, "with the exception of poor Jeff, and I only met with him once before his untimely death. He was murdered, wasn't he?"

"Are you asking me or telling me, Mr. Darling?"

"My friends call me Denny, and I hope to count you among them."

The guy was engaging, I will admit, but he seemed intent on cementing our relationship with the speed of a gigolo at a debutante ball. I could see no reason to withhold what little I knew, as the full story of Jeff's demise would be in tomorrow's papers and was probably being aired on the evening news as we spoke. Also, as a crack investigative reporter for a national magazine he would know how to wrest information out of a desk sergeant on Palm Beach island.

"Well, my friend, I would like to know why you chose me to impart information — whatever it may be — that would be of more interest to the police than to this disinterested civilian."

The waitress arrived with our drinks and Darling waited until she had served them and gone before responding. "Prior to coming here, I had my assistant check the bare facts of this Eden and one of the facts she came up with was that Archy McNally is employed with his father's law firm as a PI, not a lawyer, because Archy was bounced out of Yale for reasons unknown. His job at McNally and Son is to run interference between the swells and any embarrassing problems that might arise, like dead bodies in their swimming pools." He picked up his glass, "Cheers, Archy."

A lot of cheek but, again, the glib yet honest delivery was infectious. I would guess Dennis Darling had put together a few facts and was tossing out what he only surmised. I liked this élan and my McNally intuition told me I had found a kindred spirit. I would play it by ear and, if he didn't disappoint, count him as a friend who could be very helpful now and in the future.

I picked up my martini. "Cheers, Denny." His smile told me he hadn't missed the irony in my delivery.

"So, you are working for MacNiff," he stated.

"Could be," I said. "It depends."

"On what?" he wanted to know.

"On what you have to tell me about Jeff Rodgers."

Darling shrugged. "Give-and-take, you mean?"

"I mean, Denny, you invited me here regarding a most urgent matter, to quote you, and I'm not saying another word until you tell me what it is."

He sipped his Johnnie Walker Red and pretended to give this some thought. A moment later he was taking me into his confidence. "I didn't come to Palm Beach to write an exposé on the resort. It's been done, ad nauseam, as I'm sure you know."

"So why did you come?"

"I got a call in New York telling me that for the right price I would be told the truth about Lance Talbot."

I almost started at hearing the name and hoped Darling hadn't noticed, but I'm sure he had. Noticing such things was how he made his living. First Jeff and now Talbot. I wondered if Dennis Darling had been hanging out in my back pocket since last we met.

"I'm sure you know who Lance Talbot is," he went on, "but at the time I didn't. However, my research assistant filled me in. A rags-to-riches story is always good copy as it gives people hope. I called back and said I might be interested. My contact wanted to know how much I would pay and I told him my magazine's honorarium would be in keeping with the information being bartered.

"I didn't know if I was on a fool's errand but things were slow and a few days in Palm Beach in February didn't seem a bad way to fight ennui. In case it should turn out to be something interesting I put it about that I was here to write a piece on your popular and posh resort to throw other snoops off the scent."

"And who was your caller?" I asked, fearing the worst.

"Jeffrey Rodgers," he said, confirming my fear.

Well, that not only made the cheese more binding and the plot more thick, it also made the two cases Nifty had asked me to look into clash like a couple of rams doing battle over a four-legged temptress. Jeff Rodgers and Lance Talbot. The waiter and the playboy. They couldn't have less in common if they existed on different planets. However, they didn't exist on different planets but on one tight little island.

What could Jeff have known about Lance Talbot that would interest Dennis Darling? More to the point, what did Jeff know about Lance Talbot that got Jeff dead? That Lance Talbot wasn't Lance Talbot? How could Jeff have known what Nifty, and perhaps old Mrs. Talbot, only suspected? My medulla oblongata was trying to process too much too soon which, I have always believed, was as dangerous as coping with too little too late. Besides, Denny seemed to be enjoying watching me squirm. It was my turn to give, and not taking any chances I parted with only what would soon be common knowledge.

"Jeff Rodgers was murdered," I said. "Chloroformed before being shoved into the pool."

Denny pursed his lips to whistle but if any sound emerged it was lost to the babble as early diners began arriving to join the bar crowd. He was too much of a pro to speculate on how Jeff had been shoved into the pool while Nifty's party was in full swing, probably because he had already figured it out for himself. Who had done the shoving was the question which Denny now posed.

"You think Jeff was made redundant because of what he had on the Talbot guy?"

"I have no idea," I said, "mostly because I didn't know there was a connection between the two until you told me."

Again, he asked, "Are you working for Malcolm MacNiff?"

"I plead client confidentiality," I told him before asking, "Why haven't you told the police why you came to Palm Beach?"

"That would be revealing a source, which I never do," he said.

"Your source is dead," I reminded him, "and what he told you could help the police in their investigation of his death."

"It could also help you, Archy. That is, if you are looking into Jeff's murder on behalf of a client."

"We're shadowboxing, Denny," I said, thinking that we had reached an impasse and I was getting bored with the charade and with Denny. True, he had given me a connection between the assignments I had undertaken for Nifty — Jeff's murder and the legitimacy of Lance Talbot's claim —

but I wasn't about to tell Denny that. In fact, I was going to tell Denny as little as possible and learn as much as I could. In the game of give-and-take, the object is to take as much as you can get and give as little as you can get away with. And, lest I forget, I was playing with a pro.

Denny again signaled our waitress and indicated by pointing that we were ready for another drink. It's long been rumored that reporters are big-time boozers and Denny wasn't doing anything to dispel the supposition. "If you'd like a cigarette we could move out to the terrace," he offered.

"What makes you think I'm a smoker?"

"You're beginning to fidget," he said, mockingly.

"And you're beginning to bore, Denny. Now if you'll excuse me . . ."

"Cool your heels," he said, motioning me to stay seated. When I kept my place he leaned forward and, speaking in earnest, got down to the purpose of our meeting. "Look, Archy, I need your help and I'm willing to pay for it. What's your fee?"

"Steep, like everything else in Palm Beach, but I'm sure you, or your magazine, can afford it. What did you have in mind, Denny?"

The waitress deposited our drinks and

took away the empties. When she was out of hearing range Denny said, "I want you to find out what Jeff had on Lance Talbot. I thought I had come down here chasing a rainbow but the kid's murder changes all that. He was on to something. Something so big it got him killed. Drugs? Kinky sex? Maybe. But my guess is that Jeff Rodgers knew who Lance Talbot's father was and the disclosure would make headlines."

"So you know he was born on the wrong side of the blanket," I said, impressed with Denny's facts.

"My assistant compiled a dossier on Talbot, his mother, grandmother and the Detroit Reynolds connection. My first thought was that Jeff had learned who fathered Lance and that it was a man of note who would like to remain anonymous. It's why I came down here."

This, of course, opened a can of worms I had not even considered nor, I suspect, had Malcolm MacNiff, who was unaware of the link between Jeff and Lance. It was Lance's identity, not his father's, that worried Nifty. As for Jeff's murder, all Nifty cared about was clearing his friends of the crime. Denny, on the other hand, didn't have a clue that Talbot might not be Talbot. If I signed on with Denny for a hefty fee it would be for a completely different reason I had been engaged by Nifty — thus not a conflict. *N'est ce pas?* Greed, thy name is Archibald McNally. I was in the catbird seat and enjoying the view, which prompted me to quip brazenly, "I thought you came down for a respite from February in New York."

"*Touché*, Archy, I deserved that." He downed another swig of Johnnie Walker Red. "If I start asking questions it will draw the attention of every hack in the country and they will make a beeline to Palm Beach in search of the honey. I say that with all due modesty to my fame as an investigative reporter. Plus, I don't know my way around these parts and you do." He raised his glass in a toast. "Partners?"

I gave that a moment's thought and raised my glass. Denny had given me a connection between my two cases for Nifty that I might never have discerned on my own. I owed the man something and, let's not forget, he would pay well for my largesse.

"You said you had one meeting with Jeff. What did he tell you?"

"Not much," Denny said. "He wanted to know how much I would pay for his information. I told him, yet again, it would depend on what he was selling. He asked for a ballpark figure, as he put it, and I got the feeling that he was engaging in a private auction."

"You mean he was talking to another magazine?"

"No. I think he was talking to Lance Talbot, or Lance's dad, and using my presence as a threat. He wanted to know how much I would pay so he could tell either party it would cost him double to keep his mouth, and mine, shut. Smart kid, right?"

"So smart it got him drowned," I said, finding it impossible to believe Jeff Rodgers could know who had fathered Lance Talbot, but said, in spite of this conviction, "And if it was the father Jeff was dealing with it's very possible Lance knows nothing about the blackmail scam or who his father is."

"It's possible," Denny said, not sounding too happy with the hypothesis. Denny wanted the young, handsome and rich Lance Talbot to be the focal point of his story, not a footnote.

"Did you give Jeff a ballpark figure?"

"Guessing he knew the name of Talbot's father, and that it was a big name, I said twenty thousand was not unheard of for the right information."

It was my turn to whistle through my teeth. "Lance did not kill Jeff Rodgers," I stated for the record.

"I'm aware of that, Archy. Remember, I had an interest in Lance Talbot. I got my editor to pay big to get me invited to MacNiff's fund-raiser and Lance Talbot was never out of my sight yesterday afternoon. He never went near the pool."

"Did Jeff tell you Lance was going to be at Malcolm MacNiff's yesterday?" I asked.

"But of course."

So the waiter knew the playboy's social schedule. The more one learned, the less one knew. At this juncture I had to ask, "Tell me, Denny, are you interested in a story or justice?"

"A story, of course. If the bad guys get their comeuppance along the way, that's fine too."

"I appreciate the candor," I told him, "and I have no problem with learning the facts and reporting them, but I will have no part in *creating* a story that doesn't otherwise exist."

"Fair enough. And may I remind you that since I am your client you are not obligated to tell the police what I have told you. Client confidentiality, remember?"

I had already thought of this but insisted

on saying, "Unless withholding information endangers anyone, and I reserve the right to go to the police with what I learn about Jeff Rodgers and Lance Talbot directly after giving you your scoop."

I did not say that the police would consider Denny's information hearsay, as was Jeff's claim that he had something on Lance Talbot. Cold, hard facts were woefully lacking, which had me thinking that this could be an ingenious plot on behalf of Dennis Darling to rock the boat on a calm sea with Archy enlisted to get the wind up. *Beware investigative reporters bearing gifts* would be my mantra when dealing with Denny.

"I will pretend to be gathering information for my Palm Beach story," Denny was saying, "and continue being snubbed by all the right people and patronized by those who don't matter."

That reminded me of Lolly. "Have you met Lolly Spindrift?"

Denny thought a moment. "You mean the little guy in the white suit at MacNiff's?"

"That's him. He's our local gossip columnist," I said, "and you might interview him as part of your cover."

"He gave me the cold shoulder," Denny

complained, "like everyone else at the MacNiff party."

"I happen to know that Lolly can't refuse an invitation to be wined and dined at someone else's expense. Cafe L'Europe is his favorite."

Denny nodded. "I'll give it a try. Would you like to be wined and dined at my expense right here? The food is excellent."

"Thanks, but I have a dinner date."

At that moment, from out of nowhere, the sound of a shaky but robust tenor rose above the din, belting out Verdi's rousing drinking song from *La Traviata*. I turned to see one of the waiters, a little older and a little stouter than the rest of Daniel's crew, playing Alfredo in the middle of the small parquet dance floor and, appropriately enough, wielding a glass of champagne to the delight of his audience.

"The room's singing waiter and main attraction," Denny informed me. "They call him the fourth tenor."

Our Caruso wanna-be finished with a theatrical flourish to his imaginary Violetta and to a standing ovation. I couldn't wait to drag Al Rogoff to the next performance.

EIGHT

I crossed back to the island and drove north on Ocean Boulevard with the top of my red Miata down, under a canopy of glittering stars and a new moon. I have traveled this route countless times but have yet to become jaded to the sights and sounds and splendor of my hometown on a balmy winter night when a gentle ocean breeze sets the palm trees swaying to the music coming from my car's radio.

I drove past sumptuous white brick condos with terraces overlooking the Atlantic and grand homes with their windows ablaze as limos and sports cars with foreign plates pulled in and out of gated driveways. Further along the island widens to accommodate palatial villas on both sides of the highway and I found myself sandwiched between the rich and the richer in the land of Oz, on my way to see the Wizard.

Forgive the blather, but the easy listening music beneath the stars and swaying palms had me waxing poetic — as do two martinis, unsolved murders and singing waiters. I was actually on my way to the land of Juno to see my current flame, Georgy girl, known to her coworkers as Georgy and to her parents as Georgia. My green-eyed blonde is the happy result of a union between Ireland and Italy. I speak of her parents, not the nations. I read that this mix, especially in New York, is the most popular in our melting pot but has not, thanks to the blessed memory of Georges Auguste Escoffier, led to the joining of boiled potatoes and pasta.

Instead, it has given us handsome lads and gorgeous colleens with attitude. There are those who, in the garden of love, always manage to get hit on the noggin with a falling lemon. I was struck by a peach who packs heat and is licensed to kill. Lieutenant O'Hara, a state trooper if you please, and even if you don't please. We met over a corpse in a seedy motel room. Given that beginning I figured the relationship had no place to go but up, so I invited her to dinner. We've been an item ever since.

Georgy's electronic message this afternoon had instantly reminded me where and when I had heard the name Joe Gallo, the affable young man Holga von Brecht and I had beat two games out of three before the discovery of Jeff Rodgers's body in the MacNiffs' pool. The name came not from a wine commercial as one might expect, but from the ruby lips of Georgy girl. Gallo was her ex-lover who had forsaken her for the good life with a rich divorcée of advanced years whom I now suspected was none other than Vivian Emerson. Really! In Palm Beach in season one needs a *dramatis personae* to tell who's who, but that's what we have Lolly Spindrift for.

Driving past Mar-a-Lago, I thought of my lunch with Malcolm MacNiff, which, in turn, led to thoughts of the meeting I had just left with Dennis Darling. Odd, how all the names rattling around in my head on this enchanting evening, with the exception of Georgy girl, were present when Jeff Rodgers met his maker. Now I knew of a link, however tenuous, between the dead boy and one of Nifty's guests, namely Lance Talbot; and between Joe Gallo, Vivian Emerson and Georgy. If one dug deep enough, would everyone at the MacNiff house yesterday afternoon emerge holding hands like paper dolls stretched the distance from the tennis courts to the pool?

Today saw the first time two clients had

hired me to investigate the same person for different reasons. Nifty wanted me to prove that Lance Talbot was, or was not, Lance Talbot and, incidently, to learn what I could about his backyard murder. Denny wanted me to find out what the murdered boy had on Lance Talbot, not knowing that Lance Talbot might not be who he claimed to be.

Clearly, what I needed to learn were the elements and circumstances in which the crime was committed. In this instance, the number one element is, Why was Jeff killed? The leading circumstance is, Who was able to go from the tennis courts to the pool, without being missed or seen, to commit the dastardly deed?

I believed the answers would K two B's with one S: solve Jeff's murder and old Mrs. Talbot's tantalizing riddle, "The king is dead." The latter, I suddenly decided, would be the title of the case I would begin recording in my journal when I arrived home this evening, or, with a little bit of McNally luck, tomorrow morning.

Georgy girl lives in what was once the guest cottage of an antebellum mansion that has seen better days. Her old landlady, a recluse who is the sole occupant of the manor house, checks the traffic in the driveway leading to Georgy's digs by peering surreptitiously from behind a beaded curtain. In the months I have been calling on Georgy, the old lady and I have devised a coded form of communication. She peeks through the beads and I beep the Miata's horn in reply.

The first time I spent the night with Georgy, leaving in the early morning, I do believe the old biddy shook a fist at me from behind her beaded shield. In the weeks that followed she seems to have come to terms with the facts of life, or the facts of her tenant's life, and we are once again on nonspeaking terms.

Georgy invited me to supper, which, given her cooking skills, is tantamount to playing Russian roulette with your digestive system. Georgy holds the "Fast Food Queen of Florida" title and has been shortlisted to take the world title faster than you can nuke a weenie in your microwave.

When I entered the cottage she was at the stove in her cute galley kitchen emptying a can of tuna into a pot of cooked noodles. Turning, she lovingly greeted me with, "I hope that's not an alligator shirt."

"I hope that's not a tuna 'n' noodle casserole."

"What you see is what you get," she assured me.

What I saw was a blond creature in white shorts and T-shirt that allowed for an inch or two of bare midriff. When, as now, Georgy putters around the cottage barefoot, she reminds me of the comic strip character Daisy Mae, whose charms were lost on Lil' Abner. Georgy's allure is not lost on Lil' Archy.

Coming behind her I parted the blond tresses like a curtain and kissed the back of her neck. She smelled of jasmine-scented soap and tuna fish. "Let me take you away from all this," I whispered into her ear.

"How far?" she wanted to know.

"The bedroom?"

"That's what I thought," she replied, elbowing me aside to put the odious casserole in the oven. "Help yourself to a drink and then start preparing the salad."

Since I brought a toothbrush, shaving kit and change of shorts and socks into Georgy's home, she thoughtfully purchased a tea trolley in antiquated Formica — there truly is such a thing — on which to set up a portable bar. Remembering my two vodka martinis, I poured myself a light vodka and tonic and mixed the same for my hostess, earning me a mischievous wink of her green eye.

"Cheers," she said, taking a sip. "Hmmmm, good. I've been cruising in the patrol car all day, terrifying speeders."

"Did you catch any?"

"Not enough to justify the gas I used." She took a salad bowl from one of the cupboards and placed it on the kitchen drain board. "How was your day?"

"Lunch at Mar-a-Lago with Malcolm MacNiff and cocktails at the GulfStream with Dennis Darling of *Bare Facts* magazine."

"You poor, poor dear. Do you want me to make the salad while you take a snooze until I ring the dinner bell?"

"My job might seem like a piece of cake," I said, not for the first time, "but murder was on the agenda at both meetings. It's emotionally exhausting."

Opening the refrigerator door I knew better than to go to the vegetable bin in search of a good, old fashioned solid head of iceberg. Experience taught me to reach for a Ziploc bag of precut, prewashed mixed greens, the contents of which I emptied into the salad bowl. "You wouldn't happen to have a nice, ripe tomato I could cut up and put in the salad?"

"I don't think so," Georgy said, opening

a package of frozen crescent rolls and arranging them on a baking dish.

"Cucumber?"

"I'm a policewoman, Archy, not your Ursi," she complained.

"A tomato and a cucumber do not an Ursi make," I informed her, putting the bowl in the refrigerator. "French, Russian or Italian?" I asked, eyeing the three squeezable plastic bottles lined up on the inside of the fridge door.

She put the crescent rolls in the oven, next to our casserole that was beginning to bubble, making tiny popping sounds that could put a horse off its feed.

"This is the last time I'm making you dinner," she sassed.

"Your lips to God's ear," I said, and she burst into tears.

I took her in my arms and patted her back. "There, there, Georgy girl. I was only kidding."

"You were not. I'm a lousy cook and we both know it."

"But you have other worthy attributes," I told her.

"Name two," she demanded.

"I would rather show you than tell you."

"All you ever think of is your stomach and your . . ."

"Don't say it. I evoked God's ear and He's listening."

"You're a snob, Archy McNally. And an egotist." She paused for breath as my hand kneaded her lower back where T-shirt did not meet shorts. "And you're stuck on yourself."

"My favorite wit said, 'to love yourself is the beginning of a life-long romance.' "

Ignoring Mr. Wilde's observation, she continued her attack with, "Getting photographed in a jacket that looks like a botanical garden in full bloom and confusing me with your dog. I could scream."

Now we were nearing the heart of the matter. "You saw the interview."

"I did," she said, "and so did everyone in the Juno barracks. I am now known as Hobo, thanks to you."

Not wishing to add insult to injury, I suppressed a chuckle and suggested we sit in the parlor and enjoy our drinks while we bashed each other, like proper married folks. "You're overreacting," I diagnosed.

"Am I? Name one of Augusta Apple's films," she challenged.

"Who in the name of jumping Jehovah is Augusta Apple?"

"Lila Lee, your favorite movie star, that's who. You're a phony, McNally."

Did I mention that besides being the Fast Food Queen of Florida, Georgy girl is also the undisputed champ of movie trivia? It was a title I thought I held until meeting up with Officer O'Hara.

"She was the mother of the writer James Kirkwood," I offered.

She shrugged that off with, "Everyone knows that."

"I doubt it, but let's not argue the point." Taking her hand I proposed, again, we sit, "But first lower the oven temperature to warm, we don't want to char the tuna 'n' noodle casserole."

"The rolls won't rise," she said.

"We'll declare them crêpes and have them for dessert."

The parlor, galley kitchen and breakfast nook are all one room and take up half the cottage's square footage. The other half comprises the bedroom and bath, located through a doorway just to the left of the kitchen. We settled on the couch, which was upholstered in a tan, corded fabric; a material that is serviceable and a color that goes with everything.

"Now tell me what the tears are all about," I said, once we were side by side with her blond head resting on my shoulder.

"I just told you," she lied.

Georgy girl was a policewoman to the core, proud of the fact, and a credit to her chosen profession. This did not compromise her femininity one iota. She was any man's equal, but did not shrink from using her charisma to charm the pants off her beau. (Metaphor not coincidental.) Under ordinary circumstances, and from past experience, I knew she would register her displeasure with my interview by crowning me with the casserole after draping the crescent rolls around my neck. But tears? Never.

Voicing my suspicions, I casually inquired, "How did you know I played tennis with Joe Gallo?"

"Did you actually play with him? I knew he was at your fancy party, but I didn't know you met him."

My chin being higher than her head I couldn't see her face but I envisioned those emerald eyes, wide with curiosity. Did she imagine Joe Gallo and me doing battle across a net for her favors? And she called me an egotist? Before she had me forgetting the question, I repeated, "So how did you know I was at a fancy party with Joe Gallo?"

She mumbled something. "Speak up, missy," I ordered.

"Connie called me," she said, an octave higher, but painfully audible.

Well — am I to be spared nothing? Introduce two women and the next thing you know they are discussing you on one of those wireless contraptions while chasing vehicular speeders and, no doubt, running over au pairs wheeling prams. This, I thought, is what comes from playing goody two shoes and thinking we can all be friends. Well, it's clear, we can't.

Connie Garcia, who is social secretary to Lady Cynthia Horowitz, a septuagenarian with a face that could stop a clock and a figure that could stop traffic, and I were once an item. In fact we were a staple on the PB social scene until nasty words, like *marriage,* passed between us. When Connie told me to move in, legally, or move out, permanently, Georgy girl and I struck up a conversation over a corpse. At the same time, the gods, who work in strange ways, had Connie hook up with Alejandro Gomez y Zapata on a conga line in South Beach.

Alex is a rebel whose cause is to free Cuba from Mr. Castro. It is not clear how Alex is going to do this. In the meantime he leads political rallies, parades and conga lines. It's rumored that Alex is going to make a run for mayor of Miami. If he wins, Connie will be Mrs. Mayor. I sincerely hope Alex invades Cuba, taking Connie with him, before this comes to pass.

One evening, dining with Georgy girl at my club, the Pelican, we found ourselves at a table next to Connie and her Spanish dancer. This could happen because the Pelican is also Connie's club. Ignoring my chauvinistic instincts, I invited my former to join our table and meet my current. Now I learn they talk behind my back and, if Connie knows that Joe Gallo and Georgy were once an item, they talk quite intimately. And if Georgy talked about Joe, did Connie talk about *moi?* I think I blushed, which is not a good thing for a discreet inquirer to do.

Here you have the result of allowing women to join men's clubs, compete in manly sports, enter manly professions and vote. Wise Queen Bess said the suffragette movement would end civilization as we know it — and she was right. A pox on equality.

Probing further into this treachery, I ventured, "So how did Connie know I was at a fancy party with Joe Gallo?"

"A friend of Lady C's was there and she called Lady C to report on all the hot young men in their tennis shorts. This woman and Lady C trade, so Connie tells me."

Trade? Does the women's movement know no bounds? "And Joe Gallo was on the hot young men list, I take it."

"You know it," she said.

That I wasn't on the list was implied, if not stated. Was remembrance of things past the reason for Georgy girl's melancholia? Giving her a jolt that would either cure or kill, I said, "I also met Vivian Emerson."

Georgy sat up, reached for the drink she had deposited on the glass-top coffee table, and imbibed. "Archy, can you honestly say you never think about Connie — remembering the good times — and wondering what went wrong, and why?"

Now we were hitting below the belt, and it hurt. "I can't honestly say I don't," I told her.

"Then get off my case."

Now, that was the Georgy girl I knew and loved. Never beat around a bush when you can pull it up by the roots with a few well-chosen words. If confession is good for the soul, it also has a profound effect on the appetite. "Should we get the one-pot extravaganza out of the oven and check on the crêpes?"

"Not until you tell me about the murder. Is that why you had lunch with MacNiff? It happened at his house, right?"

"Didn't Lady C's talent scout have anything to say about it? She was there when it happened."

"She only reported that one of the caterer's boys drowned in the pool. She thought it was an accident. Now we all know it wasn't. Are you acting for MacNiff?"

I saw no harm in telling her that MacNiff had asked me to look into the matter, as it had occurred on his turf. When I get a case, such as this one, that is also being investigated by the police, I have to play it very close to the vest when discussing it with Al Rogoff and Georgy girl. Of course this did not prohibit me from asking, "What do you hear about the boy's murder?"

"Are you looking for privileged information, McNally?"

"Naturally."

"Well, save your breath. I know that the boy was chloroformed and pushed into the pool to drown."

"That, I'm sure, is in the police press release," I said.

"That's where I got it," Georgy admitted. "And it's as much as I know. It's out of my jurisdiction and unless we're called in that's where it'll stay. State troopers don't get involved in murder cases unless we happen to stumble over them. Remember?"

Indeed, I did remember. The sad truth was that the murder of a young waiter would not be given top priority by our men in blue. The venue, not the crime, was the reason Jeff's had been given television coverage and newspaper headlines. If no one was charged after a routine investigation it would go into the "open cases" file where it would remain till Lake Worth froze over. However, if the police and the press knew there might be a Talbot involved in the crime, the top brass and the national press would be all over it like ants at a picnic. Dennis Darling was very wise to distance himself from the affair, thereby avoiding a media stampede to southern Florida.

Right on cue, Georgy girl asked, "How come Dennis Darling invited you for drinks? Is he going to write about the murder for his rag?"

"He's here to write about Palm Beach and I'm on his list of tourist attractions."

"I don't believe you," she said.

"Why would Dennis Darling get involved in what appears to be a vendetta between the young and reckless of the working classes?"

"Spare me the minutiae of our caste system, McNally. That tennis party was crawling with big guns, like the hunk Jackson Barnett. He would interest Dennis Darling, especially if Barnett was interested in one of the waiters."

Not a bad guess, I thought, proud of my Georgy girl. She was in the right church, if the wrong pew, which was fine. For the time being, let them all think what they wanted as long as Lance Talbot wasn't on their most wanted list. "Jackson was asked not to leave town, as we all were," I said, "and is presently stowed away on Phil Meecham's yacht, but Lady Cynthia has invited the pro to play on her court."

"That," Georgy said, "is like being caught between the proverbial hard place and a brick wall."

"No, my dear. It's like being trapped between two flesh-eating creatures — speaking of which, shall we eat?"

We rose, kissed and headed for the kitchen. Georgy suddenly stopped, took hold of my elbow and exclaimed, "Don't open the oven."

"For Pete's sake, why not?"

"I just remembered, I forgot to put the mushroom soup in the casserole."

"What?"

"You came in just as I was about to open the can and distracted me," she wailed. "It'll be congealed."

"Congealed? Georgy girl, it will be cement."

She ran to a kitchen drawer and pulled out a stack of colorful menus. "Lee Wong's Chinese Take Out, Mama Mia's Italian Take Out, Julio's Cuban Take Out . . ."

"Stop it," I shouted. "You're making me ill."

"Lee Wong's is not bad," she recommended. "Excellent sesame noodles."

"Your landlady doesn't like it when strangers call on you after dark," I reminded her.

"Lee Wong a stranger? You must be kidding, McNally."

Georgy girl is living proof that the way to a man's heart is not through his stomach.

NINE

Breakfast not being an option Chez Georgy, I stopped at a diner on the way south and treated myself to scrambled eggs, sausages and toast, telling the waitress to go easy on the hash browns. Lee Wong's chicken and snow peas do not stick to the ribs. Georgy would pick up a container of coffee and a buttered roll at the troopers' favorite pit stop on the way to work. How she maintained that figure and flawless complexion on a diet of fast food and breakfasts on-the-go could only be attributed to youth and good genes. Georgy girl had an abundant supply of both.

I arrived at the McNally manse in plenty of time to get into a change of clothes and make a few notes in my journal before going to work on behalf of my two clients. Ursi was in the kitchen, removing the remains of breakfast; Father had left for the office and, so Ursi told me, Jamie and Mother were off in Mother's coveted wood-paneled Ford wagon in search of orphaned begonias in need of TLC.

"I made beef bourguignon last night and

those crispy roasted potatoes you like so much," Ursi informed me. "We missed you."

"Not as much as I missed you, I'm sure."

"I take it you were out on business," she said, puttering around the sink as if she wasn't curious to know where I had spent the night. The family had reconciled themselves to the fact that Connie and I were no longer seeing each other and I had told them about Georgy girl, but to date had not invited her to the house. Fools rush in, as they say, and I was no fool. Well, not most of the time.

Knowing how to divert our housekeeper from probing into my love life, I said, "A mix of business and pleasure, Ursi. I had drinks with Dennis Darling, as a matter of fact."

"The reporter for the scandal sheet," she exclaimed. "I hear he's come to Palm Beach to make trouble. What did you tell him?"

"Read all about it in *Bare Facts* magazine."

"Will they quote you, Archy?"

"I doubt it, as I didn't tell him anything he didn't already know." I poured myself a cup of coffee, which I intended to take to my room while I changed. The leader of the Ocean Boulevard domestic brigade would spread the word that I had met the enemy and vanquished him without firing a shot. "What's new with the rich folks, Ursi?" That stopped her from fussing over the sink.

"Well, that tennis player, Jackson Barnett, spent two nights on Phil Meecham's yacht, and isn't that a scandal? Mrs. Marsden tells me that Lady C has been on the ship-to-shore phone trying to get Mr. Meecham to turn Barnett over to her. Whatever happened to quality folks, Archy?"

Mrs. Marsden is Lady Cynthia's housekeeper and our Ursi's best friend and confidante. Also, Meecham's yacht is berthed in a first-class marina on Lake Worth, so the ship is not very far from the shore. "Quality folks, Ursi, have gone the way of the horseless carriage and the divorceless marriage. What do you hear about the boy who was drowned at the MacNiff party?"

"Poor child," Ursi said. "Who knows what those kids have gotten up to? Mrs. MacNiff is doing nicely, so Maria tells me. She's been in touch with the boy's father — Mrs. MacNiff, that is, not Maria — and the MacNiffs are paying all funeral expenses, though Lord knows they aren't obligated."

As happens in the land of unaffordable housing, sympathy had already shifted from poor Jeff to those his murder had inconvenienced, with the MacNiffs' show of noblesse oblige garnering all the attention and applause. Well, I care about Jeffrey Rodgers and I don't give a damn who knows it. I vowed there and then to bring his killer to justice regardless of whose toes I stepped on along the way. (Which reminded me, did Lance Talbot have nine or ten of those digits?)

Sitting at my desk I could indulge in an English Oval while sipping a cup of Ursi's home brew, after banishing the return of Joe Gallo to the nethermost regions of my mind. As a rule I am not opposed to competition, but I never play by the rules.

"The King Is Dead," I began, writing in black ink with my silver Montblanc pen. I must say I liked the title.

First question: Were these words the ranting of an old woman under the influence of a strong narcotic, administered to make her exit from this world as peaceful as possible, or was she trying to tell Malcolm MacNiff something about her newly returned grandson and heir?

Answer: To be determined.

I recorded what I had seen and heard at

the MacNiffs before and after the young waitress discovered Jeff's body in the pool, noting that Denny and I agreed Lance Talbot had not gone near the pool that afternoon. Here, I jotted down the name Holga von Brecht because she was linked to Lance Talbot. Recalling the daggers Vivian Emerson had directed at Holga across the net, I added her name to my roster which, in turn, got Joe Gallo on the list.

Next, I penned what I had learned during my lunch with Malcolm MacNiff and from my meeting with Dennis Darling. Putting it in writing, I find, is a good way to sort out the facts, refrain from jumping to conclusions and plan my next move, which, in this case, would be my first move.

I am not a believer in coincidences; therefore, if Jeff boasted he had something on Lance Talbot and was murdered, the odds were a million to one that Jeff was silenced because of what he had on Talbot. But even those odds did not rule out the possibility that Jeff was killed for reasons having nothing to do with Lance Talbot. Given similar odds, people do win lotteries and hit the jackpot playing one-armed bandits in casinos from Monte Carlo to

Las Vegas and all stops between. In short, assume nothing.

Be that as it may, if Denny and I were correct, one had to assume Lance Talbot was not the culprit, which was a pity as he was the most likely suspect. All good detectives, from Sherlock Holmes to dear Miss Marple, advise us to know thy victim. I didn't know Jeff Rodgers but I knew someone who did. A visit with Todd, born Edward, would be where I would begin my search for a dead king.

I pulled into our underground garage where Herb, our security guard, was on duty inside his glass kiosk. He waved me in with one hand while the other dialed Mrs. Trelawney's extension to report my arrival at the McNally Building on Royal Palm Way. She would record the time in her little pink book covered with forget-me-nots, a fitting symbol of Mrs. Trelawney's ability never to forget a thing she could use against me.

In my windowless glorified closet, the little red light was aglow and blinking on the machine I distinctly remember unplugging yesterday. Binky Watrous, our mail person, had no doubt wandered in to deliver my paltry assortment of fast food menus, adverts for recording devices one could hide in a hearing aid and envelopes that stated they were not to be opened by persons under eighteen. Binky reported the unplugged machine to Mrs. Trelawney — they work as a team — and she told him to reconnect me with the outside world.

Reluctantly I pressed the message button, which indicated I had two calls waiting.

"Archy. It's Denny. I'm having dinner with Lolly Spindrift tonight. He agreed as long as I didn't ask him any questions about Palm Beach socialites. I told him I used to cover Hollywood for the magazine and that we might swap stories one would never see in print. He said he could be persuaded. Cafe L'Europe at eight if you care to join us. Have you found out anything?" Click.

No, I would not care to join you and, no, I have not found out anything. I hit the vile button again.

"Connie here. Why didn't you return my call? Lady C is having temper tantrums. They say Meecham had a party on the *Sans Souci* last night that broke up at sunrise with everyone bedding down on the upper deck in sleeping bags. Two to a bag according to Lolly, who is taking delight in keeping Lady C posted on Jackson's lay-over in Palm Beach. You know Jackson was supposed to report to the coast for some kind of screen test but now we hear that the picture crew is coming here to accommodate him and Meecham has invited them all to stay on the *Sans Souci*. Lady C wants you to torpedo Meecham's yacht and deliver Jackson to her for safekeeping. Ta-ta." Click.

We'll see who gets torpedoed, Ms. Garcia. I dialed Connie, who presides over a communication system at the Horowitz mansion that would be adequate to service some small countries.

"Lady Cynthia's residence."

"Tell your lady boss that procuring is not only illegal, it's also immoral."

"Oh, simmer down, Archy. Madame just wants to make our visiting celebrity comfy."

"He seems perfectly comfy on Meecham's deck in a sleeping bag built for two."

"Who shared Jackson's bag?" Connie gushed.

"Didn't Lolly tell you?"

"No," she cried.

"Well, maybe you could speculate on it the next time you sit down with Georgy for a heart-to-heart."

Being a quick study it took Connie a beat and a half to come back with "Joe Gallo."

"Exactly. And how did you know Joe Gallo and Georgy were once engaged?" I asked, as if I didn't know.

"Georgy told me, that's how."

She certainly wasn't cowering under my interrogation, but then cowering wasn't Connie's style. She was a lovely Spanish spitfire who could make a ninety-year-old Buddhist monk rethink his vows. "I didn't know you and Georgy had become so chummy," I said.

"Just girl talk, Archy. Don't worry, I didn't mention your shortcomings."

"I wasn't aware of any shortcomings on my part," I told her.

"Well, compared to Alex . . ." She had the temerity to giggle.

"Alex is ten years younger than me."

"So is Georgy," she responded, none too kindly.

Being a gentleman I refrained from re-minding her that she was just a year or two younger than me, hence a number of years older than Alex. Instead I suggested we should refrain from double dating. "It only seems to exacerbate the difficulties we were having with our so-called open rela-tionship."

"The only thing open, Archy, was my door, and you walked out of it."

"And met Alejandro Gomez y Zapata coming in. Let's face it, Connie, you should have installed a turnstile."

"If I wasn't a lady I would tell you where to go, Archy McNally."

"I will get there without your guidance, thank you. Give my best to Alejandro and tell him I hope his invasion fares better than the last one."

"I will, Archy. And you give my regards to Lila Lee."

Click.

The woman was insufferable, but I got in the last word by pulling the plug on my answering machine. Then I pulled open the bottom drawer of my desk and removed a pile of mail I had never bothered to read. I was shocked to discover a pack of English Ovals beneath the rubble. I lit one, expediting my way to where Connie wanted me to go if she wasn't a lady, and felt immediately better.

I called the Pelican Club and heard the reassuring voice of Simon Pettibone. The Pettibone family is the mainstay of the Pelican. Patriarch Simon is our general manager, bookkeeper, maître d', bartender and bouncer. His wife, Jasmine, is our den

118

mother, and their children, Leroy and Priscilla, are chef and waitress, respectively. Mr. Pettibone is a tall, regal African American who bears a striking resemblance in looks and stature to the late performer, Paul Robeson.

"What can I do for you, Archy?" he graciously inquired.

"I need the phone number of the boy who comes in on Saturday nights to help Priscilla. He calls himself Todd, I believe."

"Has this anything to do with the young man who was drowned at the MacNiff benefit the other day? I believe Todd was there when it happened."

I have never had any reservations about confiding in Simon Pettibone, who was blessed with the tact of an ambassador-at-large. "It does, Mr. Pettibone."

"A terrible business, Archy. Hold on while I get my address book."

A moment later he was back on the line. "His name is Edward Brandt and I have a contact number for him in Lake Worth."

Edward Brandt was a fine name and Eddy was surely better than Toddy, but, as the Bard said, What's in a name? I called the number Mr. Pettibone had given me and was connected with a young lady who emoted "Hello" as if we were on intimate terms. I didn't know if I should pity or envy Todd, but leaned toward the latter. "May I speak with Todd, please?" I asked.

"Is this about a job?"

"No. It's a personal call. I'm a friend. Tell him Mr. McNally would like to speak to him."

When Todd came on the line he didn't waste a moment on pleasantries. "Is this about Jeff, Mr. McNally?"

"Yes, it is, Todd. I would like to ask you a few questions."

"The police have had us all on the hot seat for two days, Mr. McNally, and I can't tell you any more than I told them because I don't know anything about what happened to Jeff."

"How well did you know Jeff, Todd?"

"We were pretty tight," he said. "We teamed up about ten years ago when he left the Day School and got into my class here in Lake Worth."

"The Palm Beach Day School?" I blurted, unable to mask my surprise. "What was Jeff Rodgers doing there?"

"Going to school, of course," he mocked, and rightly so. "You mean, What was the likes of Jeff Rodgers doing at the posh and most expensive prep school in Florida?"

I was impressed with Todd's quick wit and politically incorrect approach to life in Palm Beach. "Okay," I said, "what was the likes of Jeff Rodgers doing at the Palm Beach Day School?"

"It's a long story, Mr. McNally."

And one I wanted to know. I was getting a tingle down my spine that told me I was on to something and I wasn't about to let it go. "You see, Todd, you know more than you think you know. Answers that shed light on a case are prompted by the right questions. Did you tell the police that Jeff had once attended the Day School?"

"They didn't ask," he said with a chuckle.

"Look, Todd, your friend is dead and a lot of people, including the police, think the murderer was one of Jeff's friends. Someone in your crowd."

"No way," he shouted into the phone.

"I agree. Help me and you'll be doing all your friends a service and maybe even get Jeff's murderer off the streets." At the time I didn't know how prophetic that statement was.

"What do you want me to do, Mr. McNally?"

"Give me a few minutes of your time, that's all. If I can come to your place now we can wrap it up in an hour."

He hesitated, then told me to hold on. I imagine he was discussing my request with his roommate. She must have agreed because when he returned he gave me his address.

"Have you guys had lunch?"

"What's that?" Todd answered with that fetching bit of mockery in his voice. I wondered if he had actually studied acting or if he possessed a natural talent for cajoling an audience. Either way, I thought Todd Brandt had star quality. I would have to remember to talk him into changing his name to Edward.

"Lunch is what happens between breakfast and dinner. How about a large pizza, half anchovies, half pepperoni, and what's your choice of beverage? I bet the police didn't treat you like this."

"Are you bribing me, Mr. McNally?"

"But of course."

"In that case I'll have a Coors Light."

"And your roommate?"

"Diet Coke," he answered without a consultation.

I filled the lunch order at the Bizarre Avenue Cafe which, bizarrely enough, is on Lake Avenue in Lake Worth, and picked up a six-pack of Coors at the local 7-

Eleven. I did not keep receipts as it is more expedient and more profitable to estimate my expenses — it also infuriates Mrs. Trelawney.

The house in the nine hundred block of South N Street was a two-story affair in peeling yellow-painted stucco. Todd Brandt occupied the ground floor. My knock was answered by a beautiful teenage girl with platinum-blond hair so straight it could have been ironed that morning. It fell to her shoulders on either side of a fringe of perfectly cut bangs. She was poured into a pair of jeans with a hole in one knee over which was a loose-fitting man's shirt with the tails hanging out. Todd was to be envied.

"Pizza man," I introduced myself.

"Hi. I'm Monica. Come on in."

I stepped into a minuscule hall before following Monica into the living room, which was furnished in things rattan, a grass rug and movie posters. The far wall was mostly sliding glass doors leading to what is called a Florida room, i.e., a screened-in patio. A long counter separated a fairly good-sized kitchen from the living room and was fronted by two backless bar stools.

Todd entered from a doorway opposite

the kitchen. "Hi, Mr. McNally. You've met Monica?" He took the square white cardboard box from me a moment before it singed the palms of both my hands and put it on the kitchen counter. Monica relieved me of the beer as she eyed my outfit, which consisted of freshly washed chinos, a black silk shirt, open collar, and a belted cord jacket. It's not easy to find a belted cord jacket and I hoped she appreciated the fact.

"Let's eat outside," Todd said. "Monica, get some paper plates and napkins. Do you need a glass, Mr. McNally?"

Not wishing to utilize anything that might need washing, I declined and, taking the six-pack, followed Todd to the glass doors, which I slid open, allowing him and the pizza to precede me. The patio boasted a redwood table, folding beach chairs in green and white nylon, and a gas barbecue minus a gas tank. "The place comes furnished," Todd said by way of telling me he had nothing to do with the decor, in or out.

Mother and I often describe people in terms of film stars, past and present. Now that Mother's memory is not what it used to be I am happy to have Georgy girl to play the game with. I would tell her that

Todd Brandt was a dead ringer for Richard Jaeckel, a boy-next-door type who played the young recruit in war films of the forties, often getting himself killed to ensure audience sympathy and sell war bonds.

Todd's hair is longish and sandyish, the exact shade depending on how much rinse he applies when he washes it and how much exposure it gets in the Florida sun. He has dark eyes, good teeth, and a smile that encourages people, especially older women, to overtip.

"How's the career going?" I asked when we were seated and the cardboard box opened to reveal the world's oldest repast — bread and cheese.

"I'm going into rehearsal for *Death of a Salesman* at the Lake Worth Playhouse."

"As Biff," I guessed.

"How'd you know?"

"Miller wrote it with you in mind."

"Thanks, Mr. McNally, only I wasn't born when he wrote it."

I wanted to say, Neither was I, but Monica joined us with the paper products and a Diet Coke, which, I suddenly realized, I had not brought. To compensate forgetting her I asked how her career was going.

"I'm on a break from the U. of Florida in Gainesville," she told me. "I came here to earn some bread working private parties and schlepping weekends at the Ambassador. I'm going back to school when the season is over."

"What are you studying?"

"Political science," she announced.

Well, whoever would have thunk it? "You have my vote, Monica."

She liked that and gave me a dimpled smile. I thought a modern day Grant Wood might preserve this couple in oil — Monica in her Holey jeans and Todd in his yellow Bermuda shorts — and call it American Neo-Gothic.

We all reached for a slice. I stuck to the anchovies as the Italian pepperoni gives me the Italian agita. Todd popped the tab on two cans of Coors Light and, the niceties out of the way, it was time to collect on my investment.

TEN

"A wiseguy and a malcontent," was Todd's take on his late buddy, Jeffrey Rodgers. "The grass was always greener in someone else's backyard and the backyard was always on the other side of the bridge in Palm Beach. He got petulant, as if he had been cheated out of his rightful place in the world, when he was a bartender and not a guest at the society shindigs we catered."

Todd's briefing was in response to my asking him to tell me what Jeff Rodgers was all about. We had all put away two slices and were now nursing our drinks as Todd spoke. My life, if nothing else, is a study in contrasts. Yesterday, lobster salad at Mar-a-Lago. Today, pizza and beer in the backyard of a furnished apartment. The latter, to be sure, had the advantage of the company of two charming young people who more than made up for the modest ambiance.

"And he worked the circuit. Palm Beach in the winter and East Hampton in the summer. He blew hot and cold with the rich, Mr. McNally. He didn't have a kind word for them but he couldn't stay away from them either. You know what I mean?"

"I think I do, Todd."

Todd sipped from his can of Coors before going on. "Then, a few months back, I'm not sure exactly when, he was all smiles and boasting that he was coming into a lot of money by way of a rich relative."

I sat forward in my beach chair. "Did you ever hear about a rich relation before this?"

"Never," Todd said. "I figured it was just more of Jeff's wishful thinking. He did a lot of that."

"He told me," Monica put in, "that when he went back north he was going to buy a house in the Hamptons and maybe open his own restaurant. He said if I wanted I could come to work for him."

"Do you think he was serious?" I directed this at Todd, refraining from asking if Jeff's supposed windfall surfaced with the arrival of Lance Talbot in our midst. I wanted neither to tip my hand nor taint Todd's memory with my input. As it turned out, Todd needed no prompting to introduce Lance Talbot as a major player in the life and times of Jeff Rodgers. If there was any doubt that Jeff was blackmailing Talbot, it would be dispelled before the remaining two slices of pizza grew cold.

"Jeff was a four-flusher, Mr. McNally. Always pointing out the guys and gals he was chummy with in his days at the Day School and telling anyone who would listen what he knew that could embarrass them. I think it was really frustrating for him when he worked parties they attended or served in restaurants they patronized. But I have to tell you, the way he was bragging these past weeks I started to believe that he was really coming into big money. He said if I came north with him, he would get me into the Actors Studio. Big deal. Who needs the method when you got a mug as cute as mine?" He laughed to tell me he was only kidding, but I knew better.

I was glad it was Todd who had brought up the Day School. It saved me from having to initiate the topic. Recalling our phone conversation, I said, "So what was the likes of Jeff Rodgers doing at the Day School?"

"Lance Talbot," Todd said, not having the slightest idea of the consequences of his disclosure.

I wanted to shout *Bingo!* but that would be gauche as well as premature. If I was about to learn the tie-in between Jeff Rodgers and Lance Talbot, my return on the cost of a pizza and a six-pack was bullish, indeed. The last thing I wanted was for Todd and Monica to guess my mission and go blabbing to their crowd that Archy McNally suspected Lance Talbot of Jeff's murder. My clients, the police and last, but most important, my father, would not be amused — nor would Lance himself, who would hire a lawyer to press a libel suit against me. Good grief, would father offer his services? I suspect he would.

This was my first break in the case and of interest to both my clients. My job now was to look, listen and make no moves until I was certain I was treading on solid bedrock and not quicksand.

"The story goes," Todd explained, "that Jeff's father was the Talbots' chauffeur. Jeff and Lance were about the same age and the boys became buddies, sharing the same sandbox on Ocean Boulevard. They were so tight that when Lance was enrolled in the Day School his mother sent Jeff along with him, picking up Jeff's tuition.

"Mr. Rodgers drove the boys to and from school and I bet from kindergarten on Jeff didn't want the other kids to know the chauffeur was his father. Given this was in Palm Beach, I would say everyone knew it.

"Then, when the boys were about ten, Lance's mother took off for Switzerland, taking Lance with her and ending Jeff's glory days at the Palm Beach Day School."

"Incredible," I uttered, and meant it. It was a story even the soaps would find too hokey to air. I could see Jeff at the bottom of the MacNiff pool, a half-smoked cigarette floating over a dead body; then I saw a ten-year-old being booted out of the only school he had ever attended. The chip on Jeffrey Rodgers's shoulder must have weighed a ton.

Was Jeff's father the chauffeur who accidentally closed the car door on young Lance's foot, causing his little toe to be amputated? I doubted if Todd knew anything about this and didn't volunteer the information. I was here to take, not give.

Thinking aloud, I heard myself saying, "Did Jeff see Lance when he returned to Palm Beach?"

Todd drained his can of beer before shaking his head and answering, "I don't know, Mr. McNally. If he did, he didn't mention it to me."

"But you do know Lance Talbot was at the MacNiff benefit you guys worked the

131

afternoon Jeff was shoved into the pool."

"Sure I know," Todd said.

"Did Jeff have anything to say about Lance that day?"

Again I got a shake of the professionally cut mop of hair. "We were busy, Mr. McNally, and had little time to do anything but our usual bitching and moaning."

I wanted to ask if he saw Jeff and Lance exchange any words that afternoon, or even if he noticed them in close proximity to each other, but didn't. I had learned enough and more talk of Lance Talbot and Jeff would only arouse suspicion. It was obvious that Todd hadn't a clue as to the connection between Jeff's alleged windfall and Lance's arrival in Palm Beach and I wanted to keep it that way for now.

"Todd," I said, "I'm sure the police asked you if you know anyone who wanted to harm Jeff, but I can't leave without asking the same thing."

"I have no idea, Mr. McNally. I swear to you, I don't. We all smoke a little pot, you know that, and we've all tried the trendy pills like Ecstasy now and again, but none of our crowd, including Jeff, is into any heavy scene in that direction. What I'm saying is, Jeff wouldn't be in debt to a dealer."

"What about a jilted lover, woman or man?" I probed.

"If Jeff was hustling, I didn't know it."

"Did you see anyone go from the tennis courts to the pool after Jeff went on his break, about the time we talked?"

"Negative," he responded before asking, "Are you looking into this on behalf of Mr. MacNiff? I mean because it happened on his turf."

"I am, Todd, but I would rather it wasn't common knowledge."

"I understand," he said. "I know it's your job, but the police have been over all this with me and the entire catering staff." With that note of mocking innuendo he added, "Have they questioned the guests?"

"I'm sure they have, and it's still going on. In fact, I'm waiting for my call. Even Jackson Barnett has been told not to leave town."

At the mention of Jackson Barnett, Todd and Monica exchanged a look that told me the name was of profound interest to one or both of them. Verifying the thought, Monica said, "Todd wants to ask you something."

"About Jackson Barnett? All I know about him is what I read in the sport pages and gossip columns."

"Me too," Todd said, "so I know he's going to do a film for a major Hollywood studio. Lolly Spindrift wrote that Jackson was staying on Phil Meecham's yacht, and that the studio is sending a crew here because Jackson can't go to Hollywood for the preliminary tests, and Meecham has invited the crew to stay aboard the *Sans Souci*."

When he paused to catch his breath, I said, "So I've heard."

"You know Mr. Meecham," Todd stated rather than asked.

With a sigh, Monica brought the painful scene to a head, saying, "He wants to ask you if you'll help him get a job on Meecham's yacht so he can be discovered."

"Can it, Monica," Todd advised.

I like Todd Brandt and he had been a great help to me today. Not wishing to rain on his parade, I didn't say I believed Lolly's story was more hyperbole than fact, but told him I would try to get him aboard the *Sans Souci* when and if the cameras began to grind.

"I would be more noticed if I was working for Meecham. Bartender, deck boy, anything like that."

"I don't think I would like to see you join Phil's crew, Todd. Believe me, it's

134

not your kind of gig."

He grinned charmingly. "I know all about Meecham and his boys and girls, Mr. McNally, but I can take care of myself."

"Really, Todd? I strongly suspect Jeff Rodgers believed he could take care of himself, too."

I had a lot to think about on my drive back to Palm Beach, not the least of which was envisioning Jeff Rodgers's frame of mind the day he was murdered. Know thy victim. "A wiseguy and a malcontent." The malcontent must have been seething as he watched his boyhood chum, now come into millions, cavorting among the Palm Beach elite with a beautiful and mysterious older woman on his arm, while the wiseguy was plotting his revenge.

Passing the GulfStream on my approach to the bridge, I thought of Denny and what a great story this was going to make for his avid readers. If rags to riches was a popular theme — rags to riches to rags would get Darling a movie deal. Pauper meets prince, pauper loses prince, pauper dies because of what he learned about the prince. Nice plot, except the prince did not kill the pauper and there was a ten-year span between the pauper's exile and his untimely death.

Jeff and Lance were friends years ago, when they both attended the Palm Beach Day School and even before that. When the boys were about ten, Lance and his mother left Palm Beach to make their home in Switzerland. If Jeff knew something disparaging about Lance it went back to the first ten years of their lives, when they were mere tots. Surely, Jeff wasn't killed because he knew Lance was a rake with the girls in the first grade or had plagiarized an essay in the fourth grade.

A detective is akin to a plastic surgeon reconstructing the face of an accident victim. The PI gathers the facts, puts them together and comes up with a scenario that he hopes is a true replica of the events as they happened. A skilled surgeon probably works from a photo of the guy going under the scalpel. In both cases you end up with a reproduction. At best, a plausible likeness, at worst, a distortion of the truth.

Excuse the analogy, but was Lance Talbot wearing a surgical mask that was a good likeness but a distortion of the truth? If Lance didn't commit a major indiscretion in the first ten years of his life, the only thing Jeff could have against him was

136

that he wasn't who he claimed to be. My rationale was Nifty's feeling that old Mrs. Talbot had some doubts about her grandson she either wasn't able to articulate or wasn't able to define. Neither Jeff nor Mrs. Talbot had seen Lance in ten years. Could Jeff have discerned something about his boyhood friend that a sick old lady could only puzzle over? If Jeff's father was the chauffeur that caused the accident, Jeff would know about the amputated toe. Could Jeff have had a look at the returned Lance's feet? Unlikely.

This line of thinking had me heading straight for the MacNiff house to report what I suspected. Purposely, I made a detour to Seaview Avenue and drove past the Palm Beach Day School. A charming, light and airy edifice surrounded by palm trees, it looks like an ideal setting for the young and privileged. Noted for their soccer team, the Bulldogs, the school recently enrolled two boys, one from Italy, the other from England, to join the varsity squad, living up to its claim that "Beyond academics, the Palm Beach Day School stresses the importance of community service, athletics, fine art and social skills." Jeff must have loved it.

I drove the Miata off the A1A, or Ocean

Boulevard if you prefer, and into the MacNiff driveway, pulling up short of the three-car garage that displayed the tails of a Rolls and a BMW. The third door was closed so one could only guess what it was hiding. My ring was answered by Maria Sanchez in a white uniform that would not be out of place in a hospital's intensive care unit. Maria is a shapely woman with the hourglass figure so popular a hundred years ago. I wanted to encourage her with the fact that what goes around, comes around.

"Mr. McNally," she said, as if I were the last person she expected to find on the MacNiffs' doorstep.

"In person, Maria. May I come in?"

"Yes. Please." She opened the door to allow me to step into the entrance foyer, which was modest by Palm Beach standards. I doubt if it could hold more than a string quartet and a dozen waltzing couples. The furnishings of the MacNiff home are not Louis Seize or Louis Didn't Say, but American and British antiques worthy of the Winterthur collection. Wood, not gilt, dominated, making the display more home and hearth than awesome. But then the landed gentry don't have to dazzle to intimidate.

"When you call Ursi to tell her I'm here, Maria, would you mention that I will be home for dinner this evening?"

Maria blushed scarlet. "Mr. McNally. I no do such a *ting*, you bad boy." My word, she sounded like Carmen Miranda.

"Before you no do such a *ting*, would you announce me to Mr. MacNiff?"

"Sí. I go now. They are in the drawing room."

When Maria returned she beckoned me onward and I followed her into the drawing room where I had commiserated with Nifty after the abrupt termination of his *Tennis Everyone!* benefit. Mrs. MacNiff was seated on a lovely couch (Duncan Phyfe) with a tabby on her lap and two other cats, a gray and a black, reclining on Mr. Phyfe's masterpiece. The three felines eyed the intruder with suspicion. I am not a cat person and suspected they could tell. Also, my lunch was beginning to talk back.

Nifty was in a wing chair (Queen Anne), reading *The Wall Street Journal*. Both were dressed casually, she in skirt, blouse and sensible oxfords, he in flannels and a rugby shirt. Nifty made a motion to rise but I stopped him with a wave of my hand. "Don't get up, sir. I won't keep you. I just wanted to report what I've learned regarding . . ." I hesitated and was saved by Mrs. MacNiff.

"Lance Talbot," she said. "I know all about it, Archy. Why don't you have a seat." She patted the space next to her on the Duncan Phyfe, annoying the cats. "Shoo, Iago. You, too, Othello." When I started at hearing the names she laughed, saying, "And this, of course, is Desdemona."

I couldn't think of a more compatible trio. "Is she married to Othello?" I asked, gingerly taking the place Othello and Iago had vacated. They had retreated to the far corner of the couch, relinquishing their position, but not their domain.

"Actually, he prefers Iago, who we discovered was a female after we had named her. Or, I should say, Othello discovered she was a female."

Looking at the two snuggling in a corner of the sofa I hoped the MacNiffs had checked for themselves and not relied solely on Othello's scrutiny. One never knows, do one?

"Can we offer you a drink, Archy?" Mr. MacNiff asked.

"No, thank you, sir. I had two slices of pizza with anchovies and a can of beer for lunch and a drink would be like trying to put out a fire with gasoline."

Mrs. MacNiff laughed heartily at my little jest. She is a small woman with dark blue eyes and a smiling face covered with nothing more than a dusting of powder and framed by a halo of white hair that showed no trace of blue.

"I swear that jacket once belonged to Malcolm," Mrs. MacNiff stated.

"I beg your pardon, ma'am?"

"She means the Lilly Pulitzer you donned for the interview," her husband explained.

I was certainly getting a lot of mileage out of that romp. "I said it belonged to my father but he swears he never owned one," I told them.

"Knowing Prescott, I'm sure he didn't," Nifty said.

"And how is your mother?" Mrs. MacNiff asked.

"Fine, except for a little forgetfulness now and then."

"Tell me about it," she said. "I walk into rooms and wonder what I'm doing there."

"Well, dear, we know why Archy is here and I would like to hear what he has to report," Nifty gently chided his wife.

"Oh, I forgot all about that," she responded, giving me a sly wink.

I waited until I was certain both parties had their say before beginning my report. "Well, sir, I fear I have some disquieting news."

Hearing this Iago arched his back — excuse me, her back — and meowed. Nifty began to fold his newspaper as if it would be some time before he could return to it. "Let's have it, Archy," he said.

"You asked me to learn what I could about the newly arrived Lance Talbot and poke my nose into the unfortunate demise of Jeff Rodgers."

"We spoke to Mr. Rodgers," Mrs. MacNiff announced. "The funeral is tomorrow. I don't know if we should attend . . ."

"Helen!" Nifty cut her off. "Please let Archy have his say."

"Sorry, dear."

"I'm afraid there's a connection between the two, sir," I related.

"Connection?" Nifty questioned, as if he had suffered a gross injustice.

"It seems, sir, that Jeff Rodgers and Lance Talbot were boyhood friends. In fact, they attended the Palm Beach Day School together, at Mrs. Talbot's expense. Mrs. Talbot being Lance's mother, not his grandmother."

"He must be the other boy in the picture," Mrs. MacNiff exclaimed. "Don't look at me like that, Malcolm. You asked me to dig up a picture of young Lance to give Archy, and I found one." The tabby flew off her lap a moment before Mrs. MacNiff got to her feet and went straight for the desk-on-frame. I will say the MacNiffs' treasures were for use and not for show.

From the drawer she removed a small photo and proudly handed it to me. I found myself looking at two boys, aged nine or ten, in baseball uniforms, their gloved hands raised as if they were shagging flies.

"The boy on your right is young Lance as I remember him," Mrs. MacNiff told me.

He could or could not be the Lance Talbot now in Palm Beach. This was the trouble I had anticipated from the start when asking to see a photo of young Lance. One changes in ten years. Especially the years from prepubescence to maturity. The other boy could be Jeff Rodgers or any other boyhood friend of Lance Talbot. But I now knew of someone who could tell me if the other boy was Jeff. In fact, it could be the person who had taken the photo. Jeff's father.

Watching me scrutinize the photo, Nifty said, "I've been looking at it since Helen pulled it out of her collection. All I can say is it doesn't disprove Talbot's claim of being Margaret's grandson. I mean he's a white, Anglo-Saxon male."

"Is that racist, Malcolm? Or sexist?" Mrs. MacNiff wondered.

"No, dear, it's a fact."

"My feelings exactly, sir," I said. "Mind if I keep the photo, Mrs. MacNiff?"

"Please do, Archy. I wish I could be of more help but you must remember that Malcolm and I were close to Margaret Talbot but seldom came in contact with Jessica and young Lance. Jessica was always a bit of a loner. Do you think the boy is an imposter? Poor Aunt Margaret was rather vague on the subject."

"My dear, she was on her deathbed," Nifty reminded his wife. "Where did you learn that Lance and Jeff were once buddies?"

"From a friend of Jeff's," I told him. Then, not wishing to prolong the inevitable, I dropped the other shoe. "I have reason to believe Jeff Rodgers was blackmailing Lance Talbot, sir."

Iago leaped from her corner onto my lap.

ELEVEN

I told the MacNiffs as much as I could without compromising Denny's position. One cannot serve two masters, especially when their interests converge. Judging by the speed with which this case was progressing, I would say Denny and Nifty were fast approaching a collision course, with Archy poised at the crossroads. In a very short time I would have to make them aware of each other, but not right now. I needed solid proof that Jeff was blackmailing Talbot and what secret he possessed that enabled him to do so. The reason for the blackmail was the crux of my case and Jeff Rodgers took the reason to his grave.

"This is very disquieting," Nifty said after listening to my spiel. "If this boy, Jeff, was killed because of what he had on Lance Talbot, we have to assume that Lance is the murderer."

"Assume nothing, is my credo, Mr. MacNiff, and remember, I said I could vouch for Talbot not being near the pool at the crucial time. You, Dennis Darling,

Talbot and I played a set just prior to the time of the murder. After our game Lance Talbot didn't stray far from the tennis courts. In fact I saw him talking on his cell phone about the time Jeff was chloroformed and pushed into the pool."

"Perhaps he hired a hit man," Mrs. MacNiff suggested. "Or should I say a hit person?"

"Helen, really!" her husband admonished.

"If he did," I reminded Mrs. MacNiff, "he, or she, was recruited from among your guests."

"Oh, dear," she lamented, "I never thought of that."

Mention of the MacNiffs' guests reminded me of Vivian Emerson and I asked Mrs. MacNiff if she knew her.

"I can't say I do, Archy. I'll have to check my guest registry. Is it important?"

"I'm not sure, ma'am. I suspect she knows the von Brecht woman and as von Brecht is staying with Lance Talbot I think I should try to learn the connection between the two women. There's no rush. At your convenience, is fine."

"Do you think Holga von Brecht and Lance Talbot are lovers, Archy? They say she's eighty if she's a day."

"Helen," Nifty sighed. "Archy is not here to gossip, and that woman's love life and age are not your business."

"Oh, Malcolm, don't be such a party pooper," she accused. "She's living with the boy who claims to be Aunt Margaret's grandson, and if we want to know more about him, Holga von Brecht is the only person who can help us. She knew him in Switzerland and none of us did."

Score one for Helen MacNiff. I nodded in agreement, but very cautiously. Iago was now asleep on my lap and I thought it imprudent to disturb her. The sages tell us to let sleeping cats lie.

"Holga and Lance are very close," I offered, "be they lovers or just friends. We must remember that she will not tell us, or anyone, anything she doesn't want known. That's why I'm interested in talking to someone who might know Holga and be willing to share."

This was not the time or place to add that I believed there were ill feelings between Holga and Vivian Emerson, which might prompt Vivian to blab more than if they were on friendly terms.

"And who is this person who told you the dead boy had information on Lance Talbot he was trying to sell?" Nifty asked.

"I'm afraid, sir, I can't divulge my source at this time. I promised him anonymity." It was as good a line as any and one people read so often in their daily newspaper they never think to question it.

"How exciting," Mrs. MacNiff said, pleased that her husband had been rebuffed. "Is your informant anyone we know, Archy?"

"Helen, we're not here to play twenty questions, either," Nifty snapped, rousing Iago, who looked up at me and meowed. "And you think Jeff had reason to believe that Lance Talbot is an imposter?"

"Just a hunch, sir. Coupled with what you told me about Mrs. Talbot's doubts, I couldn't think of anything else Jeff might have on Lance. As Mrs. MacNiff just said, Lance has been away from these parts for ten years and Jeff Rodgers has never left here. What else could he know?"

"It seems far-fetched," Nifty claimed, "that the boy would know something Aunt Margaret didn't."

"But she did know something," Mrs. MacNiff cried. "The king is dead. The king must be Lance."

Nifty shook his head. "King? Why not *prince?* Or *my grandson?* It makes no sense."

"I don't know why she used the word

148

king, sir, but I now believe that Mrs. Talbot was on to something. At first I suspected her words were the rambling of a heavily sedated old lady. But now that we suspect this person calling himself Lance Talbot was being blackmailed by a childhood friend who was as close to him then as was his grandmother, I have to conclude that Mrs. Talbot was not hallucinating."

"Archy, I appreciate the fact that you can't disclose your source, but are you certain he, or she, is reliable? Did Jeff Rodgers actually talk to this person and try to sell him information on Lance Talbot?"

"The answer is yes to both questions, sir. And don't forget, Jeff had been boasting to his friends that he was going to come into big money very soon. The connection between these facts cannot be ignored."

"Oh, I have no intention of ignoring anything, Archy. I owe it to Aunt Margaret to get at the truth, not only as the executor of her estate but as an old and dear friend. What I didn't count on was the murder of a young man in my pool. As I said, it's disquieting."

"Don't worry, dear, Archy will sort it all out," Mrs. MacNiff said with more conviction than I felt at the moment. Despite their little tiffs her words of consolation were a clear indication of the unwavering affection between the long-married couple. How like my parents, I thought. Would I, one day, be so blessed? *Tempus fugit,* Archy, *tempus fugit.*

The question I was waiting for now came from Nifty. "How much of this do the police know, Archy?"

"None of it," I said. "And until I have solid proof of the connection between Jeff and Lance Talbot I have no obligation to report what I've learned to them. Finger-pointing based on hearsay and speculation is dangerous and libelous."

Nifty liked that. Until proven otherwise, Lance Talbot was one of *us,* and if he was being blackmailed for any reason other than his true identity — well, the less the police knew, the better. Nifty's crowd firmly believed that to err is human and to forgive divine — as long as it was one of them being errant.

I hated to put a damper on Nifty's divinity but I thought I should prepare him for the worst. "Right now the police are interested in Jeff's friends and associates but when they come up with nothing, which I think they will, they'll have to look . . ."

"In our backyard," Mrs. MacNiff concluded.

I was enjoying this delightful lady's charm and wit but I fear her husband had had his fill of it. "Everyone at the benefit, Helen, wasn't a friend of ours."

"Yes, dear. But the scene of the crime was our backyard."

He couldn't argue with that, so he jumped on me. "What's the next step, Archy?"

"Well, sir, I was hoping you might give a party."

"A party? Are you mad, Archy?"

"Actually, sir, a pool party."

"The toe," the clever Mrs. MacNiff cried. "The next step is to see if our Lance Talbot is or is not missing the little toe on his right foot."

"Exactly," I said. "It will end all the guesswork and I can't think of any other way of going about it short of asking him to remove his shoe and sock. That would be unseemly."

"I think," Nifty countered, "giving a party around the scene of the crime, as Helen put it, would be unseemly."

"Nonsense," she answered. "The police have removed all their yellow tape we were not supposed to cross and the grandchildren will be here this weekend and I refuse to tell them the pool is off-limits. We can't avoid using it forever, Malcolm, and I think Archy has given us the perfect reason for doing so now."

"When we began probate with Aunt Margaret's lawyer," Nifty said thoughtfully, "Lance submitted his passport for the required identification. As I recall it passed muster, meaning it contained his picture."

"Was it a picture of his face or his foot, Malcolm?"

"Oh, Helen, for God's sake be serious."

"I am," she said, and she did have a point.

"If I may venture a guess, sir, Lance's original passport was applied for when he was ten years old. If he and his mother traveled around Europe, I imagine the photo was updated as the boy grew. The last update could have been made when he came here, at which time a new photo was taken of the man claiming to be Lance Talbot."

"Very good, Archy," Mrs. MacNiff complimented. Naturally, I concurred.

Still looking for an out, Nifty argued, "Suppose he flatly refuses to come to our pool party?"

"That, sir, will tell us a lot, too. If he knows about the amputated toe, he'll avoid being seen barefoot. If he doesn't know about it, he'll fall into our trap. If he is the real Lance Talbot it makes no difference either way, so why not have a go at it?"

"Why not, Malcolm?" my ally joined in.

"Okay," he relented. "You make the arrangements, Helen, and don't forget to ask the von Brecht woman, too. I have some papers the boy must sign, so you might use that as an excuse for the visit, then tell him to bring his trunks as we're having a few people in for lunch and a dip. If it doesn't rain that day, he'll be one of those people who swim in rubber shoes or fins."

"Your optimism is appreciated, Malcolm," Mrs. MacNiff quipped.

"May I suggest someone whom I would like to be invited?"

"Of course, Archy," Mrs. MacNiff quickly replied. "A lady friend?"

"Thank you, ma'am, I'll think about that. It was Dennis Darling I had in mind."

"The investigative snoop?" Nifty said, pulling a face. "His magazine offered my charity trust a hefty check plus an invitation to our journalism students to submit their work with a promise to publish the best of the lot. All they asked in return was for Darling to be included in the *Tennis Everyone!* event. How could I refuse?"

"Clearly you couldn't, sir," I agreed.

"Why him?" Mrs. MacNiff asked me.

Anticipating the question, I had concocted a reply that was not entirely untrue. "Everyone is aware that Darling is in Palm Beach to gather information for a so-called exposé on our town. I want to see how Lance Talbot acts in the presence of a seasoned reporter nosing around for salacious scandal. If Talbot has something to hide besides his right foot, it should be an engaging afternoon."

Seeing Nifty about to protest, I added, "I know Talbot met Darling briefly the day of the benefit, but that was on the tennis court and I doubt if Talbot knew who Darling was that afternoon."

If Jeff was using Dennis Darling as a threat, Talbot damn well knew who and what Dennis Darling was all about when he faced him across that net. I wanted Denny at the pool party for the reason I had given the MacNiffs. He was a cunning and experienced observer of scams and the people who made a living off them. I had to convince Nifty of this without outing Denny.

Nifty stated his position. "I don't want it to appear that we're encouraging a snoop and tattling on our neighbors."

Mrs. MacNiff told it like it was, saying,

"The word is out along the Boulevard to shun Mr. Dennis Darling."

I told her I knew this. "But we have a mission, and Darling can be of help to us even if he doesn't know it." Appealing to Mrs. MacNiff, I pleaded, "Let's have him for the same reason you felt it was not inappropriate to use the pool so soon after the tragedy — to learn if the man calling himself Lance Talbot is who he claims to be."

My pep talk was met with silence, except for Iago who started to purr in triumph as my eyes began to itch.

Nodding, Nifty broke the spell. "In a sense, we would be using Darling, not him using us."

"Exactly, sir," I encouraged, eager to depart the MacNiff abode and my lapmate, whom I now believed to be a witch.

"So be it," Nifty stated with a sigh of resignation.

Already planning her guest list, Helen MacNiff asked no one in particular, "Do you think we should have the tennis player, too? He was so good to help us out and now he's stuck here because of it."

"That would be very nice," I mumbled, nudging Iago before getting to my feet. She hissed her indignation before slinking back to Othello. "Before I go I would like to have Talbot's Swiss lawyer's name and his fax number. Also, Mr. Rodgers's phone number. Did you say the funeral is tomorrow, Mrs. MacNiff?"

"It is, Archy. St. Edward's on North County Road. Eleven tomorrow morning."

Well, if Jeff had been barred from joining the *noblesse* in life he was certainly having his last hurrah in their bailiwick. In the halcyon days of the Kennedy administration, when Charlie Wrightsman's mansion was known as the Palm Beach White House, St. Edward's was the place to be seen on Sunday mornings in your Saturday night attire. It made a statement.

Being given the information I requested, I took my leave. With a firm handshake, Nifty told me to keep him posted. Mrs. MacNiff asked to be remembered to my mother. Then, when I was almost out the door, she called after me. "Oh, Archy, do you know where Dennis Darling is staying?"

"The GulfStream," I responded without thinking.

"Thank you," she cooed, stroking Desdemona's back.

I was glad Helen MacNiff was on our side.

On the ride back to Royal Palm Way I decided it was time to apprise Father of what his favorite son had been up to these past two days. We talked last the night before my lunch date with Malcolm MacNiff, which now seemed aeons ago in light of all that had transpired since then. If Father was going to make a bid for Lance Talbot's business, I thought it advisable to inform him that this Lance Talbot might not be the grandson and heir of the late Margaret Talbot, thereby earning my keep.

The way to Father's executive suite is guarded by my favorite nemesis, Mrs. Trelawney.

"Well," she exclaimed as I stepped off the elevator. "If it isn't the man who does everything but windows, and where did you ever find a belted cord jacket?"

"So, you read the interview."

"Who didn't?" she said, as if I were the sole cause of a national decline in literary values. "Archy McNally attended Yale. Strange, your class year was omitted."

"He didn't ask, so I didn't tell," I tossed back. Mrs. Trelawney and I are never happier than when we are engaged in a spirited game of verbal knock-hockey. "I don't do windows because my office lacks one.

I'm the guy in the converted broom closet, lest you forget, and my jacket is from one of the better men's shops on the Esplanade, an area of our community bereft of your patronage."

Mrs. Trelawney favors severely tailored suits, usually pinstripe with padded shoulders, the skirt hemmed at midcalf. Pincenez, lapel watch and penny loafers complete the picture of a Katharine Gibbs grad from the Eisenhower era. Her grammar is impeccable, her spelling faultless and her attendance record perfect. In short, she is as indispensable to McNally & Son as the law degree hanging over my father's desk.

"The office that has a chronic problem with the answering machine recently installed at company expense?"

"One and the same, Mrs. Trelawney. The plug keeps popping out of the wall socket."

"So Binky tells me. He's had to reconnect you several times in the past two days."

"Which keeps his nose out of other people's mail."

"Binky is a great help to me," she said, as if I didn't know. Moving right along she glibly asked, "And what did Officer O'Hara have to say about your confusing her with your pet canine in print?"

Mrs. Trelawney takes vicarious pleasure, though some would say vicious, in my love life. Mr. Trelawney, who was an auditor for the IRS, filed his final return some years back, leaving his widow a modest pension and his government guide on the arts of spying, probing and harassing.

"Georgy is a good sport," I lied.

"And what did Connie have to say, may I ask?"

"Why do you ask permission after the fact, Mrs. Trelawney?" My dander aroused, I let go with another whopper. "Connie and I are the best of friends."

"With a hunk like Alejandro on her arm, Connie can afford to be generous," was her cutting reply.

Getting out while behind, I stated, "It's always a pleasure sparring with you, Mrs. Trelawney, but right now, I need to borrow a pad and pen with which to write a fax I would like you to type up and send it ASAP."

"Where is it going, Archy?"

"Bern, Switzerland. To Mr. Gregory Hermann, Esq."

"Do you have a charge number?"

"A what?" I remonstrated.

"Archy, you must start reading office

memos before stuffing them in the bottom drawer of your desk to hide your English Ovals."

There wasn't a nook or cranny in the McNally Building that wasn't subject to search by our Mrs. Trelawney. I vowed to stuff that drawer with enough unmentionables in a variety of colors and flavors to knock the intruder off her pins.

"Your father and I created a list of all possible reasons one might incur extraordinary expenses and assigned each a number," she lectured with all the patience of a first-grade teacher leading a classroom full of hyperactives. "A fax to Switzerland is extraordinary, thus I need a charge number."

Knowing better, but having nothing to lose, I ventured, "What is the number for *miscellaneous?*"

"There is no such thing as a miscellaneous extraordinary expense, Archy." She shrugged her shoulders dramatically, setting her dangling pince-nez and lapel watch in motion. "Which reminds me, the outrageous expense report you handed in last week was charged entirely to miscellaneous."

"And that should be reason enough to assign it a number," I advised while reaching for a pad and pen. Mrs. Trelawney huffed and puffed as I wrote a brief message to Hermann, stressing the urgency to contact me soonest regarding Lance Talbot and the von Brechts without so much as a hint of our doubts regarding the legitimacy of his former client. Coming on Father's stationery, Hermann was apt to think the request concerned nothing more than a routine legal matter.

Mrs. Trelawney mellowed considerably when she read my note. Impressed, she politely asked, "Lance Talbot? Are you working for him?" Suddenly, the only extraordinary thing at McNally & Son was my presumed business association with the heir apparent. Such is the power of the Talbot name in this town.

"I have a finger in several miscellaneous enterprises, Mrs. Trelawney." I do so enjoy kicking people when they're down.

"Could one of them be that poor waiter who was killed at the MacNiff fete?" she asked. "I hear you were on the scene when it happened."

"Just clearing up a few details for Mr. MacNiff. What do the papers say?"

"Not much," she answered. "They're still questioning people, mostly the catering staff, and Jackson Barnett is being detained although the police keep repeating that he's not a suspect. Is he really camping out on Phil Meecham's yacht?"

Let me make it perfectly clear that the word *camping* in Mrs. Trelawney's lexicon means sleeping under the stars and nothing more — Phil Meecham notwithstanding. "According to Lolly Spindrift, he spurns a berth in favor of a sleeping bag *à deux*," I reported.

"That sounds dirty," Mrs. Trelawney frowned, proving Oscar Wilde's assumption that if one speaks German, no one listens, and if one speaks French, everyone thinks it's naughty. Not wishing to further titillate our monarch's equerry I asked in plain English, "Is our leader in?"

"He is," she said, "and he's been asking for you. I take it you didn't sleep at home last night."

"As a matter of fact I shared a sleeping bag with Jackson Barnett."

"You are impossible, Archy McNally."

I knocked before entering the inner sanctum. Father, all prim and proper, was seated behind his desk, stroking his mustache.

"Ah, Archy. I'm so glad you're here. I have some interesting news."

162

I took a visitor's chair and waited to be enlightened.

"I received a call from Lance Talbot," he said with obvious glee. "While he intends to keep his grandmother's attorney, he wants to diversify and employ us primarily on a consulting basis. Needless to say, I told him we would be honored to be of service."

"Well, sir," I commenced, "I, too, have some interesting news."

TWELVE

"This is very disquieting," Father reflected woefully.

I seemed to be the bearer of disquieting news this afternoon, however I remembered to be thankful that the messenger of ill tidings is no longer shot for his troubles.

While Father liked nothing better than to recruit a new paying client, especially one of note as well as fortune, he would gladly surrender gain in the pursuit of justice. Prescott McNally ran an honest game and the apple does not fall far from the tree.

His grandiose mustache prevented him from exhibiting a stiff upper lip but an insistent tug on it betrayed his dismay at learning a well-heeled client might in fact be a penniless swindler. "I made no definite appointment to meet with young Talbot," he said. "We left it that he would contact me when things were more settled. In light of what you've told me, Archy, I now wonder what he meant."

"I wouldn't start looking for dark,

hidden meanings behind his every word at this stage of our inquiry. I think, sir, when he does call you should meet with him and conduct business as usual. No sense in jeopardizing what could be a lucrative liaison in the event this is all a red herring."

"Good point, Archy," he answered with an appreciative nod. While this thought didn't cajole him into stroking his guardsman's mustache, it did ease the serious tugging. "I take it this problem has gone no further than you and Malcolm."

"And Mrs. MacNiff, sir." That I confided in Father was S.O.P. for the team of McNally and son. It was not only my obligation to keep him in the loop when on a case, it was also beneficial to air my thoughts and profit from his legal expertise and learned feedback.

"Am I to understand that you have not told this reporter what Malcolm suspects regarding Talbot; nor have you told Malcolm that Darling informed you of the blackmail scheme?"

"That is correct, sir, and I have my reasons. I promised Darling anonymity because if it gets around that he's down here to investigate a blackmail threat against Lance Talbot, it will start a media stampede to Palm Beach and cost him his exclusive, if there is a story here. However, I believe Mrs. MacNiff suspects that I have been in contact with Darling."

"Helen is a very clever woman," Father said.

"And a very engaging one," I added, before continuing. "And I didn't tell Darling that the executor of Mrs. Talbot's estate is uncertain of young Talbot's claim because less said, soonest mended. The collateral from such gossip could prove disastrous."

"Very wise, Archy," father complimented. "I imagine Darling is looking for something libidinous in Talbot's past. Has he said anything about the woman who is visiting with Talbot?"

Visiting? Now there was a euphemism if ever I heard one. A true Victorian, Father always substitutes a socially acceptable word for one that might even hint at sexual impropriety. Thus, we get "visiting with" as opposed to the more brazen "living with."

"She wasn't even mentioned," I reported. "Could be that Denny doesn't even know about Lance's relationship with Holga von Brecht. He's a new arrival in town and, his reputation preceding him, people are not opening up to him, but I expect his date with Lolly Spindrift tonight will change all that."

"Denny?" Father questioned, arching one eyebrow. This is a trick he has mastered to perfection and one that escapes me.

"We got rather chummy," I admitted. "He's not at all what one would expect of an ambulance-chasing newsman, crass and overbearing. I found him very well bred and, if anything, more laid back than aggressive. I think you would like him, sir."

"Well, I hope you're still chummy when he learns you've been holding out on him."

"After the pool party it might not be necessary for Denny to know I've been less than truthful with him. If Talbot is missing that little toe — so be it, amen, and *finis* my business with Malcolm MacNiff. From that point on I'll be working only for Dennis Darling, trying to uncover Jeff's secret and perhaps his murderer."

Father eyed me thoughtfully. "Talbot's true identity, or what Jeff might have known about him that could prove pernicious to Talbot's reputation or claim, doesn't interest you as much as finding the person who murdered Jeff Rodgers. Am I right?"

"You are, sir."

"Be careful, Archy. If Jeff was murdered

because of what he knew, the murderer won't hesitate to eliminate anyone seeking to learn Jeff's secret. The closer you get to the solution, the more dangerous the game. A man who would chloroform a boy and shove him into a pool to drown is deranged and consequently a formidable enemy. As always, you have my blessing in this, but I insist you act with caution and not bravado."

We McNallys are not a demonstrative clan, so I refrained from any show of gratitude for his concern, which I knew would only embarrass him. Also, as I was arranging a pool party on Ocean Boulevard in Palm Beach, and not a breaking-and-entering raid on a harem in some unfriendly desert kingdom, any panoply of emotion would be gratuitous, if not mawkish.

On that note, I rose, saying, "Your point is taken, sir, and I will keep you posted."

It had been a day of awesome disclosures, but the best, or worst, was yet to come. The messenger was no less a personage than he who wheels his mail cart through the hallowed halls of McNally & Son, ever vigilant for homeless plugs. I speak of Binky Watrous, possessor of the doleful brown eyes of a doe caught in the headlights of a speeding SUV.

Binky and his cart entered my office like a sword being sheathed, trapping me behind my desk with my back literally to the wall. In case of fire I had the sporting chance of a snowflake.

"Hi, Archy," Binky said, placing a pathetically small pile of junk mail before me. Then, with more enthusiasm than his greeting, he asked, "Are you working on the murder at the MacNiff party? The papers are full of it. 'Waiter Wasted While Socialites Play. Jackson Barnett Detained,'" he quoted with verve. "Is there anything I can do to help, Archy?"

Binky has assisted me on several occasions, with dire consequences to his safety and my sanity. Binky Watrous stirs every dormant poltergeist. Gentle animals, like my Hobo, snarl at him. Tender two-year-olds, like my nephew, Darcy, bite him. In supermarkets, pyramids of canned tuna implode when he passes. His blender purées when it's set to chop. His microwave reduces frozen foods to ash. His checks bounce, his beach balls sink, his credit cards are maxed out and his love life is vicarious (Victoria's Secret catalogues bound in genuine vellum) to say the least.

Binky has been apprenticed to a multitude of occupations, all terminating on the unemployment line. Therefore, I had no scruples in suggesting that he assist our retiring mail person during the Christmas rush, several Noels ago, secure in the knowledge that he would be gone along with the old year. Alas, I was wrong. On the twelfth day of Christmas he replaced our retiree with the blessing of his benefactress, Mrs. Trelawney.

Binky fancies himself an incipient PI under my tutelage. What he doesn't realize is that graduation is a long way off. Not content to play Watson to my Holmes, he now wants to emulate their creator — but I get ahead of myself.

"As a matter of fact, there is something you can do for me, Binky my boy."

Standing tall, he snapped at the bait. "Name it, Archy."

"You can keep your hands off my answering machine."

"I never touched your answering machine," he assured me with the rectitude of a carny pitchman.

"Semantics," I accused. "You know to what I refer."

"If you mean your loose connection, it was a pleasure to be of assistance, I'm sure."

My, that was certainly an unBinky-like response, and he had certainly quoted those tabloid headlines with unprecedented gusto. Was I mistaken, or was there a certain swagger to his bearing today as well as a sharpness to his usually dull tongue? Even his slack blond hair seemed to have more body and less droop. Mousse? On closer inspection I noticed the cornsilk appeared to have been cut by a Worth Avenue stylist who was worth every cent of his exorbitant fee. (I should know, as he's the keeper of my mane.)

As the tunesmith said, "There's something amiss, and I'll eat my hat if this isn't love." Not that Binky hasn't been in love before. *Au contraire,* Binky is always in love, however, it is usually of the unrequited variety. Could he have found someone who wasn't made of paper to commiserate with?

"Well," I said, disregarding the affront and probing for the cause, "what's new, Binky?"

"I've joined a writers' workshop," came his unexpected reply. "I don't intend to be a mail person for the rest of my life, Archy."

I wanted to say, Thank God for small favors, but went with, "I didn't know you had literary aspirations, Binky." But I did know he was a closeted reader of lusty bodice-busters.

"I didn't either," he confessed, "until Izzy told me I was a cauldron of seething talent on the verge of boiling over."

Gadzooks! What metaphor. A cauldron of seething talent? Binky Watrous? "Izzy, I take it, facilitates your workshop."

"No, she's my squeeze," he answered with a smugness that went counterpoint to his blush. "And you might as well know before you read about it in Lolly Spindrift's column."

Before Lolly announced that Binky Watrous had a squeeze, Beelzebub would be handing out ice skates to his guests.

"Izzy is a she?" I exclaimed. Five minutes into a conversation with Binky and one begins responding in question marks and exclamation points.

"Isadora Duhane. Her mother is a Kalamazoo Battle," he said with pride.

The genealogy escaped me, but my guess was that Izzy came from a long line of lost Battles.

"Did you meet in the workshop?"

"No, at the disposal dump," he sighed, as if reliving the moment.

I guess it was better than meeting over a

corpse in a motel that rented by the hour, but I wouldn't bet my original Deanna Durbin cut-out book on it. The venue suggested that Ms. Duhane, whose mother is a Kalamazoo Battle, is a resident of the Palm Court, a unit of mobile homes on concrete blocks where Binky makes his abode and, alas, so does Sergeant Al Rogoff. Binky and Al are separated by one trailer in distance and several aeons in compatibility. Now I offered up a silent prayer, pleading with Him not to have Ms. Duhane occupy the trailer . . .

"She moved into the trailer between Al and me," Binky imparted.

Thank you, God, for your consideration and a speedy rejection. It beats the dickens out of waiting on your astute decision. The previous occupant of said trailer was a young lady with whom I was rather smitten and so, too, was Binky. I had no fear of a repeat performance with Isadora Duhane. If she saw a cauldron of seething talent in Binky Watrous I must assume that Izzy is visually challenged. Al has not mentioned Isadora Duhane to me, which implies that he is unaware or uncaring of her presence, and Al Rogoff is as cognizant of his surroundings as a territorial tiger.

After their fateful meeting, Izzy invited

Binky for coffee and a slice of her home-baked pound cake topped with a generous scoop of vanilla ice cream. I recount these details as they were given me by the moussed-up Lothario. When the talk turned to "And what do you do?" Binky told her he was assistant to Archy McNally, Discreet Inquirer, currently posing as a mail person for reasons he was not permitted to disclose.

"That," I protested, "is a flagrant lie."

"No, it's not, Archy. It's poetic license."

Give unto me a break!

Accepting a second helping of pound cake topped with vanilla ice cream, he proceeded to dazzle the lady with a blow-by-blow of our escapades. In short, the budding author verbally plagiarized Ian Fleming, Mickey Spillane, Dashiell Hammett and Conan Doyle. It was here that Izzy detected the seething cauldron and insisted that Binky join her writers' workshop.

"It's run by the best-selling author Minerva Barnes, in Lantana." Binky dropped the name like I was supposed to know it. I never heard of Minerva Barnes but I did know a psychiatrist in Lantana. Dr. Gussie Pearlberg. Gussie's age is somewhere between eighty and death and she enjoys

174

telling those who inquire after her health, "I'm alive, therefore I'm well."

So Binky joined Min's stable of scribes, but not before Izzy wheedled him into demonstrating his James Bond prowess with a femme fatale. Izzy responded with all the savoir-faire of a speeding bullet. I wanted to say "poor Binky" but he looked so damn content the thought went unspoken.

Eager to terminate this painful repartee, I was loath to ask Izzy's literary genre.

"She writes hard-boiled detective fiction," Binky informed me, right on cue. "Do you want to know what she's working on now?"

"No, Binky, I do not."

"We're collaborating," he gushed, as if I had not spoken.

My word. Cohabitating and collaborating. Binky went to the disposal dump and fell into a pot of jam.

"Now you see why it's important that you keep me abreast of the Jeff Rodgers murder," he said.

"No, Binky. The connection escapes me."

"Izzy and I are going to annotate your cases, Archy." He spoke as if he knew the meaning of the word.

Trapped as I was behind my desk, I could fall neither forward nor backward, but did manage to rise and reach for Binky's throat with intent to do bodily harm. A step backward put him out of reach and, unaware of my approaching apoplexy, he pulled a notebook out of his cart and ranted, "Remember the case that started down at Manalapan, at that big, wild party? The night you took the girl home and I had to drive her car to your place . . ."

"The night Hobo took a chunk out of your ankle," I reminded him.

"I didn't think I would mention that — but listen." He consulted his notebook and read, " 'It was a dark and blustery night . . .' "

"Blustery? In Palm Beach?"

"Poetic license. Remember?"

How I longed for a refreshing cup of hemlock.

"If you so much as mention my name I'll sue you, Izzy and all the Kalamazoo Battles," I threatened.

"I don't see what you're getting so uppity about when you got your name and your picture in the shiny sheet, wrapped in the icky jacket."

"That icky jacket happens to be a

classic," I told him.

"And so is *The Adventures of Skip McGuire*," he proclaimed, shaking the notebook in my face.

"Who?" I managed to utter as my blood pressure soared to heights heretofore uncharted by medical science.

"Skip McGuire, Archy. It's your *nom de plume.*"

Did Minerva Barnes hand out a glossary of literary terms to all her new students, or had he learned them at the knee of Isadora Duhane? I reached for the only weapon at hand and ordered, "Put that cart in reverse and get out of here before you feel the wrath of my plume."

Backing out, my Boswell challenged, "Publish or perish, Archy."

Oy vey.

"How nice you look, Archy," my number one fan noted as I entered the den.

For the cocktail hour at the McNally manse I accessorized a pair of black silk faille trousers and a crisply pressed white shirt with a tartan plaid waistcoat in blue, green and red that bore its original onyx buttons. I got this prize at a rummage shop along that stretch of the South Dixie Highway now known as Antiques Row.

The area was declared "in vogue" when Jennifer Garrigues of Worth Avenue selected it as the place for her second shop, the Dixie Monkey. Father, at the sideboard mixing our martinis, turned to see the cause of Mother's compliment, raised one eyebrow, and went back to mixing the world's wettest blend of gin and vermouth.

I kissed Mother's cheek, accepted my libation so carefully poured into a crystal stem glass, and took my seat, which is a club chair in worn dark brown leather. Father eschewed his place behind his desk in favor of a wing chair where, given his bearing and attire, he looked regal and, therefore, content. He had already served Mother's sauterne, the only alcoholic beverage she takes.

As Father and I tried to come up with a suitable subject for Mother's ears, she opened the conversation with, "I know it's not supposed to be mentioned in my presence, but I heard that poor boy's funeral is tomorrow morning at St. Edward's."

She no doubt heard it from Ursi, who got it from Maria. Father and I exchanged glances, shrugged and went with the flow. "I intend to be there," I informed those gathered.

"I'm glad you're going to church, Archy,

even if for such a sad occasion," she said.

My parents attend church every Sunday morning and I accompany them when I can't find a virtuous excuse for my Saturday night sins and seek redemption — which is very seldom. Seeing an opening, father turned the conversation to the floral arrangements at last week's service and mother was happily led from murder to marigolds with nary a backward glance. Short-term memory is not all bad.

The marigolds led to the trials and tribulations of Mother's garden club and the bad feelings created after a bitter discussion of the indiscriminate use of smudge pots. Ordering up another glass of sauterne, Mother went on about the difficulty of recruiting speakers for the Current Affairs Society, of which she is a founder and current Sergeant at Arms. Mother is a born and bred Floridian, which is rare indeed, as most Floridians are native New Yorkers.

"They all want to be paid," Mother sighed. "I think they should be happy just to be asked."

"What about Minerva Barnes?" I injected. "She's right here in Lantana." This earned me a perplexed stare from she who bore me. "She's a best-selling author," I elucidated.

"I've never heard of her," Mother said, "but then my memory is not what it used to be, and authors are so tedious, Archy. They expect you to bring their latest book for autographing, which means you have to buy the book as you can't return a library copy autographed by the author."

"Minerva Barnes writes *romans à clef*," Father lectured from his throne. "Fiction-alized accounts of the lives and loves of our more disreputable notables, all rather thinly disguised. Very naughty, I assure you."

That brought a smile to Mother's face and a glow to her florid cheeks. "Naughty, you say, Prescott? Then we must have her. The society will think I'm very with-it. Thank you, Archy."

I was too awed by Father's revelation to acknowledge Mother's gratitude. Could the sire have renounced Dickens in favor of Minerva Barnes? This was as likely as the Pope renouncing celibacy. Father appeared so pleased with himself I tried to mask my incredulity when I asked, "You've read Minerva Barnes, sir?"

"Heavens no, Archy," he said, feigning surprise that I should think he had. "She was a client some years back. It seems she didn't disguise her protagonist sufficiently enough to ward off a libel suit from the real article. We represented the defendant."

"Did we win?" I questioned, going along with the royal *we*.

"In a sense we did," he said, warming to his favorite topic. "We reminded the aggrieved gentleman that to claim he was the prototype for the dastardly character was in fact a form of self-incrimination." Father smiled as he recalled this clever maneuver. "He dropped the case."

Thinking of Skip McGuire (ugh!) I asked, "What is the line between freedom to publish and libel?"

"A very thin one, Archy. A very thin one, indeed. Can you give me an example?"

"Not at the moment, sir." But it had me thinking. Would Binky dare tell all he knew? Under the influence of Eros in the guise of Isadora Duhane, and abetted by Minerva Barnes, I believe he would. Skip McGuire had to be silenced. What did Binky say? Publish or perish? Well, the choice was clear, but who would perish — me or my clone?

Dinner was announced, ending yet another episode of *Cocktails with the McNallys*. Will the fallout from smudge pots be reconciled? Will mother get Minerva Barnes to speak before the Current Affairs Society and fool the authoress into signing a library copy of her latest book? Will Archy publish or perish? Tune in tomorrow night, when none of the above will be resolved.

If Maria Sanchez did report that I would be dining at home tonight, Ursi feted me as if I were the prodigal son. For starters, fresh crab meat, white as snow, heaped over a bed of cold, crisp iceberg lettuce and garnished with toast points and capers.

The fatted calf was a fatted *poussin* (baby chicken to you), roasted to a golden brown and accompanied with a sauce derived from a mix of minced shallots and onions blended in the bird's roasting juices and a dash of port wine. The three birds were presented with an X, fashioned by strips of grilled bacon, atop their succulent breasts.

Pommes Anna, baby peas with pearl onions and Ursi's home-baked petite cheddar biscuits completed the feast.

Father decanted a bottle of Rosso de Montalcino, a pretentious Tuscan delight, for the repast, which ended with a lemon sorbet to clean the palate and a plate of sugar cookies to go with a cup of demitasse derived from Ursi's original blend of Colombian beans.

Get married? You've got to be either kidding or *non compos mentis.*

THIRTEEN

Jeff Rodgers's murder contained all the ingredients of a pulp fiction novella, which made his funeral a media event. The mourners included a mix of Palm Beach society, an incorrigible tennis pro hunk, and a gaggle of winsome boys and girls.

The link between the newly departed and the newly arrived was still the best-kept secret of the drama, but with the number of people hot on Talbot's trail (or should that be Talbot's toe?), it was only a matter of time before he would have to make a public statement regarding his connection to the victim. When I entered St. Edward's church I had no idea the time was at hand.

Many of the young folks who filled the church to say good-bye to their friend and colleague wore the uniform of their trade and, whether because they were on their way to a job or as a tribute to Jeff, the gesture made a poignant statement. Well, if the uniformed services buried their own in full dress, why not these gallant boys and girls?

The others, accustomed to running about in shorts, T-shirts and sneakers, looked a tad uncomfortable in their trousers or skirts with a proper shirt or blouse covering their tanned torsos. The sneakers, I noted, made it to church but the surfboards did not. I saw Todd and Monica in the crowd. Todd's seat in the first row with three other young men, all wearing dark suits and ties, told me Todd was a designated pallbearer. The older man in that pew was no doubt Jeff's father.

Poor Jeff. If he were looking down on this gathering in search of his former classmates from the Day School I fear he would find that he had been snubbed in death as he had been in life. Seeing those who did come to bid him farewell, I would say Jeff Rodgers traded up when he left the Day School for a seat next to Edward (Todd) Brandt. Poor Jeff just didn't get it, and the oversight may have cost him his life.

This is not to say the gathering wasn't impressive. The press, from Miami to Jacksonville and points west, was in attendance, their accompanying photographers having the good sense to limit their photo ops to outside the church.

Representing *Bare Facts* magazine was Dennis Darling, seated next to Lolly Spindrift. Lolly possesses all the sincerity of a mole working both sides of the street. After warning us to steer clear of the man from *Bare Facts*, Lol accepts his invitation to dine, no doubt exchanging titillating gossip over the beef Wellington, and now sits before those he cautioned, and before God I might add, pointing and whispering the names of PB notables into Darling's ear. For a guy like Denny, extracting the bare facts out of Lolly was like getting a has-been ham to list his credits.

Jackson Barnett, looking like a blond Adonis and dressed like a funeral director, was with a man who exhibited all the signs of a flack. Custom-made suit, black silk tie and nervous tic. I imagine the people in New York, anxious that Jackie's involvement in Jeff's death might cost him his lucrative endorsements and their ten percent, sent down this troubleshooter to keep Barnett from doing anything foolish, like skipping the funeral in favor of sleeping late.

Phil Meecham was nowhere to be seen, which was just as well as his presence in a house of worship might well precipitate the onset of Armageddon. The MacNiffs were there, she in a deep purple frock and smart black hat. I also noticed many of the *Tennis*

186

Everyone! participants, including Joe Gallo and Vivian Emerson. He sported flannels and blazer, she a navy Chanel suit. Now aware of Joe's former involvement with Georgy girl, I scrutinized him as best I could from where I sat, seeking imperfections and finding none. This was depressing, but apropos to the occasion. The Emerson woman, as I recalled from the MacNiff gala, was a stunner.

Al Rogoff and his chief, both in civilian dress, were stationed on opposite sides of the congregation where they could not be mistaken for anything but flatfoots on the prowl.

All were present and accounted for with one glaring exception. This was a rather strange young lady seated in the pew directly across the aisle from me in the rear of the church. A few strands of dark hair fell over her forehead from beneath a kerchief that engulfed much of her face. Dark, horn-rimmed glasses and a shapeless raincoat completed the picture of a member of the royal family shopping incognito along the King's Road.

Her features, what you could see of them, were attractive, and I imagined so too was the figure the raincoat concealed. In a town where the fair sex strives to enhance their assets, she labored to be the exception to the rule — with a vengeance. Why would an attractive lass come to a funeral disguised as a frump?

Further speculation was nipped in the bud when, just at the start of the service, a young man entered the church and chose to settle into my pew. I moved to make room for Lance Talbot, who nodded politely as he slipped in beside me.

The service was lovely, if somber, and although we were reminded that Jeff Rodgers had left this vale of tears for a more affable location, I doubt if any present were eager to follow him there in the immediate future. Thankfully, no mention was made of the mode of Jeff's departure.

The four young pallbearers, Todd included, flanked the draped coffin as it was wheeled up the aisle, followed by Mr. Rodgers and, behind him, the mourners filed out of their pews to form a cortege. As the coffin rolled past us, Lance Talbot bowed his head and when he raised it he found himself literally face-to-face with Jeff's father. Mr. Rodgers paused, rudely staring at the younger man as if wondering if he should greet him. Talbot smiled, nodded and said, "Yes, Rollo, it's me."

"Mr. Lance?" Rodgers said. "Thank you for coming. He would have liked that." Then he continued to follow his son out of the church and to his final resting place.

Being in the last row we should have joined the rear of the procession to make our exit but this was not to be. Talbot sat, unmoving, hemming me in until we were alone in the church. Turning, he focused his blue eyes on me and said, "I'm keeping you prisoner."

His English was perfect but not without the trace of an accent. German, I think. Understandable considering the years he spent in Switzerland, where his first language could have been German, French or Italian. Behind us someone was closing the church doors, muting the sounds of the departing mourners.

"I've been detained in less congenial places," I assured him.

"Not jail, I hope."

"I refuse to answer on the grounds that it may incriminate me."

Talbot laughed. "I was told you had a keen sense of humor."

"To a point, Mr. Talbot, but don't press your luck. May I ask why you're detaining me?"

"I have a confession to make," he said.

"You've certainly come to the right place."

He smiled to display a set of pearly whites, then turned serious. "Jeff Rodgers and I grew up together. We were the best of friends before I went to Switzerland with mother, who died there in a skiing accident."

I offered my sympathies for his loss but made no comment on his connection with Jeff Rodgers.

"Thank you," he said before going on. "I'm sure you noticed that Mr. Rodgers recognized me."

You told him who you were, I wanted to counter, but kept my mouth shut. If he was in a confessing mood I didn't want to rattle the beads, and if his revelation was intended to take me by surprise, I thought it only fair to respond in kind. Shifting gears, I said, "I know all about you and Jeff and your days together at the Day School."

He kept his cool, but I think I got him where he lived. "Really? From who?"

"A friend of Jeff's. One of the pall-bearers, in fact."

"What did he say about me?"

"That would be telling, Mr. Talbot."

"Please, call me Lance."

"That would be telling, Lance."

"Can't we be friends, Mr. McNally?"

The guy was either painfully ingenuous or too cagey by half. This show of camaraderie was so unexpected, I wasn't sure how to handle it. Talbot was handing me, on a platter, what I had planned to force him to own up to, thereby putting me on the defensive. I recalled him saying at our initial meeting, "I'm not as clever as you, Mr. McNally." Wanna bet?

"I see no reason why we can't be friends," I said.

"Good, because I want to retain you to find Jeff's killer."

"I beg your pardon."

"It's what you do, isn't it?" Then he rattled on, "Jeff was a dear friend. His father, Ronald, was our chauffeur. I called him Rollo." With a show of impatience, he dismissed these details as irrelevant with a wave of his hand. "It's a long story, Mr. McNally, which I'll tell you at a more appropriate time. Let's just say I owe Jeff this much. Will you do it?"

Why not? I thought. I already had two clients on this case and the old adage has it that there's never a second without a third. "Have the police questioned you yet?"

"Yes. Holga, too," he admitted.

"Did you tell them that you and Jeff

were boyhood friends?"

A shrug and another irritable wave of his hand. "No. Why should I? That was ten years ago. Will you do it?" he repeated.

I was suddenly catapulted into the enviable position of being able to question my quarry, with his blessing. This, I quickly deduced, was a double-edged sword, as my questions would tell him what I didn't know and allow him to manipulate the answers to suit his purposes. To date, we had both given a little and both taken a little, so the score was one-up, and I wanted to call time. I justified what I was about to do by remembering it's not how you play the game, it's winning that matters. And I called Lolly a mole!

I gave him my standard caution. "Anything you tell me that might aid the police in their investigation of Jeff's murder, I will be obligated to pass on to them."

"I understand," he agreed.

"As you said, Lance, I think we should discuss this at a more appropriate time and on less sanctified turf." And, I didn't add, give me time to digest this newformed alliance.

"The Leopard Lounge at the Chesterfield?" he suggested.

"I can't think of any place less sanctified."

I found a note on the dashboard of my Miata. "What were you two doing in there — exchanging vows? Can't wait to hear all about it. You can buy me lunch at your Pelican Club. D.D."

Lolly. Who else? I could hear him cluing Denny. "The little fire engine belongs to Archy McNally, our resident PI, but you didn't hear that from me. His club is the Pelican, out near the airport. The food is passable, the members aren't."

I found Denny at the bar, nursing a pilsner glass of dark beer. "I told Mr. Pettibone you had invited me and he insisted I partake of your hospitality while waiting." Denny ran a finger under the collar of his dress shirt. "It was cooler in church than it is in here."

"God looks after his own," I told him, signaling to Mr. Pettibone, who was organizing his garnish set-ups before the onset of the noon rush. "Can you pull me a stout, Mr. Pettibone?"

The Pelican is located in a clapboard house converted to the needs of a social club. The L-shaped first floor is our dining room with additional tables in the ell that is now the bar area. The kitchen, greatly improved and enlarged, is in its original location, and a room that may have served as a den is now used for private parties and meetings. The Pettibone family occupies the second floor.

Priscilla, looking ravishing in skintight white jeans and T-shirt emblazoned with the club's emblem, a pelican lording over a sea of dead mullets, was placing menus on the tables and fussing over the silverware. People were beginning to drift in and a few tables were already occupied.

"A sad business," Mr. Pettibone said, serving my stout. "Were you able to contact Todd, Archy?"

"I was, Mr. Pettibone, and he was most helpful."

"The police don't seem to have any leads, if we can believe today's newspapers."

"You can believe them," I told him as he went off to greet a newcomer.

"Nice," Denny said, indicating the room in general and Priscilla in particular.

"I'm sure Lolly trashed it," I said. "You mustn't believe everything he told you."

"Archy," Denny moaned, "I couldn't remember half of what Lolly told me. He tattled on everyone and everything from the upper crust to the low-life watering holes where, according to Lolly, the twain meet.

The only thing he does more than talk is eat. You owe me big, Archy."

"I did you a favor. He now thinks you're here to write your exposé and will keep out of our way. If he even thought you were after a story on Lance Talbot he would tell Lance in hopes of getting in his good graces. Lolly, as I'm sure you now know, can't keep a secret or resist pandering to the local gentry."

Denny took the last swig of his beer and motioned to Mr. Pettibone for another. "Lolly is more interested in Talbot's lady friend than in Talbot himself. Some titled lady offered Lolly a generous tip if he can discover the location of Holga von Brecht's fountain of youth."

"Lady Cynthia Horowitz," I said. "She and Lolly are archenemies who can't keep out of each other's faces. They share an interest in athletic young men. Lady C is also offering a premium to Lolly if he can get Jackson Barnett off Meecham's yacht and into her bedroom, but he won't do it because Meecham shares the wealth and Lady C does not. Get it?"

"My, my, you are an earthy little community," Denny laughed.

"We like to keep up," I boasted. "Do you want to see a menu?"

Mr. Pettibone brought Denny's beer just as I was ready for seconds. Nothing like a funeral to work up a thirst.

"First, I want to know what you and Talbot were doing in the church for at least ten minutes after the service."

"He was confessing," I stated.

"To the murder?" Denny exclaimed, a tad too loud. Mr. Pettibone paused in his labors to stare, as did a couple of men at the bar. Priscilla, on her way to the kitchen, also stopped in her tracks to give us the fisheye.

"Curb your enthusiasm, Denny. We've already agreed that Lance Talbot could not have done it. Remember? He confessed to being an old acquaintance of Jeff's and hired me to investigate the murder."

Denny pursed his lips and exhaled a muted whistle. "Did you accept?"

"With alacrity, old boy."

Seeing the irony as well as the possibilities of the situation, Denny gave me a broad grin before raising his glass in an unspoken salute. "So they were buddies," he mused, as if this finally explained how Jeff Rodgers could know something about Talbot that might embarrass him.

"It was a while back," I said, holding up my hand to keep Denny from interrupting.

"Let me explain. You just heard Mr. Pettibone ask if I had contacted Todd Brandt. He was a friend of Jeff's. In fact, he was one of the pallbearers at the funeral."

Here I gave Denny a full report on my meeting with Todd. I had already passed on this information to Nifty and I would have to repeat it for Lance this evening at the Chesterfield. When dealing with multiple clients it would help to write up reports and photocopy them for distribution.

"I was right," Denny said, visibly excited by my tale. "If they were tight when they were boys there is every reason to suspect that Jeff knew who fathered Lance. Boys talk, you know. They share secrets." Then he grabbed my arm and gushed, "Good Lord, Archy, maybe the chauffeur is the father. Jeff and Lance were brothers. The prince and the pauper."

"Blessed mother of Samuel Clemens, will you calm down, Denny. You're beginning to believe your own copy."

"Am I?" he questioned. "Remember the New York deb — what was her name? — Gamble, Gamble Benedict, that's it. She ran off with the family chauffeur. It was in all the papers."

"Jessica Talbot didn't run off with

anyone, nor would she retain her son's father as her driver. Jeff Rodgers was a frustrated playboy. If he had any proof that he was Lance's brother he might try to sue for his share of the estate and his rightful place in society, not pussyfoot around with some inane blackmail scam to raise a few bucks. Ditto, Mr. Rodgers, the elder."

Denny looked disappointed, but contrite. "You must admit it would have made a smashing story. Maybe even a film or a TV series." However, he continued to pursue the father angle with, "But I still think Jeff knew the identity of Lance's father and it's either a married Palm Beach big shot or a politico. It has to be someone who would be embarrassed by the disclosure." Denny, I believe, was hoping for a politician, preferably one who touted the virtues of family values.

I felt a twinge of guilt at not being able to tell him what Nifty and I suspected — that Talbot was an imposter. But that would be premature and guilt is a destructive emotion, so I turned to more pressing matters for solace. "Should I get a table or do you want to eat at the bar?"

"Here is fine," he said. "A burger or sandwich will do for me."

"Leroy makes the best burgers in

Florida, if not the world. Fries?"

"Can we share? I've got to watch the calories and the cholesterol. My doctor gave me six months to live."

"Really? When was that?"

"Six months ago." Denny sighed.

"We've never had anyone expire at the Pelican, but we do have a contingency fund to cover those who pass out at the bar. You might be covered."

"Thanks, Archy." Seeing Priscilla approaching he said loud enough for her to hear, "Will this lovely lady take our order?"

"I would be happy to oblige, Mr. Darling," Priscilla cooed.

Denny must have introduced himself to Mr. Pettibone, and Priscilla had gone running to her father the first chance she got to learn the name of the handsome guy waiting for Archy McNally. Need I add she knew who Dennis Darling was?

"I subscribe to your magazine, Mr. Darling, and read every word," she flattered. "Your stories, especially."

"Aren't you nice," he said.

"This is Priscilla Pettibone," I introduced the two, "who is here to take our lunch order and not to hit on guests."

Priscilla stared hard, blinked, then exclaimed, "Why it's Archy McNally. I didn't recognize you without your Lilly Pulitzer trappings."

"What did you think of the interview?"

"Like they say, fools' names and fools' faces often . . ."

"That's enough, young lady," I said, cutting her off and sparing us the obvious. "It's not original. Mr. Darling and I would like the hamburger, medium rare, with sliced onion and kosher dills on the side. We'll share Leroy's fries."

She winked at Denny before sashaying off to the kitchen.

"She's adorable," Denny commented, watching Priscilla's retreating derriere.

"Don't encourage her," I warned him. "She's a minx and loves the attention. One day we'll lose her to a traveling talent scout on the lookout for a stand-up comic with the looks and magnetism of Lena Horne."

Mr. Pettibone was setting us up with place mats and cutlery when Denny reflected, "So Talbot confesses that he knew Jeff Rodgers but he seems reluctant to let the police in on it, and Jeff was bragging to his friends about coming into money. Blackmail, Archy, no question about it. I want to know what Jeff had on Lance

Talbot and I'm not leaving Palm Beach until I find out."

"I may have the answer for you first thing in the morning."

"You mean . . ."

"I mean I'm meeting with Talbot this evening, and I'm going to tell him everything Todd told me and ask him what he knows about Jeff's supposed windfall. Talbot is courting me because he knows my father is Malcolm MacNiff's attorney and, in case you don't know, MacNiff is the executor of the old lady's estate. Talbot even called my father, waving an offer to do business with him. Lance Talbot wants to know what the executor is saying about him to father and me." That was as much as I was willing to tell Denny at this point in the investigation.

"Talbot must suspect that MacNiff engaged you to look into Jeff's murder and he hired you to keep an eye on you," Denny chuckled. "He's hiding something, Archy."

"No doubt," I said. "But you have to admire him, Denny. He's gutsy." I was thinking of the way Talbot had handled Mr. Rodgers at the funeral, carefully skirting an awkward moment.

"Whatever you do," Denny warned,

"don't blow my cover."

"Not to worry. I won't lay down all our cards. Not yet, anyway. But I did arrange for you to meet with Lance. You're going to get a call from Mrs. MacNiff to invite you to a pool party at the scene of the crime."

"Sounds ghoulish," Denny said.

"Perhaps, but I arranged it. Lance will be there and I insisted you come, too. If Jeff dropped your name as a threat, I want to see how Lance acts in your presence. I told the MacNiffs you were interested in doing a story on his charity." Lies fall from my lips like honey sifting through the comb.

"Talbot hardly noticed me at the MacNiffs' the other afternoon," Denny recalled. "Do you think his lady friend will be there?"

"Holga? I'm sure she will. What did Lolly have to report on her?"

"She's a baroness who's seventy — at least. The Baron is a vampire who's a thousand — at least. He operates a rejuvenation clinic high in the Alps where he injects his followers with — well, I don't want to spoil your lunch."

Unbeknownst to either of us my lunch was already jeopardized when a young lady entered the club and followed Priscilla to a corner table in the bar. It was the strange girl I had seen in church. As soon as she was seated, I beckoned to Priscilla. "Who is that?" I whispered.

"Binky's fiancée," Priscilla announced with glee. "She has carte blanche on his account. Don't you love it?"

Before the shock wore off, Denny turned to look at the subject of our conversation and said, "She was at the funeral. After Lolly showed me your car he spotted her coming out of the church and went rushing off to talk to her."

Priscilla caught me as I slid off my bar stool.

FOURTEEN

The Leopard Lounge is a popular oasis for cocktails after sunset and a nightcap before sunrise. In season the bar is particularly crowded and boisterous with tourists showing off their newly acquired tans and joyfully exchanging the exciting news of blizzards and cold fronts pummeling the northeast. Their drinks come in tall, chilled glasses filled with a variety of fruit tidbits and often topped with miniature parasols.

The Palm Beachites labor to look bored and pray the tourists' chatter doesn't tempt the gods to blow a little of that cold front our way. It has been known to happen. Their drinks, except for the occasional olive or pearl onion, are unadorned.

Going to the Leopard Lounge affords me a chance to wear khakis with a safari jacket I purchased from Abercrombie & Fitch in the days I spent more time browsing around New York than frequenting lecture halls in New Haven. But that, like the heyday of Abercrombie & Fitch, is a thing of the past.

I was happy to see that Lance Talbot had secured a table far from the madding crowd where we could hear ourselves talk and enjoy our libations, of which I was in desperate need. It had been, as you may have guessed, one hell of a day. One would imagine that starting with a funeral, things could only get better, right? Wrong!

After learning that Binky's squeeze (what a loathsome idiom!) was the mystery woman I had seen in church, I was told that she was pursued by none other than Lolly Spindrift. Is it any wonder my brain short-circuited? It will be rumored that Archy McNally fainted at the Pelican bar while talking to Dennis Darling. This will lead to speculation that Darling had just treated McNally to the more salient paragraphs of *The Palm Beach Story* exposé. Finally, the news will reach Ursi before I reach home.

Nonsense. I didn't faint. I simply took a *turn,* as they say, and teetered off my stool and into the arms of Priscilla Pettibone. I can think of less harmonious places to teeter into. I rallied in time to stop her from shoving a vial of smelling salts under my nose, which Mr. Pettibone had produced from his cache of restorative aids beneath the bar. The incident was over in a matter of minutes, drawing a minimum of attention from the lunch crowd. Ms. Duhane, I noticed, was busy scribbling away in a notebook she had produced from her handbag.

I wasn't about to tell Denny, and especially not Priscilla, that Ms. Duhane was recording the occurrence for inclusion in the next chapter of *The Adventures of Skip McGuire*, and that I was Skip's archetype. At times like this I longed to be in a monastery, sporting a hair shirt and reclining peacefully on a bed of nails.

Lunch was served and it helped to keep my mind off the scribe but I think Denny surmised the connection between my *turn* and Isadora Duhane's appearance. No fool Dennis Darling. Ms. Duhane was having herself a hot lunch, with wine, on Binky's account. What cheek. Binky's account was, as always, in arrears, and I had generously advanced him a few quid to tide him over and keep him from the embarrassing position of being *non grata* at the Pelican until his anemic exchequer showed signs of recovery, which would be never. Steady employment at McNally & Son and a profusion of credit cards had enabled Binky to keep up with the Joneses, all merrily skipping along the yellow brick road to bankruptcy.

Now, it seems, I was feeding Ms. Duhane. If the writing team of Watrous and Duhane intended to reimburse me with the advance from their first tome, I would see the money when Alejandro Gomez y Zapata invades Cuba. And why did Lolly Spindrift accost Isadora Duhane? All in all, it was a most disconcerting repast.

Then, a funny thing happened between lunch at the Pelican and cocktails at the Chesterfield. Namely, a fax from Switzerland that awaited me in my office. To wit:

Dear Mr. McNally:

Herr Hermann is in Berlin attending to business. He returns when I am not sure. I will to him convey your request when next I see him here. He is sure to respond most soon. Thank you.

Greta Gottenburg,
Secretary to Herr Gregory Hermann.

Translation? The fickle finger of fate had entered the fray and denied me the information I needed from the Swiss lawyer before my meeting with Lance Talbot. Here begins the all too familiar if-only mantra. If only Herr Hermann had not gone to Berlin on business. If only I had delayed seeing

Lance Talbot until I had talked to Hermann. If only hindsight were foresight — and all that jazz.

Unable to resist, I called Lolly Spindrift at his office and, surprisingly, got him. "I'm just putting together my copy on Jeff Rodgers's funeral for tomorrow's edition. I haven't seen so many names in the same place at the same time since Lady Cynthia's reception for Bonnie Prince Charlie."

Lolly does obits for extra moola, also weddings and bar mitzvahs.

"As I recall, Lol, the bonnie prince was a no-show."

"Yes. How sad. He was up all night nursing his polo pony."

"Really? I heard he declined her invitation."

"No?" Lolly gushed. "Where did you ever hear that?"

"I read it in your column."

Lolly does not like to be reminded of his more base literary offerings, so the faux royal affair was forgotten but not the fact that I had rung him up. "Did you call to make trouble, Archy, or to beg me for a date?"

I called to learn what he knew about Isadora Duhane, but with Lolly it's always best to put him on the defensive before asking a favor, otherwise he'll try to extract payment for his trouble. "I was surprised to see you rubbing shoulders with the Philistine in our midst. You know, the guy you nominated as the most worthy recipient of the PBCS."

It took Lolly about ten seconds to think of a rebuttal. "You mean Dennis Darling? Oh, I've had a change of heart. After all, he is a colleague and I thought it in the best interest of the community to open up to him instead of having him ferret out misinformation from malcontents who are only too ready to feed us to the lions. Dennis is really a dear man. So giving, if you know what I mean."

I knew, all right. Dinner and drinks at Cafe L'Europe. "If he has your blessing, Lol, we'll roll out the red carpet for Mr. Darling. The one Lady Cynthia purchased for the prince."

"Shame on you," he tittered. "Now, about that date. I'm free for cocktails and dinner, after which we can jump aboard Meecham's floating circus and mix with the bad and the beautiful. You game, Archy?"

"Sorry, but I'm booked this evening, Lol. Can I have a rain check?" It's always best to humor Lol, but to my everlasting ignominy I admit to having had some interesting evenings on Meecham's yacht.

"Don't be morose, Archy. It never rains in Palm Beach."

"Tell that to Dennis Darling. Now I must go — oh, I almost forgot. There was a young lady in church this morning wearing a kerchief and raincoat . . ."

"Isadora Duhane," he shouted, almost rupturing my ear drum. "I couldn't believe my luck when I saw her coming out of church. I didn't get much out of her, but . . ."

"Whoa," I cut in. Lolly sounded as if he had accidentally encountered the missing link coming out of a church in Palm Beach. "Who in blazes is Isadora Duhane?"

"Who is Isadora Duhane? Her mother is a Kalamazoo Battle, that's who."

I found myself reaching for the bottom drawer of my desk, but as Lolly expounded on the history of the Battle family I feared I needed more than a nicotine fix to survive the ordeal.

The first Battle was a forty-niner who struck a vein that made Fort Knox look like a piggy bank. Hankering to become a gentleman rancher, he used a portion of his loot to buy a rather large hunk of

Texas. While his son ran the ranch, daddy went off to the Klondike, where he struck a vein that made the California mine look like a piggy bank.

"His name," Lolly said, "was Ezra M. Battle. It was rumored the M stood for Midas."

Meanwhile, back at the ranch, Ezra's grandson, weary of dehorning cattle, got a team of wildcatters to see if there was anything interesting under the sod and, as the Midas touch would have it, the ranch was soon pumping a million gallons of black gold a day with no end in sight.

The family grew and spread, until they could be found in cities from coast to coast, running giant holding companies that were the invisible owners of businesses as diverse as department stores and oil tankers.

"Isadora's mother married a Duhane of Kalamazoo and resides there when not cruising on one of the Battle liners. Isadora attended Rosemary Hall, which is the distaff side of Choate and . . ."

And on and on. The nitty-gritty being that Binky Watrous, who owed me three hundred bucks, was cohabitating and collaborating with a zillionaire, and I wanted my money back.

"They call Isadora Izzy," Lolly was saying as if he were on intimate terms with the woman. If Lolly knew who held that position he would be writing his own obit for tomorrow's edition.

"Izzy is the family black sheep, you might say. She's always running off to weird places like Timbuktu and Bora-Bora," Lolly raced along, hardly pausing to breathe. "As if Kalamazoo wasn't weird enough for her. And she's into projects. Women's lib, conservation, archaeology, criminology, zoology, the list is endless. There was a rumor that she was in these parts but I didn't believe it until I saw her myself this morning, and coming out of church, of all places. Any idea what she was doing at the funeral service, Archy?"

"Writing a book," I answered.

"Oh, Archy. Be serious. I would be on every A-list if I had Isadora Duhane on my arm. She gave me the brush-off this morning but that won't stop me. She's the hottest thing to hit this town in years and I want an exclusive. I might even hire you to find out where she's staying."

"Try the Palm Court trailer park," I told him.

"That's not even funny, Archy."

Like I always say, if you don't want

212

people to believe you, tell the truth and your secret is safe.

"Now I must fly," Lolly gasped as if he just saw his train leaving the depot. "Babe Evans is giving a tea party to show off the abstract oils she purchased in Florence last summer."

"I didn't know that crowd was into art," I said.

"They're not," he prattled. "Babe also brought back the artist. It was a package deal, I'm told. Everyone says he's absolutely delicious."

If he thought I was going to fall for that one, he was barking up the wrong pant leg. "Arrivederci, Lolly."

My English Oval kept me from banging my head against the wall. The signs were not auspicious. In the good old days I could sacrifice a bull to allay the gods. Right now all I wanted to sacrifice was Binky Watrous and his solid-gold squeeze. If Isadora Duhane was all Lolly claimed she was — and when it came to delineating the rich and famous, Lolly Spindrift was a walking *Who's Who* — I was in deep doo-doo.

I had thought that Binky went to the disposal dump and fell into a pot of jam. I now knew he went to the disposal dump and fell into an American dynasty. If a publishing company, or two, was among the Battle family holdings, *Skip McGuire* would be published and this discreet inquirer would be as discreet as Old Glory on the fourth of July. My clients would not be amused to find themselves the thinly disguised characters in a *roman à clef*, to say nothing of Father dearest.

While Binky cruised the seven seas on a Battle liner, Archy would be delivering the mail at McNally & Son. To keep the quo status, the dynamic duo of crime fiction had to perish before they published.

Georgy called to invite me to dinner. She promised to remember to put the can of mushroom soup in the tuna 'n' noodle casserole. I told her that tunas were an endangered species and mushrooms were a fungus. "I have a business meeting at seven and can be at the Pelican on or before nine. Meet me at the bar and I'll buy you dinner."

"Nine is late for a working girl, Archy," she protested.

"Trust me. I'll have you in bed before midnight."

"If that means what I think it means . . ."

"Georgy girl," I pleaded, "it's just a figure of speech."

"So is buzz off, buster."

"Nineish at the Pelican?"

"What's on the menu?"

"Tuna 'n' noodle casserole with real frozen crescent rolls," I told her.

My wry humor not withstanding, she exploded, "And you know where you can go, Archy McNally."

If Satan asks who sent me I will have a long and prominent list for his perusal.

I called Malcolm MacNiff to relate the disappointing results of my fax to the late Jessica Talbot's Swiss lawyer. "We'll just have to wait for his return before we get a detailed account of Jessica's last days. I also want to know if he can tell us anything about the von Brecht woman."

Knowing that the MacNiffs had taken financial responsibility for Jeff Rodgers's funeral, I also told him I thought the service, flowers, et al., were fitting and most moving.

"Thank you, Archy," he said. "So many young people there. How sad to see them at such a lamentable gathering. And so many from my tennis benefit. I don't know if I'll ever have another now that it's been tarnished with this memory."

All Nifty wanted was a noble excuse not to cancel his prestigious *Tennis Everyone!*

affair, and I gave him one.

"Please reconsider, sir. The fund does so much for young people, I think you should continue it in Jeff's memory."

He pounced on it like Othello being tossed a sack of catnip. "What a splendid idea, Archy. That's just what I'll do."

Jeff would adore having his name on the guest list of a classy Palm Beach happening as opposed to being part of the wait staff. In memoriam, true, but better late than never. I was honored to be the catalyst of the tribute.

On a roll, I said, "And you can announce the concept at the pool party, lending dignity to the occasion and making the event more palatable. Your pool, sir, becomes a symbol of hope, not a coffin."

"I like it better all the time, Archy. My gratitude. As you know I just hated opening the pool again, but it must be done and what better way than this?"

I must say there are times when I astound myself. A little corny, I daresay, but it's all for a worthy cause.

"Which reminds me," Nifty said, "the gathering is set for tomorrow at one. Helen left a message for Mr. Darling at his hotel and we're waiting for his call. We also contacted Lance and he'll be there with Ms.

von Brecht. Helen has invited about a dozen of her crowd to make it look less like an inquisition. Anyone you want to add?"

"Why not Lolly Spindrift to give it the flavor of a press conference."

"Another good idea, Archy."

Having put together a lethal mix of snoops and suspects for our pool party, I asked, "Did you know Lance was in church this morning?"

"I saw him as we were leaving. I believe he was seated in your pew."

"Indeed he was. In fact, sir, he asked me to look into Jeff's murder. To find the murderer, as he put it."

It took him a moment to reflect on this before responding. When he did it was the same response I got from Denny a few hours ago. "And did you accept?"

"I did, sir."

"Did he tell you he was an old school chum of the murdered boy?"

"Yes, and that's about all he told me. Given the time and place our conversation was kept to a minimum. I have an appointment to see him this evening when I hope to learn more about Lance Talbot. I believe he suspects that you have hired me to look into the murder. He also called my father and proposed a business meeting in the near future."

"What's the boy up to?" Nifty mused.

"I think he wants to see what we're up to. This is his way of being kept informed and he's willing to pay for the privilege. Lance Talbot has something to hide, sir."

"Confound it, Archy, you have no idea how I detest all this clandestine nonsense. I've lived too long, I have. In my day you didn't need to see your neighbor's passport to know his name, and poseurs were black-balled from the club."

"You sound like my father, Mr. Mac-Niff."

"A good man, Prescott," he said.

Father would be pleased to have Nifty's endorsement.

"Thank you, sir. I'll see you tomorrow at one. Do you think Holga von Brecht will wear a thong?"

"Archy!" Mrs. MacNiff scolded. Good grief, she had been on the extension listening to our conversation.

I returned home in time for my swim before dressing for cocktails with Lance Talbot. I covered my patriotic Mark Spitz red, white and blue bikini Speedo with a black hooded terry robe. All I had to do to stop traffic was step out onto Ocean Boulevard and raise my hands. With a nod of thanks, north and south, I hobbled my way to the Atlantic.

I showered, got into my safari togs, and stopped in the kitchen to tell Ursi I would not be home for dinner.

"Don't fall off any bar stools," she advised.

FIFTEEN

As I approached his table, Lance Talbot appraised my raiment thoughtfully and, as if suddenly getting the joke, tossed back his head and laughed. "An avant-garde Beau Brummell," he said, pointing. He had either memorized my interview or read it again before our meeting.

"The leopards have already been shot, Archy, but you get an E for effort. Do sit." He beckoned to a waiter. "I'm having a gin martini. Very American, *ja?*"

In spite of Talbot's chummy use of my given name, his dress and deportment marked him as Eurocentric. His white, open-collar shirt was silk. His navy blazer was perfectly cut to accentuate the classic male torso: broad shoulders tapering to a narrow waist. A red handkerchief hung rakishly from his jacket's breast pocket. And, perhaps because of the German *yes,* his accent seemed more pronounced than when we last talked. Too, he exhibited the haughty air peculiar to Europe's upper classes — or Eurotrash mimicking their betters.

Conversely, our landed gentry bend over backwards to make us believe they are just one of the boys, which is why Nifty orders a modest wine while feting me at his immodest club.

"A bourbon and branch water," I said to the hovering waiter as I took my seat.

"Have you ever been on safari?" Lance asked.

"No, but I've ambled through the brambles in New York's Central Park and I once toured our Everglades on a boat called the *African Queen*. Does that count?"

"I'm afraid not," he said amiably. "Mother and I went on safari in Kenya. You know, of course, the British tried to turn it into England's breadbasket before the big war. Baronets by the dozens bought up land to farm and proceeded to turn the natives into indentured servants while indulging themselves in an orgy of drugs, booze and wife-swapping that the English label *affairs*. I believe an earl was shot dead by an irate husband and the murder never solved."

Rather than rehash the saga of poor Josslyn Victor Hay, Earl of Erroll, I asked, "Did you bag anything in Kenya besides the country's sordid history?"

"Heavens no," he protested. "We would

never kill for sport. A safari these days is more like wandering around a zoo where the animals roam freely. We were sightseers and picture takers and nourishment for the mosquitoes."

"Now that sounds like our Central Park," I offered as the waiter served my drink.

Talbot raised his martini. "Here's to money and the time to spend it."

Coming from him, the toast was almost apocalyptic. Given his inheritance and age, he certainly had plenty of both to spare and then some. I tried not to forget that what Lance Talbot lacked in years he more than made up for in experience. Safari in Kenya? What other exotic ports of call did he and his mother frequent in his teen years? What forbidden fruits had he indulged himself in before he had reached his majority? Was Holga von Brecht one of them? Was Archy overreacting or envious? I savored my bourbon. It helped, but not enough.

Talbot's cobalt blue eyes always seemed to be smiling at his surroundings in a most condescending manner. *Been here, done this,* they signaled with a yawn. In short, Lance Talbot was a colossal pain in the you-know-where. How I longed to pull off his right shoe (John Lobb loafers, no doubt) and shout *j'accuse,* punk! But in the Leopard Lounge with the moon on the rise the gesture might be misconstrued.

"So," he began our meeting, "why did you ask this friend of Jeff's questions about me?"

"I didn't," I answered. "He volunteered the information."

"More to the point, Archy, why were you asking questions about Jeff Rodgers?"

The use of my given name without permission to use it continued to irk me. "That, Lance, is none of your business."

He started, then laughed. He had taken a cigarette from a pack of Gauloises and was holding it, unlit, between his fingers. The very gesture seemed to show his irritation at not being able to smoke in a bistro. In Europe, I imagine, one could light up in church if the need arose. I was so glad I had given up the weed — almost. However, I longed to show off my English Ovals.

"I thought you were working for me," he insisted.

"I've not formally taken the assignment," I reminded him. Here I baited his fancy with, "And should I accept your commission, that does not mean I can divulge information gathered for another client."

He tapped the imaginary ash off his unlit cigarette. If I was beginning to decompose his composure, it was not unintentional.

To accentuate his frustration, I advised, "You will have to get used to the new rules that govern smoking in our republic, Lance. It's now something you do outdoors."

With an arrogant air he waved the unlit Gauloises at me and stated, "I have to get used to nothing, my friend. I have no intention of making my home in Palm Beach, or anyplace else in America. I consider Switzerland my native land and Europe my playground. Here, I am a rich bastard. There, I am only rich."

He waved to a passing waiter and pointed at our drinks. Being behind, I tossed back my bourbon to catch up. His stand-up martini was already down to a landlocked olive.

I was tempted to ask if his mother had ever revealed the name of his father to him but thought better of it. If, as Denny suspected, Jeff had known who it was, I deemed it best not to even hint that others had picked up the scent. Also, the label *bastard* had become synonymous with scoundrel as well as illegitimate. How embarrassing if I popped the question and Talbot was not referring to the circumstances of his birth. But surely he was aware that he carried his mother's maiden name and not his father's.

"Then there are others interested in finding Jeff's murderer?" he posed.

"The Palm Beach Police Department, among others," I asserted.

Waving this aside, as was his annoying habit, he said, "There is an investigative reporter in town who is with a particularly odious tabloid. We played tennis against him and Malcolm MacNiff, as I'm sure you know. Is he interested in Jeff's murder?"

Were we dueling with rapiers instead of words, it would be time for someone to shout *en garde*. Any doubts that Lance Talbot was fishing were now dispelled. Did he know that he had given away more than the question warranted? I think he did. I also thought he had no choice in the matter.

As Denny and I suspected, Jeff must have put Lance's secret on the auction block and was waiting to see who, Lance or Denny, would make the winning bid. Lance was now desperate to know how much Jeff had told Denny. If not, why

Lance's interest in the reporter from the odious tabloid?

"If he is here because of Jeff, he would have anticipated the murder," I said, "which is very unlikely. Dennis Darling arrived in Palm Beach a few days before Jeff was shoved into the MacNiff pool."

"How silly of me," he apologized.

To let him know that I was not oblivious to his concern with Denny's presence, I added, "Unless you have information that links Darling's visit to Jeff's murder."

He leaned toward me across the small table, bringing our faces very close indeed. I took the moment to notice that the area abutting his hairline was noticeably whiter than his tanned face. I concluded that his crew cut was recently acquired, and exposure to our Florida sun had not as yet darkened the skin beneath his newly cropped hair to match his handsome puss. Interesting?

It was then I remembered that I had forgotten to bring the photograph of Lance and the boy we thought was Jeff Rodgers for show and tell. The oversight would prove providential.

The waiter brought our drinks, forcing Lance to pull back, making his body language less foreboding. When he spoke, his words were less curt than they would have been had the waiter not forced him to reconsider.

"Let's cut the crapola, Archy. I haven't got the time or the patience for it. I told you I wanted to hire you to find Jeff's murderer, and I told you why I wanted the fink caught. I was sincere. If you have a client after the same thing, that's fine. My guess is that it's Malcolm MacNiff, as the crime was committed on his turf. I know he paid for the funeral. I offered to do the same and was told it had all been taken care of. Use what you've already learned and build on it at my expense. I'm willing to pay you double your going rate."

My going rate, even by Palm Beach standards, was usurious. Doubled it was delightfully iniquitous. Who knows, I might yet get to like Lance Talbot.

"The clock is ticking," I warned before going in for the kill. "Jeff Rodgers was boasting that he expected to come into a huge chunk of money, compliments of Lance Talbot. I also learned that Jeff was being paid to keep his mouth shut."

Much to my chagrin, Lance looked amused. "Keep his mouth shut? About what?"

"You tell me. You were the supposed banker."

He sighed, looking relieved. "Is that what all the fuss is about? Really?"

"Fuss?" I exclaimed. "The guy is dead. Murdered. He threatens you and he's wasted. That's not exactly much ado about nothing, my friend."

He shook his head as I spoke. "No, no. This is all a gross misunderstanding. Jeff never threatened me. That's preposterous."

"Had you talked with him since you came back to Palm Beach?" I questioned.

"Naturally. Why not? We were old friends. Classmates at your quaint Day School."

Quaint? There, yet again, was that continental put-down of things American. And it wasn't *my* Day School. It was *his*. Or was it?

"Jeff was always a bit jealous of me, Archy," he explained. "Correction. Let's be honest. Jeff was always incredibly jealous of me and anyone else who was rich. In this town, that's a hell of a lot of folks. I was too young to recall exactly how Jeff and I teamed up. I believe his father brought him to the house one day when his own sitter was unable to care for Jeff. Rollo was a widower. After that we were insepa-

228

rable. At the age of four, one bonds very quickly.

"I told you his father, Rollo, was our chauffeur. When my mother enrolled me in the Day School, she enrolled Jeff also, paying his fees. Rollo took us to and from school. Poor Jeff made me promise not to tell our classmates Rollo was his father. He had pretensions, Archy. Pretensions far above his station in life. When my mother took me to live in Switzerland, Jeff was left without a benefactress. Tuition at the Day School was beyond Rollo's means, so Jeff got dumped."

He paused long enough to sip his gin martini. So far, Lance's account of his association with Jeff Rodgers corroborated with Todd's version.

Lance continued: "Dumped is the operative word, Archy. It was a bum thing to do to my best pal. But remember, I had no say in the matter. I was a kid, too. When next I saw Jeff, we were no longer children and I had come into my inheritance prematurely. I found Jeff waiting tables, which did nothing to inhibit his pretensions. I owed him, Archy. I owed him big time. He talked about buying a restaurant or bar in New York. The Hamptons, I believe, where he worked summers when things were slow here.

"As I will always be a rich bastard in Palm Beach, so Jeff would always be someone the rich tipped. The Hamptons was his escape. I told him I would act as his silent partner, putting up all the cash necessary for his enterprise, give him an allowance until the business began to pay, and even throw in a house to sweeten the deal.

"And there's the answer to Jeff's newly acquired wealth, compliments of Lance Talbot." Still holding his Gauloises, he opened his arms wide and finished with, "Case closed."

It's closed only because a rebuttal from Jeff Rodgers was impossible, due to circumstances beyond my control. Talbot didn't know if Jeff had actually talked to Denny, but he was betting the farm that Jeff had not. I would apprise Denny of Talbot's account of Jeff's windfall and watch the fur fly when the two faced off at the MacNiffs' tomorrow afternoon. Would Denny bare what he knew, which wasn't much? Or hint that Jeff had sold his story? That, to be sure, was up to Denny. My sage father had said that if Jeff had been murdered for what he knew, the murderer wouldn't hesitate to eliminate anyone seeking to learn Jeff's secret. Beware,

Dennis Darling — *et tu,* Archy McNally.

After a moment's contemplative thought, I offered, "How very altruistic of you."

He nodded as if in agreement. "Thank you, Archy. Are you satisfied now that you know the facts?"

"Me?" I said. "It's the police you'll have to satisfy."

"Do they know about Jeff's boasting?"

No, but they soon will. After listening to Talbot's story, I had decided it was time to bring Al Rogoff into the picture. The stakes were high and getting more dangerous by the moment. I enjoy going with the flow, but after sparring with Lance Talbot I saw a tidal wave on the horizon.

"If the police don't know about Jeff's claim, they will when they finish questioning his friends. As I said, he bragged about his expectations."

"Then perhaps I should tell them the truth before they jump to the wrong conclusion. You think, yes?"

His English seemed to deteriorate under stress. "I think, yes, Lance. The sooner, the better."

"The Baron arrives tomorrow," he said. "Holga and I must meet him at the airport. He comes here from Zurich via New York. In the afternoon is the MacNiff gathering.

After that I will go to the police. I see no reason to alter my plans over this misunderstanding. It has nothing to do with Jeff's murder."

The statement left me nonplussed. If the Baron was who I thought it was, the ladies who lunch would be queuing up for his services, led by Lady Cynthia Horowitz. "The Baron?" I tried to raise one eyebrow and failed.

"Holga's husband," he said with nary a blush. I guess they had never heard that two's company and three's a crowd in the snowy Alps, but perhaps, over there, husbands don't count. The tongue waggers would grow hoarse over this trio.

"The title is a little joke between Holga and me," he elucidated. "Uncle Claus is not from a noble family, although he likes to play the part. He is a renowned doctor of surgery, specializing in reconstruction. He operated on my mother some years ago and during her convalescence at his clinic they became good friends and remained so. He and Holga became our extended family."

So the late Jessica Talbot had had a facelift and got tight with her Svengali and his spouse. "The von Brechts have no children?" I ventured.

"No. I'm their surrogate son," he said, seemingly proud of the fact.

How much of this should I believe? I wondered. The guy's imagination was as rich as his wallet. And was he taking some kind of warped pleasure in the fact that his supposed mistress's husband was coming to live with them? This was beginning to make the British colonization of Kenya look like a church picnic.

"I had the pleasure of drawing Ms. von Brecht as a partner at the MacNiffs' benefit," I told him. "From her speech I gathered she was American."

"By birth only," Lance informed me. "True, she was born in America. Maine? Vermont? It's never discussed. After college she took the tour, as it was called, met and married Uncle Claus in Switzerland and never returned here. She is as Swiss as the Alps, believe me."

Then I asked something that I would later regret. "We played opposite Vivian Emerson and her escort, Joe Gallo. I got the impression that Ms. von Brecht and Ms. Emerson were friends."

With an emphatic shake of the head he denied this. "Holga knows no one here. If she did, I'm sure she would have mentioned it to me. What made you think

Holga knew this woman?"

I wasn't about to give him any more than I already had, but even at that point it was too late to undo the damage. "Nothing, really," I said with an uncaring shrug. "Just an impression which was obviously false." Quickly changing lanes, I told him I would be at the MacNiff shindig on the morrow.

"Then you will meet the Baron, if he chooses to come. You don't think a social gathering so soon after the tragedy is a bit macabre?" he asked.

"Mr. MacNiff is using the occasion to announce that in the future his scholarship fund will become a memorial to Jeff Rodgers."

"Again Mr. MacNiff outmaneuvers me. I was going to establish something like that in Jeff's memory."

"Perhaps you can make an annual donation to the MacNiff charity on Jeff's behalf."

"I'll do just that," he said. "Would you care for another drink?"

"No, thank you. I have dinner plans."

"And do you accept my commission?"

"At double my fee, I would be crazy to refuse."

He extended his hand. "The name Archibald is derived from the German. It means 'distinguished and bold.' I enjoy researching the origin of names to see if they are an apt description of the bearer. Lance comes from the Arthurian legend of Lance-of-Lot or Lancelot. The knight who gained the Holy Grail."

I took his hand and shook it with gusto. "Afraid not, kid. Galahad gained the Holy Grail. Lancelot was caught in bed with Guinevere."

SIXTEEN

"The king is dead." The rambling of an old lady, or the solution to this case? Which was the answer? More to the point, what was the question? Was I looking for the true identity of the man calling himself Lance Talbot, or for the secret that got Jeff Rodgers killed? It didn't take an Einstein to conclude that the two might very well be opposite sides of the same coin.

Denny believed that Jeff knew who sired Lance and the absentee daddy preferred to remain anonymous. Denny wanted to believe this because it would make the most sensational story, especially if Lance's dad was a household name who was as pure as a babe in arms. The purer the better, because such falls from grace are the meat and potatoes of the tabloid press.

Denny's zeal for a kinky headline had clouded his otherwise clear vision. If Jeff knew who the man was, and if the man did not want the fact known, Jeff would have blackmailed the father, not the son. And Jeff would have done it years ago, not now, as if Lance's return spurred his memory. But suppose the man's position made him incommunicado to lesser mortals, making it necessary for Jeff to bargain via Lance?

Then again, could Lance's father have also recently returned to Palm Beach? Or would, shortly? Lance wouldn't pay to protect a father who had abandoned him. Did Jessica Talbot go to Switzerland, taking her son, because her lover was there? The Baron? Why would the doctor wish to remain anonymous, and where did that leave poor Holga?

Sorry, Denny, all of the above are possible, but surely not plausible. However, I'm sure that if Denny knew about the grandmother's doubts as to her heir's identity, he would give up the search for Lance's father and pick up, with me, the search for Lance himself.

The two people who knew Lance Talbot for the first ten years of his life were both dead. One by natural causes, after she may have expressed doubts as to his legitimacy. The other murdered, after he had allegedly leaned on Talbot for hush money. With Mrs. Talbot gone, Jeff was the only other person who could spot Lance Talbot for a phony — if that were the case.

Some secret shared by the two boys the

returning Lance failed to remember? A word, or phrase, tossed at him by Jeff that required a response Lance had not tossed back? Ten toes, when there should be only nine? It could be any or all of those things. Or, if one believed Lance, none of them.

I had just come from hearing Lance's side of the story and could find no concrete reason why I should not believe him, while believing what Jeff had told Denny. Todd had labeled Jeff a wiseguy and a malcontent. Certainly not the kind of recommendation that inspired confidence in the boy's integrity. Was Jeff getting a generous handout from Lance while using the celebrated Talbot name to lure Dennis Darling to Palm Beach with the hope of selling a story to Denny that was either trumped-up or fatuous?

After our chat in the Leopard Lounge only one thing was now certain. Lance Talbot had something to hide and he was afraid Dennis Darling knew that, or might even know the secret itself. My money was on old Mrs. Talbot. "The king" — meaning her grandson — "is dead." So who had stood me two bourbons at the Leopard Lounge this evening, and who wanted me to find Jeff Rodgers's murderer? The killer himself? But Lance had close to a hundred reliable witnesses, including Denny and Archy, to swear he was nowhere near the scene of the crime. I have looked upon many a well-turned ankle in my time but I never thought I would live to see the day I lusted after the sight of a guy's foot.

Thus was my mind occupied as I drove to the Pelican. I took the Royal Palm Way Bridge on this balmy winter night with the temperature in the seventies and a breeze off the Atlantic making a cashmere wrap appropriate for the ladies and jackets more serviceable than show for Madame's escort. The lit windows of the new steel and glass office buildings in West Palm reflected playfully on the dark waters of Lake Worth, and I imagined I could hear music coming from the Governor's Club in the penthouse suite atop the opulent tower it called home.

My red Miata raced through an animated picture postcard of Palm Beach in season, in all its flamboyant splendor — and how I loved it. Also, I was very hungry.

Georgy girl was seated at the Pelican bar. So too were Binky Watrous and Isadora Duhane. They were chatting like old friends and drinking what I thought to be champagne cocktails. The dining room was hopping and I spotted Todd working the floor along with our Priscilla.

Georgy looked gorgeous in one of those sack dresses she favored. This one in white, with a silk paisley scarf cinching her waist. White flats adorned a pair of gams that did not need the classic high heel to show off their allure. Her emerald eyes lit up at my approach and my silent admiration was rewarded with a kiss.

"You're not late," Georgy said, "I was early and Binky and Isadora were good enough to keep me company before going off to dinner." Turning to Isadora, she went on, "This is the famous Archy McNally. Archy, this is Binky's friend, Isadora Duhane."

"Our paths have crossed three times today, Mr. McNally. It was inevitable that we finally meet," Isadora said, eyeing my safari jacket as if memorizing the tiniest detail for reproduction in prose.

Unlike Georgy, Isadora was not the girl next door most likely to be voted Homecoming Queen or the sweetheart of Sigma Chi. Far from it. I would classify Isadora Duhane as striking. Good skin, not yet tinted by our tropical sun. The dark hair I had seen under the babushka was cut as short as a man's and fringed with bangs. The eyes behind the no-nonsense specs were as dark as the frames. In the makeup department, Ms. Duhane believed that less was better. Lipstick and perhaps a dusting of face powder proved her right.

Her figure, sans the shapeless raincoat, was impressive, if a bit on the lean side for my taste. Tonight she wore a straight gray skirt in Ultrasuede with a black jersey mock turtleneck. Her only jewelry appeared to be a single strand of pearls that looked ultrareal and probably were.

"Do you usually go to morning services at St. Edward's, Ms. Duhane?"

"You may call me Izzy," she said, as if I should be grateful for the honor.

"And you may call me anything *but* Skip McGuire," I retaliated.

"Oh." She smiled. "Binky told you about our little project?"

Glaring at my friend, I told her he had. "And I'm not thrilled at the prospect of being parodied in a murder mystery."

"Lighten up, Archy," Georgy said. "They told me about it and it sounds like fun."

"You wouldn't think so if you were in it," I answered.

"But she is," Izzy cried. "We're calling her Sam. Short for Samantha. Get it?"

I got it all right. Was there no end to Izzy's cleverness? And what did she see in Binky? I mean, he's okay, if you like your men average height, blond and bland. Poor Binky just didn't have the wherewithal to please the opposite sex — if you get my drift. Looking at him now, as he tried to avoid my irate gaze, I hardly recognized my old friend. Besides the manicured hair, he was decked out in a double-breasted Armani suit and a white-on-white shirt with French cuffs and pearl links. Who did he think he was, me? And were the links from a matching set to the strand hanging from Izzy's neck? What next? A diamond-studded yoke?

I must remember to tell our mail person that he who marries for money, earns it.

Mr. Pettibone was now before us, asking, "Will you have the same, Archy?"

"Who's paying?" I wanted to know.

"Archy!" Georgy chided me, and Izzy laughed.

"My treat," said Diamond Jim Watrous. "Champagne cocktails all around, Mr. Pettibone."

"What are we celebrating?" I asked.

"The opening lines of *The Adventures of Skip McGuire*," Izzy announced in triumph.

"In that case, I'll abstain," I told Mr. Pettibone.

"Don't be a spoilsport," Georgy nagged. "It's really very good."

Shocked, I asked, "You've read it?"

"Just the very beginning," Georgy said. "Binky read it aloud."

"You know, Ms. Duhane . . ." I began.

"Izzy, please," she broke in.

"Okay, Izzy," I began again. "It may interest you to know my father was called upon to defend your mentor, Minerva Barnes, in a libel suit brought on by a person she had maligned in her last romantic extravaganza."

"Sabine maiden," Binky murmured with reverence as he watched Mr. Pettibone pop the cork on a bottle of pricey Brut. I didn't know if he was referring to the title of Minerva's book, ancient Rome or his rich squeeze.

"Him!" Izzy said, naming a film star of note. "He was my second cousin's first husband, and everything Minerva wrote about him was true. When I decided to try my hand at fiction I came here just so I could join Minerva's workshop. She's a real pro."

"Then why don't you emulate your teacher and stick to romance?"

"Romance is not my strong suit," Izzy pleaded, and I wondered if Binky had heard the comment.

"But when Binky told me about your adventures as a discreet inquirer, I knew I had found my forte," Izzy rhapsodized.

It seems romance is not the tie that binds this literary couple, but Binky's spilling the beans on his pal Archy. Or should that be former pal? Like the Arabian princess, Binky had to keep talking to keep his love alive, and I shuddered to think what poetic license he would take with my life. He continued to avoid my gaze as Mr. Pettibone poured our cocktails. I have always thought a champagne cocktail was a waste of good wine, but when you're out with amateurs you take what's being offered.

Should I expose Binky here and now? Tell Izzy the man she bought the Armani suit for was our mail person, and send him back to his paper dolls, where he belonged? Seeing him all gussied up and afraid to look at me, I just didn't have the heart. You're a sentimental sap, Archy McNally.

Then Georgy got on my case. "Don't rush to judgment, Archy. Keep an open mind. I wonder who will play me in the movie," she chatted like a magpie.

"Augusta Apple," I told her.

"Augusta Apple is dead," she protested.

"And so will you be if you persist in endorsing this inane idea," I threatened. My gentle nature was being provoked by these women and the friend who refused to look me in the eye. "My livelihood depends on discretion. I like to keep a low profile, thank you."

"So why did you give Michael Price the interview?" Georgy countered.

"So I could confuse you with my pet canine, that's why."

Izzy chuckled. "I like that. Binky, make a note and put it under gross mishaps, like the time his lady friend emptied a dish of eggs Benedict down the inside of his trousers, and the night he went skinny-dipping and a crab bit his . . ."

"Enough!" I cried. "Binky, you are history."

Georgy picked up her stem glass. "Cool it, Archy, and drink up. Here's to a best-seller."

They picked up their glasses as I folded my arms across my chest. Needless to say I was dying of thirst. "I'll sue," was my toast to the best-seller.

"Binky, read Archy our opening," Izzy

requested. "You'll love this, Archy."

"Don't you dare," I cautioned the traitor.

Defiant, he pulled a page of notepaper from his jacket pocket and emoted.

As she walked into my office I caught the odor of expensive perfume and trouble. Outside my window the first two letters of the Essex Hotel's blinking neon sign had blown a fuse, as if heralding her arrival. She saw it and smiled. "Are you for hire?" she asked in a voice that was as smooth as velvet and as tough as nails.

"Depends on the job, Miss . . ."

"Mrs. Rich. Ivy Rich."

She opened her fur coat and sank into my visitor's chair, crossing her legs so that the hem of her black silk dress slithered above her knee. "I want my husband followed."

"Why?"

"Because I think he's cheating on me."

"If he is, he must be nuts."

"My, aren't you nice, Mr. McGuire."

"My friends call me Skip."

I clicked on the intercom and spoke to my secretary. "Milly? I'll be working late, honey, and I won't be needing you. Nighty-night."

Binky turned to his audience as if expecting a standing ovation. What he got from me was a Bronx cheer.

"James Cain is turning over in his grave," I moaned. "It's dreadful."

"Really?" Georgy said. "We think it's great." She tried to look like she meant it but when Izzy and Binky burst into laughter, Georgy joined in.

Even Mr. Pettibone was smiling as he dropped a cherry in an old-fashioned. "Did you read it to him?" he asked.

"Don't you see, Archy? We composed it while waiting for you to arrive," Georgy said between bursts of laughter.

"Blame me," Izzy confessed. "When Binky told me you weren't happy with our proposed book, I thought it would be fun to give you the worst possible preview of what we were up to."

"And you succeeded," I told my antagonists. "I can take a joke and I congratulate the authors." I wasn't exactly thrilled at being the target of a charade, but when you're out with amateurs, etc., etc., etc. It did, however, give me an excuse to finally raise my glass and one should always be thankful for small favors. "I rather liked the Sex Hotel. Does Skip live there?"

"No," Georgy answered, "he lives at home with Mumsy and Dada."

I could have brained her but the others laughed and I went along for the ride. I was painfully aware that I was a decade older than each of them and any show of sour grapes would be attributed to my antiquity. I drank more of my champagne cocktail.

"I'll strike a bargain with you, Mr. McNally," Izzy offered.

"Please, call me Skip."

That got a laugh, as intended, further abating the charged atmosphere that had encompassed our party before Binky's performance. Even Izzy appeared to be more regular and I now saw that her earlier, rather haughty manner was part of the show. This pleased me. If Binky married money I wanted to be comfortable with the lady of the mansion, as I would like to visit my old friend often.

However, I ruminated, eyeing Izzy, I have taken women away from Binky before and why not again? What a cad to have such a thought with the lovely Georgy girl at my side. But, alas, I had such a thought.

"Binky and I will continue to work on

our book and when it's done we will turn it over to you for comment. I promise not to publish without your consent."

"I say no and you trash it?"

"You have our word," Binky pledged.

Knowing what Binky's word was worth, I eyed him with a scowl, but he didn't cower. Remarkable what an Armani suit and a rich lady friend could do for a guy. Sensing my doubt, Izzy also gave me her word.

"Now tell me, what you were doing at Jeff Rodgers's funeral services this morning?"

"I've been reading about the murder," Izzy replied, "and I wanted to get a look at the cast of characters. Binky and I have been discussing it and we have some ideas. I know Binky is undercover at the moment, so he couldn't accompany me."

Even Georgy girl winced at that one.

"I think you had better stick to your fiction," I advised Izzy with yet another menacing look at Binky. This time he cringed, making me feel better. "Meddling with murder can be dangerous."

"Are you on the case?" Izzy asked with obvious envy.

"Let's say Skip is on top of things," I teased, giving Izzy my thousand-watt smile.

Georgy's glare had me canceling my plans to marry for money. Lieutenant O'Hara, let's not forget, carries heat and qualifies at the firing range monthly. Connie, my former flame, often threatened me with a carving knife. Did I have to be in harm's way to fall in love? With Izzy's loot, she probably owned an arsenal of assault weapons.

"How thrilling," Izzy said. "I'll try to keep out of your way. Now Binky and I must fly. Mother keeps an apartment at The Breakers and most of my wardrobe is still there. I have to pick up a few things and I thought we would have dinner at Flagler's Steakhouse. Binky adores dining at The Breakers."

The blushing undercover agent signed the bar tab and fled with his Mata Hari. "See you, Archy," were his parting words.

"I can't wait, Binky — I can't wait," I called after him.

SEVENTEEN

As they waltzed out the door, Georgy exclaimed, "Her mother keeps an apartment at The Breakers and she's living next door to Binky?"

I filled her in on Izzy's heritage. "She's the black sheep of the Battle clan."

"That explains those pearls," Georgy said with awe. "They were real, you know."

"I know. And so were Binky's cufflinks. The guy is a kept man, Georgy. He's been looking for a lucrative career for ten years and he finally found one. I believe the job description can be summed up in one word: gigolo."

She laughed. "I believe Archy is jealous."

"I won't deny it. I want those cufflinks."

"To go with that jacket? Where did you ever get it, Archy? From an extra in an old Tarzan movie?"

"No, I bought it in a smart trading post in Kenya." I signaled Priscilla who was just passing our way. "Can we get a table?"

"Your favorite in the corner will be available in five minutes. Todd is just clearing it." Priscilla was wrapped in one of those sarong dresses in beige, which is her color. Her hair hung loose, one side swept back from her face with a lovely gardenia covering the clip that held it in place.

"Do you have a Hula-Hoop to go with the frock?" I asked.

Addressing Georgy, she said, "What's a nice girl like you doing with Jungle Jim?"

Naturally, Georgy all but applauded. "I told you," she mocked me.

"Did he read the opening lines?" Priscilla asked, still directing the conversation at Georgy.

"Don't tell me you were in on it, too?" I groused.

"*Her black silk dress slithered above her knee* was my contribution," Priscilla recited, with a show of pride.

"That figures," was my comment.

"Izzy thinks I have talent," Priscilla boasted, as if Izzy were a literary scholar.

"She thinks Binky has talent, too, so consider the source, Missy," I told her.

"Meow. Meow. I think Jungle Jim is jealous," Priscilla ridiculed, wagging a finger at me. "Binky's girl is a looker and as rich as Leroy's *mousse chocolat*. If I owned those pearls, Georgy honey, I would sell them and buy Denzel Washington."

Priscilla Pettibone didn't need the price of Izzy's pearls to tempt Denzel Washington, or any heterosexual male for that matter. She's had her share of offers from some very eligible bachelors, but she's holding out for a modeling career and doesn't want to be saddled with any extra baggage when Lady Luck beckons. She's done some work for a fashion photographer in Miami in return for a composite that is now making the rounds of the New York agencies. We all wish her well but would hate to lose her.

"Not me, Pris," Georgy replied. "There isn't a man who's worth that much — present company excepted."

"That," I said, "saved you from buying your own dinner."

"Speaking of dinner tabs," Priscilla confided, "Binky is now a solvent Pelican, thanks to Izzy."

Not true, of course. It was I who had paid Binky's bill at the club, but being a gentleman I didn't tattle. I did wonder, though, if having your lady friend pay your club bill was any less embarrassing than having your male friend write the check? Binky, to be sure, couldn't care less who bailed him out as long as the wolf left his front door so he could go out and run up another tab.

If Isadora Duhane was as fickle in her endeavors as Lolly had implied, what would happen when she abandoned Skip McGuire and moved on? Would Binky trade his Armani suit for a palimony suit? With Binky, as with Jesus, all things are possible.

"Don't look now," Priscilla warned, "but here comes the conquistador and his sassy señorita. My, what a pair they make," she gloated.

I turned to see Connie Garcia and Alejandro Gomez y Zapata make an entrance that lacked only a rose between Connie's teeth to make one think the curtain had just gone up on Bizet's opus. They headed straight for the bar and I immediately took hold of Georgy's elbow, endeavoring to lead her to our table before the Cuban encroachment on our territory.

"Wait, Archy," Georgy urged, "they've seen us. It would be rude not to say hello."

I was not in the mood to be polite, but did as I was told. It was difficult for me not to do Georgy girl's bidding. Her gold hair and emerald eyes made Izzy's string of pearls look like paste. What a lovely thought. I must remember to whisper it into her ear at the appropriate moment.

Better than *sweet nothings* any day.

Connie and Don Alejandro looked like the winning contestants in a cha-cha contest. Her green sheath ended in a fringed hem that played peekaboo with her knees as she walked. Her dark hair was pulled back from her face and knotted into a bun. Connie was not a petite woman but even in her stiletto heels she was a head shorter than Alex.

It only upsets me to delineate Alex so I'll pass on Georgy's opinion of the guy, *gorgeous hunk,* and leave it at that. He was very South Beach this evening in jeans (too tight) and a white dress shirt (too tight) with a navy ascot. He dangled a light-weight jacket over his shoulder à la a matador's cape. It's a wonder the entire dining room didn't stand up and shout *Olé!*

I am a founding member of the Pelican and, being a closeted chauvinist, voted against admitting women on the grounds that a guy should be able to wine and dine a new acquaintance without fear of running into an old acquaintance who believed you were at home nursing a head cold.

I was overruled, as Connie's arrival with her guest shows. Liking the amenities the Pelican offers, Georgy is now thinking of applying for membership. I proposed a moratorium on new admissions on the grounds that our exclusivity was being compromised, which sent the sitting board members into raucous laughter from which they have yet to recover.

The girls touched cheeks and kissed the air over their heads, telling each other how pretty they looked. Alex gripped my hand and, I think, broke it.

"Have you guys been to the Leopard Lounge?" Connie asked.

"No," Georgy told her. "Why do you ask?"

"The safari jacket," Connie tittered, "he always wears it when he goes there. Right, Archy?"

"Afraid not, Consuela. I also wear it when I go to the zoo."

"I like it," Alex said. "You know, Archy, if you were a little taller and a little broader in the shoulders, I would borrow it."

Really? Well, if I were a little taller and a little broader in the shoulders, Alex, I would punch you in the nose.

Sensing my thoughts and thinking a quick parting of the ways was the better part of valor, Georgy announced that we were just going to sit down to dinner.

"Don't let us keep you," Alex said. "We just stopped in for a quick one before heading south. My cousin is getting married on Saturday and I'm in the wedding party, so we're starting the weekend a few days early."

Alex is first-generation American and therefore more American than apple pie. Between them, Alex and Connie have about three thousand cousins in Miami, making weddings, christenings and funerals a weekly occurrence. Being a political columnist for a Miami Hispanic daily seemed to give Alex enough free time to practically commute between his hometown and Palm Beach. But when the imminent invasion of Cuba is your sole topic, you can afford to play the hook. One hour in Cuba and Alex would come running back to the comforts of Miami if he had to swim all the way.

"Archy," Connie said in that voice I knew only too well meant a major grievance. "My lady boss is furious with your pal, Lolly Spindrift. She wanted to entertain Dennis Darling, but Lolly forbade it on the grounds that Darling was here to trash us and anyone associating with him would be social poison in this town. Now we hear Lolly and Darling were chatting it up over dinner at Cafe L'Europe."

"Do as Lolly says, not as Lolly does," I quipped, unmoved by Lady Cynthia Horowitz's plight. I find it difficult to get sentimental over a lady with ten million bucks, ten acres on Ocean Boulevard and six ex-husbands. Lady C's passion for gorgeous hunks made Alex most vulnerable. Connie must be keeping her new love as far from the Madame as possible, but Lolly certainly gave Lady C all the ribald details just to goad her.

"If we all did as Lolly does we'd all be at the Colony right now," Connie said. When this got her three blank stares, she told us that Thursday night at the Colony was now where the boys gathered in rather large numbers. "Lolly is probably holding court as we speak."

What was this world coming to when you had to check what day of the week it was before you went out for a few pops? The right pub on the wrong day, or the wrong pub on the right day, and you become suspect. Georgy and Alex were listening to all this with rapt attention. They both enjoyed hearing the Palm Beach scuttlebutt, which had as much impact on the real world as an elephant delivering a mouse.

"And," Connie went on, "the Hollywood crew has arrived to screen-test Jackson Barnett. Read all about it in tomorrow's dailies."

"Are they staying on Meecham's yacht?" I asked.

Connie shook her head. "At the Colony. And make of that what you will."

Mr. Pettibone arrived to take their drink order, giving us the opportunity to relinquish our stools and head for our corner table. The girls touched cheeks and kissed the air over their heads. I waved bye-bye at Alex to avoid serious damage to my hand.

"You make a handsome foursome," Priscilla said when she presented us with menus. "A study in contrasts, if you know what I mean."

"Yeah," I answered. "The sublime and the ridiculous."

"Archy, that's not kind," Georgy reprimanded, as if I didn't know.

"Meow. Meow," Priscilla meowed.

"Are you auditioning for *Cats*, Missy? If not, kindly take our drink order."

"Are you sticking to champagne cocktails?"

"No, but I'm sticking to wine. I've already had two bourbons." Without consulting the wine list I ordered, "A bottle of our best *Pouilly-Fuissé*." To Georgy, I said, "Does that suit, or would you prefer a proper drink?"

"I'm in your hands," she acquiesced.

"You might want to reconsider, Georgy," Priscilla suggested.

"Hush, and go fetch our wine," I barked.

She performed a perfect curtsy before scurrying off, leaving Georgy and me alone for the first time that evening. It was now close to ten and the late diners were just settling in as the early crowd began to make their exit. Couples and singles greeted each other in passing and Mr. Pettibone's bar was standing room only. Alex and Connie, I noticed, were now part of a group of revelers. We were a congenial crowd at the Pelican with an eclectic mix of guys and dolls who believed in life, liberty and the pursuit of different strokes for different folks, regardless of what day of the week you felt like doing your thing.

"Alone at last," I sighed.

"Where did you have those bourbons?" Georgy grilled me.

"Don't you have to read me my rights, first?" I objected.

"This is off the record, McNally."

"At the Chesterfield," I admitted.

She thought a moment, looking adorable, then said, "Isn't the Leopard Lounge in the Chesterfield?"

"Off the record, yes."

"Then Connie was right," she concluded. "Why didn't you admit it?"

"I wouldn't give her the satisfaction," I sulked.

Georgy and I had met on the rebound. Me, from Connie's demands to legalize our open relationship, and Georgy from Joe Gallo who had succumbed to the lure of a rich Palm Beach widow. What neither of us expected was to be confronted with our past loves and our reaction to it. We had run into Connie and Alex at the club where I was forced to introduce them to Georgy.

Out of curiosity, I think, the girls had become wary friends. Georgy, because she was curious about her predecessor, and Connie because she wanted to see just who had taken her place. As the fates would have it, I got to meet Joe Gallo and Vivian Emerson on a tennis court, of all places. I didn't know who he was at the time, but Georgy reminded me with a reference to Gallo's masculine appeal.

Georgy, as she just made clear, is quick to tell me how well Connie knows me, which suggests a former intimacy, and I now wonder how often Georgy dwells on Gallo's manly charms. Furthermore, I am discourteous to Alejandro Gomez y Zapata for no reason other than his affair with the woman I willingly gave up. What we obviously need is Minerva Barnes to sort it all out in twenty-five steamy chapters with a happily-ever-after ending. The only happy ending I see at the moment is me walking off into the sunset with Izzy Duhane in a pearl necklace and me in matching cufflinks.

"You're pouting," Georgy accused.

"I'm thinking about Binky's cufflinks," I said, in all honesty.

"They make a cute couple, Binky and Izzy, don't you think?"

"No, I do not think any such thing. She's interesting, in a way, and he's in over his head. All she wants from him is info on me for her book. Lolly told me she's a sucker for causes and hops from one to another like a bee in a garden. When she loses interest in this writing project she'll leave Binky, move her clothes back to The Breakers and hightail it out of Palm Beach. As Lolly would say, you heard it here first."

"Promise me you won't tell her Binky is not undercover on a case," Georgy requested. "It would break his heart."

"I want to break his neck, but I won't rain on his parade. The day of reckoning is near enough."

"You're a softie, McNally."

"And you are the prettiest cop in Juno."

"What about the rest of Florida?"

Todd brought a bucket of ice on a tripod to our table and greeted me. I introduced him to Georgy.

"Handsome," she dubbed our sommelier when he went off to get our wine.

"He's spoken for," I told her. "Her name is Monica. She's a political science major when she isn't waitressing at the Ambassador Grill."

"How do you know all this?" Georgy wondered.

"A lot has happened since last we met, Georgy girl. Do you want to hear what Skip McGuire has been up to?"

"I'm listening, Skip."

Todd brought our wine, did the honors and poured. "I'm working the MacNiff party tomorrow, Mr. McNally. You going?"

"I am, Todd."

"A little creepy, don't you think? Jeff was just buried today and now they're having a party around the pool he drowned in."

That gave Georgy a start. "What's this?"

"Mr. MacNiff is going to announce that

his scholarship fund will be renamed in memory of Jeff Rodgers. I think you'll find it all in good taste, Todd."

"If you say so, Mr. McNally." He withdrew, unconvinced of Nifty's good intentions.

"Jeff Rodgers is the kid who got done in at the charity party," Georgy said. "Was he a friend of Todd's?"

"Cheers," I toasted, and proceeded to tell her all the salient facts of "The King Is Dead."

Georgy's position makes it possible for me to confide in her, trusting that she would not repeat what she heard. Her keen assessment of the facts was always welcome as well as helpful. It's the same relationship I am lucky to share with Al Rogoff, but I must say that Georgy girl offers additional tangible assets that Al could not possibly compete with.

Georgy heard me out like the pro she was and interrupted only to clarify a point I had not made clear. When done, I refilled our wine glasses and waited for her learned commentary. Not exactly unexpectedly, she opened with, "Have you told the police this?"

"Not yet, but after talking to Talbot tonight, I decided to call Al Rogoff and share with our boys in blue."

"You should have done it sooner," Georgy said. "I'm not telling you how to run your business," she added, telling me how to run my business. "I hear the Palm Beach police haven't got a thing out of the boy's friends, and they have no reason to suspect any of the guests at this point. Your story changes all that. You could have saved Al and his partners a lot of sweat, tears and shoe leather."

"Please, don't lecture," I complained. "What else do you hear?"

"The chloroform has them puzzled. It's a controlled substance but readily available in hospitals. Any nurses at the party?"

To the best of my knowledge, there were no nurses at the party and Holga's doctor hubby had not yet graced us with his presence.

"Georgy girl, if I had a buck for every controlled substance on the open market I could buy Binky's cufflinks."

"You and those cufflinks, McNally. You're obsessed."

"Okay. If I had a buck for every controlled substance on the open market I could buy you Izzy's string of pearls."

"Now you're talking my language, McNally. But before you run off to Harry

Winston's emporium, go to the police and tell them what you know."

"I will after the pool party tomorrow. With any luck I can get Talbot into a pair of trunks and count his toes. If he is Talbot, I won't worry the police on that score, and we can look elsewhere for the key to Jeff's blackmail scheme."

"If Jeff was blackmailing Lance Talbot," Georgy said. "And if he isn't Lance Talbot. What then?"

"Malcom MacNiff, the executor of old Mrs. Talbot's estate, goes to the police and motive is established. Then all we have to do is find out who done it on behalf of the faux heir."

Georgy smiled thoughtfully. "Is there a butler on the list of suspects?"

"Nary a one," I lamented. "What's your take on all this?" I asked, looking for a fresh angle on the case.

"Let's toss it around over dinner," she said. "I'm a hungry working girl and it's after ten."

I signaled Priscilla and she came to take our order and impart the specials.

"Osso buco, served over polenta with grilled peas and prosciutto. Calf's liver, sautéed with onions and bacon. New York steak with fries and corn niblets."

"I want them all," Georgy said. "But osso buco is something I seldom do at home, so I think that's what I'll have."

Osso buco is a veal shank, braised in a vegetable and herb broth. Loosely translated it means a hollow bone. Properly cooked, the meat is so tender and savory it needs no knife to accompany your fork. I didn't think Leroy's presentation would be disappointing.

Polenta is Italian-style cornmeal, combined with water and cooked slowly to create an unctuous, creamy base for the meat drippings. It's often compared, erroneously, to grits.

"You'll find it a tad better than Mama Mia's Italian Take Out," I assured her. "I'll have the same, Priscilla. Any suggestions for starters?"

"Being in an Italian frame of mind, Leroy has stuffed artichokes to die for," the chef's sister recommended.

"Let's go all the way," Georgy exclaimed.

"Well, aren't you nice," I teased. I love to see Georgy girl blush. The color begins at her lily-white throat just before two patches of pink appear on her cheeks like a Raggedy Ann doll of yore.

"You're hateful," she cried.

Priscilla laughed as she asked if we cared for a salad before or after dinner.

"After," Georgy declared, "and then espresso with *dolci*. If we're going to dine Italian we . . ."

"Might as well go all the way," Priscilla finished when Georgy hesitated. "We have fresh spinach with chives, leeks and tiny tomatoes, topped with an olive oil and balsamic dressing."

"Sold," I said.

"And another bottle of wine," Georgy ordered.

"You'll get tipsy, Officer," I cautioned.

She shrugged. "When in Rome, McNally. When in Rome."

Todd brought our bread basket and a saucer of oil for dipping, along with a plate of green and black olives, chickpeas, carrot sticks and mini celery stalks.

As we dipped and nibbled, Georgy asked, "Where did that crab bite you, McNally?"

"I'll show you when we get home."

I love to see Georgy girl blush . . .

EIGHTEEN

"I have my own taxi now," Mr. Rodgers said. "Been working for myself since Ms. Talbot went off to Switzerland, taking the boy with her. She gave me the money to set up in business. Severance pay, she called it. Very generous lady, she was."

We were sitting in Rodgers's kitchen in a neat bungalow located just off Lake Worth Road in Greenacres. The neighborhood was similar in look and affordability to Palm Springs, Lake Clarke Shores and Glen Ridge. A bedroom community far enough west of Palm Beach and Lake Worth to be affordable and close enough to the Gold Coast to keep its inhabitants employed.

Ronald Rodgers was a thin, bespectacled man who was approaching or just past the half-century mark. He had kindly offered to brew a pot of coffee, which he served in mugs that now sat before us at the breakfast table. As he spoke, he clasped his mug between the palms of his hands as if trying to warm them.

I had had my usual breakfast on the run after leaving Georgy's cottage this morning, stopping at home only long enough to change my clothes and visit with mother in the greenhouse to assure her that I was still alive. She reported, thanks to Ursi to be sure, that the MacNiff pool party was the talk of Ocean Boulevard, coming so soon after the tragedy. I told her it was for a good cause but did not mention that her favorite son was the catalyst of the shocking affair.

I had called Mr. Rodgers from home, telling him that I was looking into his son's death on behalf of Malcolm MacNiff and would like to see him at his convenience. He said this morning was as good a time as any. I got into a pair of smart, white bell-bottoms with a buttoned fly and a madras shirt in anticipation of the afternoon gathering. Shoving a pair of black-and-white-striped trunks in a leather tote bag, I drove the Miata to Lake Worth, thinking of Denny as I sped past the GulfStream, hoping he had remembered to pack his bathing togs.

I apologized to Rodgers for disturbing him so soon after his son's funeral. He told me he had gone back to work directly after the interment because "working keeps my mind off thinking on what happened to Jeff. He wasn't perfect, Mr. McNally. Don't know anyone that is. But he didn't deserve what they done to him."

Ronald Rodgers had a midwest accent with a slight drawl that made me think of supporting actors in old Western flicks. He was in black trousers and a black tie, a uniform he was unwilling to give up when he stopped driving for others and bought his own cab. I pegged him as a hard working, sincere, kindly man who had spawned a rebel and didn't know quite what to make of it.

"Have you any idea who murdered your son, Mr. Rodgers?"

He shook his head. "The police have asked me that over and over and I'm telling you what I told them — I don't know. Like I said, he was no angel. Discontent with his lot and always looking over the fence for greener pastures. I figure he got in with a crowd of punks who made him believe they could make big bucks with some half-ass scam that blew up in their faces, and my Jeff took the fall. Either they turned on him and put him in that pool or the people they were stinging done it."

"What makes you think that, Mr. Rodgers?"

"My boy was a braggart," he admitted. "He was always talking about some get-rich-quick scheme that was in the works and almost ready to pay off. But these last few weeks he sounded as if he really did have something in the fire. I mean he was walking around like his ship had come in and it was loaded with ready cash. He even promised to buy me another cab, although I don't know who he expected would drive it. Not him, that's for sure."

Jeff had something in the fire, all right, but he was working alone and his patsy was Lance Talbot or Dennis Darling, or maybe both of them.

"I wanted him to come in with me," his father said. "We could work two shifts, I told him. Days he covers the airport, train depot and hotels. Nights, I work the bars and restaurants. In no time we could have had that other taxi and . . ."

He shrugged his thin shoulders in a hopeless gesture.

"Jeff had other ideas," I prompted.

"Fancy ideas," he said. "And maybe I was to blame."

"You mean introducing him to Lance Talbot?"

"You know about that?" he asked.

"I talked to Lance," I said. "Do you

272

mind telling me how the boys came to be such good friends?"

Rodgers got up to pour himself another cup, bringing the Mr. Coffee carafe to the table. I refused seconds. He took out a pack of unfiltered Camels and asked me if I minded. I had puffed one English Oval while dressing and making notes in my journal this morning and vowed not to have another until after dinner when I reported to father over a glass of port.

I told Rodgers to light up, resigned to inhaling what he exhaled, which I understand is just as harmful as going all the way. (Thinking of Georgy girl, I suppressed a foolish grin.)

His story was similar to what I had heard from Todd and Lance Talbot, except that now I was given more pertinent details. Rodgers was chauffeur to old Mrs. Talbot. Her daughter, Jessica, and her boy, Lance, lived in the house on Ocean Boulevard. Rodgers was a widower who employed a sitter for his boy, Jeff, who was four at the time. On a day when his sitter was unable to take Jeff, Rodgers brought the boy to the Talbots' and asked if the child could sit up front with him as he had no place to leave him.

Mrs. Talbot insisted that the child would

be happier spending the day in her home, in the company of her grandson. "And that was the start of it," Rodgers said.

Like many an only child growing up in a house full of adults, Lance was lonely and bored. He was delighted to make a friend and begged to have Jeff visit daily. His request was granted and a year later, when Lance went off to the Day School, Jessica Talbot sent Jeff along and picked up the tab.

"Lance called me Rollo, and so did Jeff. Never *Dad* or *Father.* You see, Mr. McNally, my son was ashamed of me. I should have taken a belt to his behind but I didn't because I loved him. We do some terrible things in the name of love."

Having been down that road I could empathize with poor Rollo. My romantic adventures, to date, had not got me chloroformed and dropped into a pool to drown but I wasn't counting my chickens.

"Do you know why Jessica Talbot decided to live abroad, Mr. Rodgers?"

He puffed on the Camel and I noticed his fingers were stained yellow from the weed. "Young Ms. Talbot was a rebel with a cause," he said with a smile. "She wanted a child but she didn't want a husband. She moved to New York, the Village I think, where it wasn't hard to find someone willing to accommodate her. Old Mrs. Talbot blamed it all on women's liberation.

"When Lance was born she came back home but not with her tail between her legs, believe me. She refused to name the father, and old Mrs. Talbot, who was a proper Victorian lady, never got off her case. I know all this because Ms. Talbot used to talk to me about the old days and how unhappy she was then and how miserable she was now. She used to smoke dope in the back seat of the Rolls while I drove her around town. She couldn't do it in the house, you see."

"Why do you think she came back to Palm Beach?" I asked.

"Because of the boy. She was a Talbot and he was a Talbot and she was going to see that he was raised proper, not in some fleabag apartment full of junkies. She was wild, Mr. McNally, but no fool."

"Did she tell you who fathered Lance?"

"No, sir. She did not. Meaning no disrespect, I would guess she didn't know herself, if you get what I mean."

I got it and, I expect, so did grandma. "Why did she suddenly decide to live abroad?" I asked again.

"It wasn't sudden," Rodgers said. "She talked about it often. Then, one day, she couldn't take her mother's lip no more and off she went, taking the boy. The old lady was mad as hell because she loved Lance, regardless of where he came from, and when they were gone she was alone. I believe Ms. Talbot was independent financially, having been left a trust fund by her father."

"Did old Mrs. Talbot dismiss you?"

"No, sir. I quit, thanks to Jessica Talbot's generosity, and got my own cab."

And poor Jeff got kicked out of his ivory tower and landed in a seat in the Lake Worth elementary school next to Edward (Todd) Brandt. If life was a crapshoot, Jeff had rolled snake eyes at the ripe old age of ten.

"Mr. Rodgers, I know you liked Jessica Talbot." These words are always the precursor to something the listener would rather not talk about and from the look on Rodgers's face he guessed what was coming. "However, I must ask a delicate question. Mr. MacNiff is eager to help the police find the person who killed Jeff. Because the crime took place in his home, he feels he owes it to Jeff, and you, to learn just why this happened."

"Mr. MacNiff has been very kind," Rodgers said. "He paid all the funeral expenses. Do you know how much it costs to get buried in style, Mr. McNally?"

I nodded, knowing it cost more than Mr. Rodgers was currently worth. "Was Jessica Talbot a drug addict?" I finally got out.

He stubbed out his own addiction in an ashtray and, without looking up, answered in the affirmative. This explained Mrs. Talbot's concern, which probably led to her harping on Jessica to seek help. It also told me why Jessica fled to Europe.

I showed the photo Mrs. MacNiff had given me to Ronald Rodgers. He removed his glasses and dabbed at his eyes with a paper napkin. "Jeff and Lance," he mumbled, his voice cracking. "I took that after a ball game. They were on the team at the Day School. I think I have the same picture someplace around here."

The nostalgic reverie was just the lead-in I needed to comment, "I guess his missing toe didn't prevent Lance from participating in sports."

"You know about that? It happened before I started working for the family. I heard one of the help accidentally shut the Rolls door on the boy's foot. They had to amputate the little toe on his right foot.

No, it never slowed Lance in any way."

Moving right along, and before he started to wonder about my mission, I said, "Was Jeff in contact with Lance Talbot since Lance returned to Palm Beach?"

"He was. Jeff said they had met and talked, and it was Jeff who told me about Ms. Talbot's being killed in a ski accident."

"Did Jeff's talk about coming into money coincide with Lance's return?"

He pondered that a moment and then, as if suddenly realizing what it implied, cried, "Are you saying Lance Talbot was going to give my Jeff money? A lot of money?"

"Lance told me he was going to bankroll Jeff in a bar and restaurant business up north, in the Hamptons."

Rodgers looked stunned. "I know that was one of Jeff's pipe dreams. He talked about it often. But he never said anything about Lance Talbot giving him money. No, Mr. McNally, he never said that. Is that why Lance has been so generous? Because he couldn't give it to Jeff, he gave it to me?"

"Lance has been generous," I remarked.

"Yes, sir. He called after the funeral. He said he wanted to pay all the expenses but

Mr. MacNiff had already taken care of things. He asked me where I banked and said he was going to transfer money to my account in memory of Jeff."

"And did he, Mr. Rodgers?"

"I called the bank this morning and learned I was ten thousand dollars richer. Everyone is being so kind, Mr. McNally."

Speaking of altruism, I thought it the right moment to mention Nifty's grand gesture. "I'm at liberty to tell you that Mr. MacNiff is going to dedicate his scholarship charity to the memory of Jeffrey Rodgers."

The man was truly awed. "How can I ever thank him?" he asked.

"You've been very helpful, and that's thanks enough, I'm sure." Affecting a blasé air I asked, as if it were a trivial detail, "Was the man you spoke to in church yesterday, calling you Rollo, Lance Talbot?"

Rodgers looked puzzled. He was a bit slow on the uptake but sooner or later he could put two and two together and come up with something resembling four. "You're asking me more questions about Lance Talbot than about Jeff. The police never asked me about Lance or my time working for the Talbots. What's this about, Mr. McNally?"

"It's about finding your son's murderer. The police are questioning all of Jeff's friends but haven't as yet made the connection between Jeff and Lance. However, they soon will."

"How do you know that?"

"Because I'm going to tell them. Please answer my question, Mr. Rodgers. Was that Lance Talbot who spoke to you in the church yesterday?"

"Was it Lance? Sure it was. Who else could it be?"

The group gathered around the MacNiff pool acted more like they were there for a memorial service than a party. Thankfully, the area was no longer surrounded by a yellow ribbon emblazoned with the words POLICE LINE DO NOT CROSS, but the memory lingered on. There were about two dozen people milling about in clusters of two, four or more, speaking in hushed tones and avoiding eye contact with the watery centerpiece.

I recognized many faces from the *Tennis Everyone!* affair, which was unfortunate as well as unavoidable. They were the MacNiffs' social set and, like most social groups, limited in number. People like Lady Cynthia Horowitz, who were more glitter than substance, did not bend elbows with this crowd, who were all substance and rather lackluster.

The MacNiffs had done it up in style because I doubt if they knew how not to put on a good show. There were "His" and "Hers" pavilions for changing, their colorful red and white satiny facades billowing in the breeze coming off the ocean under a cloudless sky and radiant sun. It was a perfect afternoon for a swim but the pool, which had been drained, scrubbed and refilled, was conspicuously empty.

The caterer had set up a buffet table presided over by two waitresses, and there was the obligatory portable bar being manned by our Todd. Lolly Spindrift, in his Panama hat, was scurrying like a mouse in a maze between Dennis Darling and Isadora Duhane. Yes, you heard right — Isadora Duhane. I knew why she was here, but had yet to learn how she got here, and was too busy trying to get this show on the road to care at the moment. If we didn't get people into the pool this would all be for naught and the MacNiffs would have my scalp for saddling them with a Stella Dallas flop so soon after having hosted a murder.

Things perked up with the arrival of

Jackson Barnett. I could have kissed Helen MacNiff for having remembered to invite him. He was in (what else?) tennis shorts and a polo shirt with crossed rackets over the breast. I believe he endorsed the shirts as well as the white sneakers he was parading around in, shaking hands, smiling, and looking like a Greek god among us mortals.

He was accompanied by his agent and a group of Hollywood types, recognizable as such by their wraparound sunglasses, closely cropped hair in a variety of shades Mother Nature never dreamed of inflicting on her children, and Gucci loafers. Nifty, I noticed, greeted the Guccibaggers as if they were the great white hope. The agent wore his custom-made suit, black silk tie and nervous tic.

Mrs. MacNiff told me later that she had invited Barnett, telling him the purpose of the gathering was to establish the Jeffrey Rodgers memorial, and he was more than happy to do his share. I imagine Jackson Barnett would go to the opening of an envelope if he thought it could get him some press. Lolly was now bouncing between Denny, Izzy and Jackie like the silver ball in a pinball machine going for a grand slam.

None of the celebrated arrivals was toting a tote, so if they didn't have their swimsuits under their trousers they had no intention of taking a dip.

This was not going well.

I went to the bar for a much needed jolt to my system and as Todd mixed my gin and tonic he nervously asked me if I knew any of the men with Jackson Barnett. "The guy in the undertaker garb is his agent, I'm sure, and the others must be the Hollywood contingent." I recalled that these were just the people Todd wanted to meet and hopefully impress.

"Do you know any of them, Mr. McNally?"

"Sorry, kid. But look, when they come for a drink dazzle them with your charm and give them a few of Biff's lines from *Salesman*."

"They won't know I'm alive, Mr. McNally."

My experienced eye told me that some of them would certainly know Todd was alive, but it was best the boy didn't know this — or was I being naive?

Denny, Jackson, Izzy and Lolly were in a huddle, and I think Izzy was playing cruise director. How did that girl do it? She was in shorts with a sailor's middy that was rather fetching. No neckerchief and no pearls.

I found our host and told him it was time for him to make his announcement and rally the troops into the pool.

"What should I say, Archy?"

"Something on the order of Marc Antony's eulogy for Caesar."

"You want me to say I come here to bury Jeff Rodgers, not to praise him? You're daft, Archy."

"No, sir. Say we're here not to mourn, but to celebrate the memory of a young man who was the victim of a heinous crime and to establish a memorial to Jeff Rodgers in the form of ongoing scholarships to worthy young men and women."

I rambled on extemporaneously, which is my forte, as Nifty listened, nodded, and finally whispered, "Let's get our feet wet."

I clapped my hands to draw the attention of those gathered who were only too happy to stop pretending to be having fun and assemble around Nifty and me.

Nifty cleared his throat, opened his arms and began his oration with, "We're here not to mourn . . ." and in a few well-chosen words, some of them mine, got the message across with a minimum of schmaltz and a plethora of showbiz pizazz.

He was politely applauded and the ice was broken, which saved me the trouble of fetching a blowtorch.

Seeing Dennis Darling holding up his recorder to tape Nifty's speech, Jackson Barnett couldn't resist getting in on the act. In a voice trained for television commercials, Jackson announced, "I will donate one thousand dollars to the scholarship fund for every person who jumps in the pool in the next ten minutes."

Amid an outbreak of screams, giggles and friendly moans, there began a mad scramble to the changing pavilions.

This was the scene that welcomed the arrival of Lance Talbot, Holga von Brecht and *Herr Doktor* von Brecht.

NINETEEN

In the mad scramble to donate a thousand bucks to Nifty's philanthropic cause without opening their wallets, no one took much notice of the new arrivals. I did see the MacNiff housekeeper, Maria Sanchez, puttering around the buffet table and watched as she took off for the house to call Ursi and report that the husband of the ninety-year-old lady with the twenty-year-old lover had just landed.

Thus began rumors of the most titillating domestic triangle since the Windsors shacked up with playboy Jimmy Donahue at the Donahue Palm Beach mansion. Then, as now, who was doing what to whom was the question. Lolly, who never removes his white suit and hat except to don his silk jammies, looked like a man on the verge of expiring from sheer bliss. A celebrated journalist, a Battle offspring, a tennis pro who looked like Adonis and, now, the Michelangelo of cosmetic surgery, all in the same place at the same time, and all within arm's reach.

Dr. von Brecht was an inch or two over six feet and carried himself so ramrod straight I thought he might be wearing a corset under his beautifully tailored light gray suit. His fair hair was parted on the left and cut short enough to lie dormant in a wind tunnel. He didn't click his heels together when he took Mrs. MacNiff's hand, but he did bow and say something that seemed to please her. He was as good-looking as casting directors allowed German officers to be in old World War II movies. The only thing missing was a monocle in his left eye.

Holga von Brecht looked the quintessence of the Palm Beach socialite in a navy, knee-length dress with spaghetti straps that alternatingly hung and clung as she walked. A wide-brimmed white hat protected her delicate skin from the sun and a pair of dark glasses shielded her eyes.

Lance was in jeans, a pocket tee and sneakers, but not the brand Jackson Barnett endorsed.

As the MacNiffs performed their hosting chores, I lolled in the background. Denny got himself a drink from Todd and then surreptitiously meandered to where I was standing. "I was afraid he wasn't going to show up," Denny said, extending his hand as if introducing himself.

"He was at the airport picking up Holga's husband," I reported, shaking Denny's hand. I wondered if we looked as silly as I felt. "That's Dr. Claus von Brecht of the clinic high in the Alps where he injects patients with something unmentionable at the dinner table."

"We all know who he is," Denny said.

"Really? How?"

"Mrs. MacNiff," he answered with a smile. "She told everyone that the famous doctor would make his Palm Beach debut right here this afternoon. That's how she got all the ladies to come. And, she told Jackie Barnett that I would be here to cover the christening of the newly named charity event for *Bare Facts*. Sassy lady, no?"

"Yes. And I'm glad she's on our side," I said.

"So what's new?" Denny asked.

"Lance explained Jeff's bragging about coming into money by saying that he had offered to financially back Jeff in buying a bar and restaurant business up north. He's also curious as to what you're doing here. Worried might be a more apt description than curious.

"I got the impression that Jeff threatened

Lance by telling him he would sell his story — whatever that might be — to you and Lance wants to know just how much Jeff told you before he met his untimely death."

"You don't believe that Lance was going to back Jeff?" Denny said.

"After talking to Lance, I wasn't sure who to believe, Lance Talbot or Jeff Rodgers. This morning I talked to Jeff's father. He said Jeff boasted of coming into money, but he didn't say where it was coming from. Why? I mean why wouldn't he tell his father that his rich boyhood buddy was playing Father Christmas? Everyone who knew him says Jeff wasn't reticent when it came to boasting about his expectations, real or imagined, and of his former but brief enrollment at the Day School.

"If Lance was backing him, Jeff would have taken an ad in the shiny sheet to announce the union. Instead he calls you and wants to know how much you'd pay for a tell-all story on Lance Talbot."

"Conclusion," Denny concluded. "Jeff was blackmailing his old buddy."

"I don't think there's any question about it. Lance also gave Mr. Rodgers ten thousand dollars in Jeff's memory."

"To atone or to keep Rodgers silent, in case Jeff confided in his father?"

"Perhaps hedging his bets," I answered. "I don't think Rodgers suspects a thing, unless he put on a good show for me, which I'm not buying. The man is painfully credulous."

"In case you haven't noticed," Denny said, "Lance Talbot can't keep his eyes off us."

"Oh, but I have noticed, Denny. He looks like a kid who wants to get away from the adults and have some fun."

"That's exactly why I chose to engage you in private conversation in the broad light of day. I want him to wonder and worry what we're up to. Give him another minute and he'll join us to try and find out."

The guests were now coming out of the changing rooms and jumping into the pool. Barnett was making a display of counting heads as his agent ticked off the time. I saw Izzy take the plunge in a two-piece affair, showing off a girlish figure that was still a bit too lean for my taste. When the agent called time, Barnett was ten thousand bucks poorer. To show what a sport he was, Jackie pulled off his polo shirt with the crossed rackets, yanked off his sneakers and, holding his nose like a kid at a swimming hole, went feet first into the deep end of the pool. For the second time that day the guests burst into applause.

"What is Isadora Duhane doing here?" I wondered aloud.

Denny shrugged. "I think she's a guest of one of the MacNiffs' guests. Lolly told me her mother is a Battle. Big bucks there, Archy."

"She's a pain in the lower regions," I told him. "She wants to write a book based on my cases, and has managed to seduce a friend of mine into telling tales out of school."

Denny started. "Seduced as in debauched?"

"I think so, Denny, but I don't know what she sees in him."

"Men seldom do know what a lady sees in the competition, or prefer to ignore it. I think she's cute."

"So does Jackson Barnett, I noticed."

"He has no choice," Denny said. "Lolly told me one of her mother's holding companies manufactures the shirts and sneakers Barnett endorses."

At any Palm Beach gathering, sooner or later, the talk turns to money and its source. With Lolly Spindrift playing Virgil to Denny's Dante, Denny was now acquainted with the cash flow of most of the people present, and from whence their cash flowed. It was money, I daresay, that kept the MacNiff crowd, all of a certain age, looking so trim in their swimsuits. Personal trainers, golf, tennis, a stress-free existence and the occasional nip, tuck and chemical peel was the secret of their success.

When the hoopla over Jackson's largess simmered down, the now motivated partygoers could turn their undivided attention to Holga von Brecht and her creator. As the von Brechts, led by Nifty and Mrs. MacNiff, began their rounds, the ladies climbed out of the pool and reached for their robes. The men, seeing von Brecht's stance, pulled in their tummies. Lance took the moment to make his break and head our way.

"Here we go," Denny whispered.

"I'll hang around long enough not to appear rude, then leave you to your investigative prying. I think he would rather tackle you alone, and I'm on his payroll, remember?"

"You're on my payroll, too, McNally, remember that."

"Welcome to Palm Beach, Denny Darling."

"May I join you?" Lance said, as he approached.

"Be my guest," I invited. "This is Dennis Darling, but watch your manners. He's here to tell lies about us and anything you say will be held against you."

Lance held out his hand languidly and I wasn't sure if he expected Denny to shake it or kiss it. I was happy to see Denny give it a manly squeeze that had Lance Talbot wincing. I must remember to introduce Denny to that other bonecrusher, Alejandro Gomez y Zapata.

"We met on the tennis court right here," Lance said to Denny. "Do you recall?"

"It was a day not easily forgotten," Denny responded, unobtrusively bringing the subject of Jeff's murder into the conversation.

How clever. I used Denny's opener to further my own cause. "You missed it, but Mr. MacNiff made the announcement I told you about last night. Everyone is taking a swim to commemorate the occasion and Jeff's life. I hope you'll join in, Lance."

"I would, Mr. McNally, but I'm afraid I didn't bring a proper swimsuit."

I wanted to stamp my feet, jump up and down, and *scream*. I had dared the Mac-Niffs to put on this show in the face of adversity for the sole purpose of getting Lance out of his shoes and socks and into the pool. Or out of his shoes and socks, period. As he didn't appear to be wearing socks, I was halfway there, but halfway didn't cut the mustard. I was skunked.

"Jackson Barnett took the plunge in his tennis shorts," I said, avoiding Denny's baffled stare.

"Are you suggesting I drop my jeans and do the same in my underpants, Mr. McNally?"

"Please," I stammered. "That would be inappropriate."

"Good," Lance said with a chuckle, "because I'm not wearing any." He winked at Denny, and the two burst out laughing, as if the joke were on me — and I guess it was.

"You were a friend of Jeff Rodgers?" Denny asked when civility was restored.

"I was. Did Jeff tell you that?" Lance asked, as if it were common knowledge that Jeff and Denny had spoken.

Denny, as well as I, realized at once that Lance was openly admitting that he knew Jeff had communicated with Dennis Darling. He had not admitted this to me, but under Denny's scrutiny he was doing an about-face, which was just what I had hoped for. You win some and you lose some.

Or had Lance been advised not to match wits with Dennis Darling? I glanced at the von Brechts who were now on the business end of a receiving line, emulating royalty at a command performance.

"He told me you two were old friends," Denny said. "So did Mr. McNally."

Lance turned to me. "You told Mr. Darling about Jeff and me?" It was half question, half accusation. This guy had the *cojones* of a brass monkey.

"I did. I also told him you thought he might be here because of Jeff's murder, which we agreed was impossible given the murder took place after Mr. Darling's arrival."

"Then why did you mention it at all?" Lance snapped.

"In hopes of learning if Mr. Darling is here to write about Palm Beach in general or one of our citizens in particular," I goaded. "You seemed to think his arrival had something to do with Jeff Rodgers and I'm looking into Jeff's murder. Does that answer your question?"

Before we came to blows, Denny held up his hands like a teacher intervening in a schoolyard brawl. "Gentlemen, please. Why don't one of you simply ask me what I'm doing here?"

"Thank you, Mr. Darling," Lance said. "What are you doing here?"

Dropping the other shoe, but not the right one, Denny disclosed, "Jeff Rodgers invited me to come to Palm Beach with a promise of giving me information concerning Lance Talbot for which he expected a gratuity. A very large gratuity."

Lance Talbot actually looked relieved. "Thank you for your frankness, Mr. Darling. I wish you had come to me sooner." To me he said, "Would you excuse us, Archy." It was a command, not a question.

With pleasure I left the vain Lance Talbot in Denny's shrewd clutches and made myself scarce. Was Denny going to learn Jeff's secret, or a version thereof? Right now it looked as if I wasn't going to learn how many toes Talbot had nestled inside his sneakers. Seeing me straying from Talbot and Darling, Helen MacNiff intercepted me to ask, "Is he going to swim, Archy?"

"I fear not," I told her. "He didn't bring his trunks."

"I thought not when I saw he wasn't carrying a tote or duffel bag," she said, trying to mask her disappointment with a careless shrug. "Everyone else did." She nodded toward the pile of carryalls scattered around the changing rooms, then asked, "Did you bring trunks, Archy?"

"My tote's there," I said.

"I did tell Lance it was a pool party. Do you think he forgot his trunks on purpose?" she suggested.

The thought had occurred to me. "I have no idea. Dennis Darling is grilling him, as you can see, and we may learn something from him."

"Dennis Darling is the person Jeff tried to sell his story to, isn't he, Archy?"

It was now so obvious, it would have been foolish to deny it. "He is, and we may soon know what Jeff was trying to sell."

"Did you tell Mr. Darling we had doubts as to Lance Talbot's true identity?"

"No, ma'am, I did not."

She let out a sigh of relief. "Thank goodness. It would be terrible to put that idea into the hands of a man in Darling's position. What Jeff had on Lance Talbot and who killed the poor boy is a matter for the police. Malcolm's chief concern as Aunt Margaret's executor is to establish Lance's identity. I wish he had never heard the old lady mumbling nonsense about dead kings."

But he did hear it and it impressed him enough to think Mrs. Talbot was trying to tell him something. I told Mrs. MacNiff as much. "Mr. MacNiff might just have to ask Lance to show him his right foot."

"I hope not, Archy. If he is truly Lance Talbot, it would create such an atmosphere of distrust between Malcolm and the boy, and they must work together as they begin probate."

I was hired to settle the question of Lance Talbot's identity, and I had put together this party as a means to that end. Now, by God, I was going to do it. How, I wasn't sure, but I would get those sneakers off Talbot's feet if I had to take them off myself.

"Which is your tote?" Mrs. MacNiff suddenly asked.

"The monogrammed leather Coach bag. Why?"

"Excuse me, Archy." And off she ran to help her husband cope with a group of ladies surrounding the now barechested Jackson Barnett like he was dessert on the hoof.

The crowd around the von Brechts was

dispersing and I thought it was time to renew my acquaintance with Holga.

"I hope you remember me, Mrs. von Brecht," I presented myself.

She extended her hand in queenly fashion (it must run in the family) and answered, "But of course I do, Mr. McNally. You were my partner on the court and I think we took all three sets."

"Two out of the three," I reminded her. "We were up against Vivian Emerson and Joe Gallo."

"Yes. A charming couple," was all I got out of her before she introduced me to Claus. "This is my husband, Dr. Claus von Brecht."

I got a handshake and a bow from von Brecht. "I have heard much about you, Mr. McNally." His English was perfect, if heavily accented.

He looked as sharp as the crease in his trousers, and she was bewitching. What a trio. The handsome doctor, his beautiful wife and their rich, adopted son. Characters out of a Minerva Barnes novel. Were they too good to be true, or too true to be good?

"I told Claus that you are helping Lance with his inquiry into Jeff Rodgers's murder." Holga explained her husband's familiarity with the McNally name.

"Yes," von Brecht said. "I understand this boy and Lance were friends many years ago. I can empathize with Lance's concern but I do not wish him to get involved in this affair. This boy, Jeff, has been abusive . . ."

"Claus, please," Holga interrupted.

"No," he stated. "If Mr. McNally is in Lance's employ, he should know the truth, *ja?*"

Resigned, Holga took off her glasses to confront me and, as she did this, glanced down the length of my body in a manner so blatant I felt myself redden like a schoolboy. The gesture was so swift that when her gaze returned to my face I thought I had imagined it.

Well!

"Lance told you he had offered to finance Jeff Rodgers in a business venture," she stated. When I nodded, she continued. "Jeff also called this Dennis Darling reporter and tried to sell him information regarding the Talbot family."

"Why would Jeff do such a thing if Lance had offered to back Jeff?" I asked.

"Because the boy was a bastard, Mr. McNally," von Brecht cried. His wife again tried to silence him but this time it didn't

300

work. "He wanted Lance to not only finance this absurd restaurant but to endorse it. That is, lend his name to the venture in order to attract a smart clientele, socialites, to ensure its success. He talked of a similar adventure here in Palm Beach. The name was to be Talbot's, of all things."

"Lance was appalled," Holga picked up the story. "He refused. That's when Jeff called this reporter person and threatened Lance with a scandal if he didn't comply."

"What was the threat, Mrs. von Brecht?" I asked.

She raised her hand to let her husband know the ball was in her court. "If Lance wants you to know, he will tell you. It's not our place to speak of private, family matters when we are not blood kin.

"I believe Lance is now opening up to Mr. Darling. Claus and I suggested that he do so. After talking to you, Lance realized this business has festered long enough to become malignant. We discussed it on our way here from the airport and were very pleased to see Mr. Darling present. It saved Lance the trouble of contacting him. The truth should clear the air and we count on Mr. Darling's discretion. Perhaps you can have a word with him, Mr. McNally."

When the rich put you on their payroll they expect value for their money. "I will try," I said, making no promises. "I also advised Lance to tell the police of his relationship to Jeff Rodgers. This was before I knew about the blackmail threat. Now it's most urgent that Lance talk to the police."

"It puts Lance in a very awkward position," von Brecht cried.

"That's the understatement of the new millennium," I assured him.

"Nonsense," Holga broke in. "Lance was with me when the murder occurred, in full view of everyone at the party."

"Then he has nothing to worry about, Mrs. von Brecht. *Ja?*"

She touched my bare arm with the tips of her perfectly manicured fingers and I felt a pleasant tingling creep across the nape of my neck. "I trust you will be with us throughout this disturbing ordeal, Mr. McNally. If Claus must go back to Switzerland, it would be comforting to have a man to lean on."

Well!

Nifty came over to introduce more of the curious to the von Brechts and I headed straight for Izzy Duhane. "Just how did you manage to get here, young lady?"

"Hello to you too, Skip. I'm a guest of

Mrs. Cavendish and she brung me."

"How do you know Mrs. Cavendish?"

"She's a second cousin," Izzy said.

"The one who married the actor Minerva Barnes trashed?"

"No, that's another one."

"How many second cousins do you have?" I questioned.

"I never counted," she rebutted, with attitude. "I came to get a look at the scene of the crime and I have some ideas . . ."

"Izzy," I cut in, "I think you should know . . ."

"That Binky is not your partner and not undercover," she cut in. "I know that, Archy."

"Then why are you stringing him along?"

"Because I think he's cute. Because his ego needs boosting. And because he's a tiger in the bedroom," she ticked off.

"I believe two out of the three."

"Okay, so he's not so cute," she grinned.

A young man joined us whom she introduced as Max Sterling. "He's with the Hollywood crew," Izzy said. "Max and I met when I did time in L.A."

"Izzy broke my heart," Max told me.

"But not your spirit," she teased. "Max is an assistant director waiting for a break."

Todd Brandt is also waiting for a break, I thought, and then a thousand-watter lit up in the balloon over my head. "Would you do me a favor, Max?"

"If I can, Archy."

"The kid working the bar wants to get into films. Would you introduce yourself to him and say a few encouraging words? Maybe give him your card. You can say I told you he was an actor. His name is Todd Brandt."

Max looked amused. "Brandt is not bad, but the Todd has to go. Sure, why not? I used to tend bar and still do between jobs."

"You're a bleeding heart," Izzy needled when Max sauntered off toward the bar.

America's philosopher laureate, Dorothy Parker, said, "The do-gooders of the world are the louses of the world." Pray she wasn't always right.

"As I was saying," Izzy rattled on, "I have some ideas . . ."

Next time I looked, Lance and Denny had parted and Lance was reporting to the von Brechts. I saw Helen MacNiff enter the scene and take Lance's arm. In a jovial manner, she began leading him toward one of the pavilions. I do believe she located my tote and was opening it. I left Izzy talking to herself and, trying not to run, got to Mrs. MacNiff just as Lance went into the pavilion carrying a pair of black-and-white-striped trunks.

"How?" was all I could say.

Arms folded in triumph, she gloated, "I told him I wanted a picture of him and Jackson Barnett cavorting happily in the pool to attract support for our cause in the local gazette. Lolly's photographer agreed to do the honors.

"When he said he didn't have trunks, I told him where he could find a pair and dragged him away from the von Brechts. They weren't too pleased," she giggled.

"I could kiss you," I cooed.

"Go right ahead."

I did, just as Nifty came to join us. "She did it," he bragged, obviously knowing the game plan. "Let's try to keep our eyes above his waist when he comes out."

"You're kidding, my dear," his wife said.

The surrounding banter seemed to abate, as if someone had lowered a radio. I saw Max talking to Todd. Denny chatting with the Hollywood boys. Jackson Barnett laughing at something Izzy was saying. The von Brechts, isolated from the other guests, staring at the pavilion that now hid Lance.

The MacNiffs and I waited in rigid silence, as if a false move would alert our quarry. When the tent flap parted, Mrs. MacNiff grabbed my hand. A smiling Lance walked toward us. Three pairs of eyes focused on his advancing feet.

I counted. One, two, three . . .

TWENTY

"Four, sir."

"Are you sure, Archy?"

"Positive. And remember, I wasn't the only one counting toes this afternoon. The MacNiffs confirmed my addition."

Father and I were in the den nursing our ports, he with his cigar and me with my much-needed, and -deserved, English Oval. I related the events of the day, from my visit with Ronald Rodgers to Lance Talbot emerging from the changing tent, the elastic waistband of my trunks clinging to his hips for dear life. After counting, I vowed to give up eating.

"And Malcolm is satisfied that the boy is Lance Talbot, heir to the late Mrs. Talbot's fortune?" Thus spoke my father, the lawyer.

"He is," I answered, "and I believe Mr. MacNiff is relieved."

It took the three of us seconds to see that the small toe on the right foot walking toward us was missing. Did Lance see us looking? Did he suspect that this was the reason Helen MacNiff had forced him into a pair of trunks that were dangerously too large? I really can't say. He made a joke of the baggy boxers, saying if they went any lower, the resulting photo might exceed Mrs. MacNiff's promotional expectations.

After that the party took off in a most indecorous manner, or as indecorous as this crowd ever gets. It was as if a weight had been lifted from the shoulders of our host and hostess, who joined in the fun, determined to accentuate the positive and eliminate the aura of doom and gloom that Jeff Rodgers's murder had cast over their domain. Their exhilaration appeared to be infectious. The guests began to line up for the eats and Todd, elated after his chat with Max Sterling, was happily filling requests for beverages. Nifty's words, "We're here not to mourn," became the order of the day, not mere rhetoric.

Even Lance Talbot went meshugah. He romped in the pool with Jackson Barnett to the joy of Lolly's photographer. The obnoxiously pompous Talbot was now the clown, clutching his trunks as if fearing they would fall, and at one point swimming to the far end of the pool where he could be seen waving the swim suit over his head. The crowd loved it.

Holga and Claus von Brecht now mixed and mingled with the common folk, the ladies buttering up to Claus and the gentlemen attending Holga.

Observing the Swiss trio I was reminded of the old saw, *People don't change, only the roles they choose to play change.*

And whoever would have thought that for want of a little toe I would lose a client?

"It's him, Archy," Nifty said as Lance walked off to have his picture taken. "I appreciate your help."

"Mrs. MacNiff did it," I answered modestly.

"But the party was your idea," Nifty responded.

I deferred to my host. Helen MacNiff could not have gotten Lance into the pool if I hadn't arranged the party and brought my trunks. Any thoughts of offering Nifty a discount were banished. I told Nifty that the von Brechts had admitted to me that Jeff Rodgers was blackmailing Lance and that they had counseled him to open up to Dennis Darling. "You may have noticed that Lance and Darling had a long private chat shortly after Lance and the von Brechts arrived." I gave Nifty a brief account of what I had learned from Holga and Claus.

He listened politely and then repeated, in theory if not verbatim, what Helen MacNiff had said to me earlier. "What those boys had gotten up to, Archy, is no concern of mine. I have enough to keep me busy for a month of Sundays just doing Aunt Margaret's bidding as executor, and blackmail and murder are not on my agenda. That's a matter for the police, or you if you want to pursue it on your own. I hired you to prove Lance Talbot was Lance Talbot and you did. Now I can get on with my job.

"If Jeff was a blackmailer, there's no telling who else he had his mitts into. We know Lance didn't kill him, and I'm sure none of my guests did either, and that's that. My money is on one of the catering staff."

"The king is dead?" I questioned.

Nifty shook his head as if this were no longer germane to his dealings with Lance Talbot. "Archy," he said, "a lot of kings bit the dust in Aunt Margaret's lifetime. The medication had her indulging in a remembrance of things past, as some writer put it."

Proust, if my brief but memorable stay at old Eli served. I recalled a classmate who had actually read Proust. For penance he served four years, graduated summa cum laude, and made millions as a pioneer in waste disposal. I read *The Power of Positive Thinking* and am now eking out a living counting toes. Is there a lesson to be learned in this?

One down and two to go. I had lost Nifty but, as far as I knew, was still on Denny's and Talbot's payrolls. Or was I? If Denny was satisfied as well as uninterested with Lance's explanation of the blackmail scam, would he check out of the GulfStream and look to more fertile pastures for sin and corruption? And now that Lance had written a check and gone skinny-dipping in honor of his old friend, would he concentrate on collecting his half-billion bananas and return to the snowy Alps with Holga and Claus?

Well, folks, Archy is staying right here and going after Jeff Rodgers's murderer with or without the reporter and the playboy. I am many things but a Discreet Inquirer *manqué* is not one of them.

Todd was all over me like a cheap suit when I went for seconds. "I'm going to send Max my credits and head shots, Mr. McNally. He's a second unit director and he's here to do the screen test of Jackson Barnett, which he says is all pure hype."

My, my. Five minutes with Max Sterling and he's talking Hollywoodese. "Don't get your hopes up, Todd. Guys like Max Sterling invented hype."

Unheeding, Todd rambled on, "And he invited me to come to Mr. Meecham's yacht tomorrow to watch the crew work. What do you think I should wear?"

"A chastity belt."

"You're a cynic, Mr. McNally, but a gentleman. Thanks for putting Max on to me. If there's ever anything I can do to help you, just holler."

For the second time in as many days, Edward (Todd) Brandt and I exchanged words that would play a vital role in the final solution to an old lady's dying pronouncement.

"What do you think of 'Rick'?" he asked.

"I don't know him."

"For me," Todd said. "Max thinks 'Todd' sucks."

"What about 'Edward'?" I proposed.

"Cute, Mr. McNally. Real cute."

On my way in search of Denny, I ran into the real Lance Talbot, of all people.

"I understand this potato sack belongs to you, Archy," he kindly reminded me.

"It must have stretched in the laundry," I apologized.

"Don't be embarrassed, Archy. You have a fine physique for a man of your age. Even Holga thinks so."

And she should know. I decided not to lose sleep over the wily dig at my age. After all, he may yet be a client and the executor had just validated his claim to the Talbot fortune.

"I had a talk with Mr. and Mrs. von Brecht. They told me that Jeff was leaning on you but refused to say why."

"They respect my privacy," he said. "I have told the reporter, Darling, all the facts and I will tell you when next we meet. Now is neither the time nor the place."

"Agreed. And I trust you will also tell the police. You realize it puts you in a rather awkward position. When a black-mailer is murdered his mark is usually suspect number one, and for good reason."

"Do you really think I engaged you to hunt me down? Or do you think it was a not so clever ruse for the guilty party to initiate an investigation into the crime? Really, Archy. I did not kill Jeff Rodgers."

"I know you didn't. You were in plain sight of me and a hundred other tennis players when the murder occurred, but that doesn't prove you weren't implicated in the crime."

"You are a trusting soul," he said. "I know no one in Palm Beach other than the MacNiffs, and I challenge the police to connect me with any accomplice. Also, I had no reason to kill Jeff. If his offensive gossip were made public it would prove an embarrassment, but nothing more. That's why I would not give in to his foolish demands. Ask Mr. Darling. He assured me the disclosure wasn't worth a drop of printer's ink. Am I glad Jeff is dead? As a matter of fact, I am."

Feisty guy, I must say. There he stood, holding up my trunks, and telling me, the police, and the horse we came in on to get out of his face. Too, I couldn't fault his case. If he told Denny, and was willing to tell me and the police, what Jeff had on him, why would he kill Jeff to silence him? As Nifty had so eloquently put it, "and that's that" — *if* Lance Talbot was telling the truth. It always came down to his word against the word of a dead man.

"Then you have nothing to fear but losing your pants," I assured him. Wondering if client number two was discharging me, I asked, "Do you want me to continue my investigation into the murder?"

"But of course," he answered. "Perhaps I

314

spoke too quickly and too rashly. You must understand that Jeff was overbearing. He was insolent as a child and never grew out of it. As the French say, he had the *idée fixe* that I was the reason for his lot in life. I offered to make amends but he wanted more than I was willing to give. Jeff Rodgers wanted to be me. No, I'm not happy that he's dead and I apologize for saying so. I want you to find his killer."

How touching. Did this guy never run out of convincing excuses for his harsh words and furtive actions? If I hadn't come upon the connection between him and Jeff Rodgers, and if Denny hadn't come here in response to Jeff's call, would Lance Talbot have publicly acknowledged the relationship or given a damn about Jeff's murder? Doubtful. Would he tell the police what he knew if I hadn't coerced him into it? Never.

"Now that I've lost my chief suspect, I have very few leads to go on," I said, hoping to vex him, and succeeded.

"Your humor escapes me, Archy. Perhaps I've been out of the country too long." Pointing to our bartender, he said, "That young man was also working here the day Jeff was killed. Is he the friend of Jeff's who gave you the information about Jeff and me?"

"Yes, he is. Would you like to meet him?"

"No. But perhaps you should question him further. He seems to know so much about Jeff that I wonder if he knows even more than he's saying. In your quest for leads, why not start where you began — with him?"

With that he hoisted his trunks and marched off to the changing pavilion. Only my upbringing and respect for the Mac-Niffs prevented me from giving him a good, swift kick in the arse.

I joined Denny at the buffet table where he was putting together a plate (china, not paper) of lobster salad, potato salad and cole slaw. "You'll O.D. on mayonnaise," I warned.

"One thing about this crowd, Archy, they know how to put on a good spread. If I hang around much longer I'll fit into your trunks."

"Everyone is a comedian. Who told you the trunks were mine?"

He added a pickle and a few olives to his already crowded plate. "It seems to be common knowledge, and stop looking so put upon. The kid is half your age and as slim as a reed. How come you were so anxious to get him into the pool?"

Nothing escapes Denny's notice, which is the art of his trade. Remembering my vow, I went for a dollop of crabmeat and the mixed greens. "How did you get here?" I asked.

"Taxi, why?"

"I'll give you a lift to the hotel and we can exchange notes."

"You'll tell me why you wanted to get the kid in the pool?"

"Only if you tell me why Jeff Rodgers was blackmailing him."

"You got a deal, McNeil."

"McNally. The name is McNally."

We hung around just long enough not to be faulted for eating and running. Izzy, thankfully, was surrounded by Jackson and the Hollywood crew, so I managed to get away without being harangued by the young lady. We did pay our respects to the MacNiffs, von Brechts, and assorted pillars of society before becoming history. Holga von Brecht gave me a warm handshake and a reminder that she was counting on me. Well, well!

The bridge was up, which happens, and as the Miata idled, Denny told me that Lolly had invited him to a reception at the home of Lady Cynthia Horowitz. "He said Barnett and the von Brechts would be there."

"And he told them that you would be there," I expounded. Wise to the ways of Lady C and her chief gofer, I surmised that Lolly saw a chance to ingratiate himself to our hostess-with-the-mostest and put the cart before the horse, if you'll excuse the banality. First he extended bids to this season's most sought-after VIPs, telling each that the others had already accepted, after which he would tell Lady C he had them on tap, and she would toss the party. What a pair. "Are you going?"

Not looking very enthused, he said, "Depends on how long I'll be here. What would I miss if I skipped it?"

"An old lady trying to get Barnett to seduce her, von Brecht to inject her and you to write about her."

The bridge lowered, traffic moved and Denny thought about packing his valise.

We sat on the hotel's terrace, fanned by a refreshing breeze coming off the lake. The lunch crowd had long gone and the cocktail imbibers had not yet arrived. A waiter asked us if we wanted anything, hoping we would say no, and we obliged.

Lance had told Denny very much what the von Brechts had told me, adding only Jeff's supposed threat.

"Jessica Talbot was a drug addict. She smoked dope in front of the boys and on more than one occasion snorted coke in their presence. Under the influence, she told Lance his father was either of Italian descent, Irish descent or a titled Englishman."

This corroborated what Jeff's father had intimated. "Not very pretty," I noted.

"Not very newsworthy either," Denny said, obviously disappointed.

"Do you believe him?" I prodded.

"No," he replied.

"Good. Neither do I. What's your rationale, Denny?"

"Jeff said that he had information that could ruin Lance Talbot. The fact that his mother was a promiscuous junkie could embarrass him, but certainly not ruin him. Jeff was a hip kid, like they all are today. When was the last time you went to the movies? Drugs and sex are the rule, not the exception. He was also a reader of *Bare Facts* so he knew it would take more than that to whet my interest. Presto, Talbot is lying."

I told Denny I agreed and added, "We didn't want to get Lance into the pool, we wanted to get him out of his sneakers."

When I finished with that disclosure,

Denny accused, "You were holding out on me, Archy."

"Client confidentiality," I pleaded.

"I'm your client, too."

"Yes. But Mr. MacNiff is by far a richer client."

"You're a tart, Archy."

I did not report this last observation to the sire, who was nodding thoughtfully as I spoke. When I was done, he asked, "And where does this leave your investigation, Archy?"

I told him I was no longer concerned with Lance Talbot's identity, but still determined to learn the nature of Jeff's secret and who murdered him. "Denny is going to stay in Palm Beach a while longer and see if he can still muster a story out of this. He thinks the blackmail scam and the murder are connected."

"What you mean, Archy, is Dennis Darling hopes there is a connection as it will provide the story he came down here to get. Please don't allow this to color your investigation. Lance Talbot did not commit the crime. That's a fact. He has given you a plausible explanation of the blackmail threat, which you and Darling arbitrarily refuse to believe. Perhaps it is time to focus your attention elsewhere."

Father was protecting his new client, which was only right. To say I had a gut feeling that Talbot was a liar would never hold up in father's eyes, or in a court of law. Instead I promised to broaden my inquiries in the direction of Jeff Rodgers's social set, adding, "I intend to see Al Rogoff tomorrow and tell what I've learned to date. Hopefully, he'll share with me. Maybe the police are on to something, or someone, that has completely escaped my notice."

Father stroked his moustache. "Good. Now what's this I hear about a Battle in our midst? You said she was at the MacNiff gathering."

At cocktails all the talk was of the pool party and Dr. Claus von Brecht. "They say he's as handsome as a film star," Mother informed us. *They,* of course, were Maria Sanchez and our Ursi. I played the devil's advocate and gave them a blow-by-blow of the event, leaving out the toe count and the baggy boxers. With Ursi serving, it would be all over Palm Beach before the cock crowed.

What Ursi served was a fillet of salmon done on the outdoor Weber, which is fired with hickory chips. Her trick is to grill the fish, never turning it, until the under-skin is dark and crusty and the interior rare. At just the right moment it's removed from the fire and placed in a warm oven.

As the salmon slowly bakes from rare to medium, the family is attending to starters, which tonight was a vichyssoise garnished with fresh herbs and accompanied by crusty chunks of a hearty French loaf. When Leroy put this fine potato and leek soup on the Pelican menu, many diners sent it back to the kitchen for heating. Well, it could be worse. Binky once ordered his steak tartare medium rare.

The salmon was served on a heated platter, surrounded by wedges of lemon and sprigs of parsley. The vegetables were chilled beets and steamed green beans in a spicy ginger dressing, and new potatoes in their skins, split and splashed with olive oil and sprinkled with black pepper and fleur de sel. Father went to the wine cellar and emerged with an '84 Graves that was the perfect complement to our simple fare. The baggy boxers were still so vivid a memory, I eschewed a slice of Ursi's Black Forest chocolate cake in favor of a tea biscuit with my coffee.

"Isadora Duhane," I told Father, "is a Kalamazoo Battle. She is currently the inamorata of your mail person."

"Binky Watrous?" Father almost choked on his port.

"One and the same," I said, before giving him the details but sparing him the Skip McGuire association. Father is of an age and I wasn't sure how much of this his heart could tolerate.

"How extraordinary," he muttered.

"We must all be nice to Binky," I apprised, "as we may all be working for him in the near future."

I left Father tugging on his whiskers and retired to my penthouse digs where I undressed, washed, brushed and donned a silk kimono in white with a scarlet obi. This was presented to me by a lady friend who was a Shintoist. I was a convert for the duration of our relationship, which was conducted on a mat. She left me for a karate instructor who came with his own mat, and I was left holding the kimono.

I sat at my desk to record in my journal, and no sooner did I unscrew the top of the Montblanc than the phone rang. I shuddered. No one calls after ten in the evening bearing good news. With trepidation I picked up the dastardly instrument.

"Archy McNally here."

"Georgy O'Hara here."

"Georgy? What's wrong?"

"I'm not sure. Joe Gallo just called me."

"I thought he was out of your life."

"He is. And it seems Vivian Emerson is now out of his life."

"She left him?"

"You might say that. She's disappeared, Archy, and Joe is scared."

TWENTY-ONE

"I ought to run you in, pal."

"What for?"

"Obstruction of justice, that's what for."

Al Rogoff and I were seated on a bench at the Lake Worth pier, holding containers of coffee purchased from the breakfast emporium just across the A1A. It was a sunny Saturday morning and the beach was swarming with locals as well as visiting firemen. The surfers were out in force and the teenyboppers in thongs were roasting in the sun like sausages on a spit. It was a scene right out of a Hollywood beach film of a bygone era. Life imitating art.

"I told you everything I know," I said in my own defense.

"After the fact," Al countered. "Before I left the palace this morning the captain told us Lance Talbot was coming in with information about the swimming pool murder. As we speak, he's telling the captain what you just told me."

The palace is Al's pseudonym for the PBPD headquarters, which some say resembles a French château. I always thought the Bastille was a more likely metaphor. The police like to label their cases for easy reference, hence the swimming pool sobriquet for obvious reasons. I believe Sergeant Rogoff was a tad chagrined because I had not powwowed with him sooner. The big lug would never admit it but he prides himself on usually being one step ahead of his colleagues in cases involving the gentry, thanks to me.

Seeking to placate my sidekick I said, "He's not telling them that Malcolm MacNiff doubted his claim until yesterday, because he doesn't know it. That's just between us."

"Also after the fact, or should I say after the toe count? What a collection of clues," Al moaned. "Nine toes, blackmail, drugs, sex and . . ." — he paused, thoughtfully — "did I leave anything out?"

"The dead king," I hinted.

I had contacted Al at the palace just as he had come off the graveyard shift, therefore he wasn't in uniform. For this reason we could meet openly instead of in our more clandestine venues, like supermarket parking lots. We weren't doing anything wrong, but a man in blue conversing with a civilian cannot help but draw an audience, which we neither wanted nor needed. When cases finally go to trial, it's not kosher for a potential witness for the prosecution to be asked by the defense what he was doing in private conversation with the arresting officer.

"You think that king business means something, or nothing?" Al pondered.

"I thought the king might be the old lady's grandson, and she was trying to tell MacNiff that her grandson was dead and the guy calling himself Lance Talbot was a phony."

"But he ain't no phony," Al stated, in his endearingly prosaic prose.

"No, he ain't," I answered. "Everything checks. His passport, his appearance, and his feet. When Mrs. Talbot got the second call saying her grandson had not been killed along with his mother, she wired him to return to Palm Beach immediately. He responded to that wire and rushed to her bedside. And the von Brechts, who were friends of his mother, are now with him. So who else could he be?"

"She's some looker," Al mused, sipping his coffee between chomps on his cigar butt. I wish he would toss the things after smoking them, but he once told me the only reason he smokes them is for the pleasure of noshing on the butt. Al also break-fasts on footlong hot dogs and Michelob while humming along with Placido Domingo. I try not to think of these things when I'm with him, but fail miserably.

"When did you see her?" I asked.

"They got to the palace just as I was leaving. The husband looks like a storm trooper."

"He was born well after the big war, Al."

So the von Brechts had accompanied Lance to his meeting with the police. Were those three joined at the hip?

"How does a king talk?" Al wondered as he watched two bottle blondes roll over to toast their backs.

One of them unhooked her bra, as those in search of a seamless tan often do, and I theorized upon what would happen if I went down there, tickled the sole of her foot, and caused her to jump up, scream-ing. Why do I harbor such thoughts? But then, why shouldn't I?

"For one thing, kings never say ain't," I told him.

With a menacing stare, he puzzled, "She said he don't talk like no king. If he ain't no king, why should he talk like one?"

I tried to count the grammatical errors in those two sentences but couldn't keep up with the deluge. "MacNiff now thinks it's all blather, Al."

"What do you think?"

"MacNiff's suspicions were all based on believing the old lady was trying to tell him the boy wasn't her grandson. Now that we have a positive ID on him, her words make no sense. What do the police think?"

"Us?" Al boomed. "We weren't apprised of this privileged information, remember? We don't know beans about Lance Talbot, his grandmother or his nine toes."

"I mean what have the police learned about Jeff Rodgers's murder?"

"You want me to tell you what we know in exchange for diddlysquat." He dropped the cigar butt into his coffee container. I assumed he didn't intend to drink any more.

Going on the offense, I retaliated. "You haven't been very forthright with me, Al."

He gave this a moment's thought, then smiled. "You've met Izzy."

Al Rogoff is a quick study and the department's most valuable asset. He never rose above the rank of sergeant for the simple reason that the noncom status suited him. Al was a servant of the people, as he liked to boast, and his favorite poet was that champion of the common man,

Rudyard Kipling, who defined a veritable man as one who could walk with kings and not lose the common touch. Al had seen too many of his superiors fail that test.

"The last time we met you knew she had moved in next door and was running around with Binky."

"They don't do much running, if you know what I mean."

"I know," I maintained. "And why didn't you report this?"

"Because I ain't Lolly Spindrift, and because she's got a jones on for Binky. I didn't want you raiding the love nest wielding your six-shooter."

Working all night had certainly fueled his powers of suggestive imagery. "She's not my type, Al."

"But her bank balance is."

"You know she's loaded?"

"Binky has mentioned the fact. She likes to shop and Binky is the willing benefactor of her conspicuous consumption."

Al borrowed the phrase from me and used it whenever possible. "She bought him an Armani suit," I said, masking my envy with a show of disdain for a man who would allow a woman to dress him at her expense. Binky had become a Pal Joey, as John O'Hara had labeled such a cad —

and I begrudged him every thread of that suit, and the pearl links to boot.

"He's looking at Ferraris," Al said, like they were shopping for an electric can opener.

Out of control, I shouted, "A what?"

"Don't bust a gut, pal. Izzy thinks it'll go with her Maserati. Cute, no?"

"No! And I think you're deriving some weird vicarious pleasure out of this romance."

"If that means I'm liking it, the answer is a big yes. It keeps Binky out of what's left of my hair, and he don't come calling every morning in search of a teaspoon of sugar or a dram of milk. I hope they marry and settle in Kalamazoo."

"You know they have literary aspirations, Sergeant."

"I figured they was up to something. They keep asking questions about the murder."

I was relieved that he didn't know they were snooping on behalf of Skip McGuire and kept my own counsel on that score. Al would razz me like a dog gnawing a bone. "Don't tell them anything, Al," I ordered.

He pulled a face. "I don't know nothing to tell," said the champ of the double negative. "We questioned everyone that was at the party and came up with nothing. Not even a long shot. Now, all that's changed. You've given us Lance Talbot."

"Correction. Lance Talbot has come forth as a concerned citizen — and you never questioned me."

Al folded his massive arms across his massive chest, which was covered in a blue shirt embossed with palm trees. His silence spoke volumes, as the hacks say, which, like most trite locutions, says it all.

"My name was on your list and to save yourself time, effort and shoe leather, you crossed it off because I'm your friend and above suspicion. Obstruction of justice, Sergeant. If you don't squeal on me I won't squeal on you."

"I'm questioning you now, pal, and look what I got out of you."

I waved that off. "After the fact, Sergeant. The guy at the palace is giving your chief the same information, and what do you think they will do with it?"

"Take notes," Al answered. "You think he done it, Archy?"

"With his own hands? No. I can swear to that. But Dennis Darling and I think there's a link between the blackmail and Jeff's murder. There has to be."

"Dennis Darling," Al guffawed. "Do you

call him Darling, Archy?"

"Only when we're alone, Sergeant."

"You said Jeff never opened up to Darling?"

"Never. And I'm not holding anything back, Al. My word of honor."

"You got anything better to swear on, Archy?"

"My virginity?"

With a yawn and a shrug he sallied, "You wanna try again, pal?" I remembered that he had been patrolling our little island all night and had yet to close his eyes. Returning to business, I stated, "Lance Talbot is now your number one suspect, yes?"

"By his own admission he's elevated himself to numero uno," Al said. "Not to mention that there ain't no numero dos. But handing him the blue ribbon is another matter. You and a hundred other solid citizens are his alibi. You say the fancy broad was also in the immediate vicinity and nowhere near that pool?"

Al means no disrespect for the fair sex. He thinks "broads" and "dames" are complimentary terms. "Aren't you interested in knowing the true reason Jeff was blackmailing Talbot?"

"Not really. Talbot was being blackmailed and he killed the guy trying to milk him for big bucks. The reason ain't relevant, like they say. Besides, it's you and your Darling who think Talbot got more to hide than he's fessing up to."

"But what Talbot is admitting to is no reason to kill for. It's got to be more than that," I argued.

Al remained unimpressed. "Maybe he thought it was reason enough to kill Jeff at the time, and when he discovered Jeff had tipped his hand to the reporter guy, Talbot thought he better come clean and pretend he wasn't worried about his mother's reputation or his family's good name. He ain't got nothing to lose because he has people like you to swear he didn't do it."

It made sense and I offered no rebuttal — but I wasn't convinced.

"You get an answer from the lawyer in Switzerland?"

"From his secretary," I reported. "He's in Berlin and she didn't know just when he would be back. We're closed today but I'll stop at the office and check the machine."

"What we gotta do," Al preached, forecasting his colleagues' stratagem after hearing Lance Talbot's story, "is link Talbot to someone at that party. Someone who could have acted for him. I think we'll have another go at the catering staff. Talbot is rich and those kids are always looking to make a fast buck. MacNiff's guests ain't in need."

I had been debating on whether I should tell Al Rogoff about Vivian Emerson's supposed disappearance before I learned more than Georgy was able to tell me last night. Hearing Al dismiss the MacNiff crowd as innocent by divine right, I changed my mind. Also, if her disappearance was connected to Jeff's murder, I didn't want Al to again accuse me of purposely keeping him, and the police, ignorant of the facts.

"Speaking of MacNiff's guests," I started, "one of them has gone missing."

That revived his interest in what Archy had to say. "How so?" he questioned.

I had neglected to tell him of my encounter with Vivian Emerson and Joe Gallo at the MacNiff benefit, and now I did.

"You think this von Brecht dame and the Emerson dame knew each other?" Al asked.

"I wouldn't swear to it in a court of law, but Vivian Emerson looked daggers at Holga von Brecht when we all shook hands across the net. Gallo called Georgy last night telling her that Vivian Emerson had disappeared."

"Back up, pal," Al directed, as if he were on traffic duty. "Did this Gallo call the troopers? Is that how Georgy got in on it?"

I didn't want to go into the nitty-gritty details, but one couldn't get away with glossing over the facts with Sergeant Rogoff calling the shots. "Actually, Gallo and Georgy were tight at one time."

"How tight?"

I sighed and capitulated. "He used to live with her."

Al looked pensive before snapping his fingers as if he had come up with a formula for curing patent baldness. "Euphemism," he barked in triumph. "You are full of euphemisms, Archy. Tight? He was your girl's boyfriend."

"Which has nothing to do with the lady's disappearance, Sergeant."

Not unexpected, the next query was, "What's Emerson's relationship to this Joe Gallo?"

Knowing when to concede to the inevitable, I briefed Al on the shoddy details of Joe's leaving Georgy's cottage for Vivian's commodious villa.

"You people got the morals of the barnyard," Al criticized.

Why I was counted among the iniquitous I don't know, and did not ask. When Al pontificates I lie low, but I couldn't help zapping his holier-than-thou gambit with, "Didn't someone say something about casting the first stone?"

Al pulled a stogie out of his shirt pocket and stuck it between his teeth. I didn't know if he was going to smoke it or eat it. "I ain't casting no stones, pal, just calling it like I see it. So what happened to this Vivian Emerson?"

"Joe said she went out Thursday night, about six, and never came back. He called Georgy last night about ten. She's been gone for over twenty-four hours."

"Did she tell Gallo where she was going when she left?"

"I don't know any details, Al. I'm going to see Georgy this afternoon. She gets off duty at four. I told her to call Gallo and have him meet me at her place. I'll get the facts from him."

"Funny he didn't call the police," Al speculated. "They could check to see if she had an accident and was laid up in a hospital."

"I expect Georgy did that first thing this morning," I said.

"You think this has something to do with

the swimming pool murder, Archy?"

"Right now I don't know what to think. But Jeff was blackmailing Lance Talbot and he got wasted. Vivian Emerson looked askance at Holga von Brecht and she disappears. Would you say it was worth your hindquarters to cross paths with our Swiss visitors?"

"Could be," he said, looking at his watch.

"You wanted a link between Lance Talbot and someone at the MacNiff benefit. This could be it."

"Suppose Vivian Emerson had designs on the young, handsome and rich Lance Talbot, and the von Brecht dame didn't like it. Woman are very territorial when it comes to sons and lovers."

I remember thinking the ladies were squabbling over Joe Gallo. Chances were Vivian Emerson had spent the night with a friend and forgot to tell her roommate her plans, or Gallo wasn't listening when she told him.

I had kept Al long enough. I promised to keep him posted on anything Denny or I picked up regarding Jeff's murder, and what I learned from Joe Gallo that might connect Vivian Emerson to Lance or Holga von Brecht.

"Before you go, have a look at this, Al." I handed him the photo of Lance Talbot and Jeff Rodgers. "It was taken when they were enrolled at the Day School."

Al put on his specs, looked at the photo and handed it back to me. "They're dressed *pour le sport*," was his keen observation.

Herb, our security person, was off for the weekend as was most of the office staff, but there was a number of cars in the underground garage of the McNally Building, which was not unusual for a Saturday. Those working on cases found it expedient to labor at the office on a day when they would not be interrupted by ringing telephones and gabby cohorts. I went directly to the executive suite to check Mrs. Trelawney's fax machine. The basket that holds the incoming faxes as they fall from the printer was empty.

I doubted the Swiss worked on weekends either, so I was resigned to waiting until Monday to send Herr Hermann a reminder if I had not received his reply by then.

The morning sun and surf vistas had me thinking about putting in my two miles before meeting with Georgy. Leaving the office, I decided to pick up a newspaper and stop at the club, where I could indulge myself in a leisurely read while nibbling on one of Leroy's light lunch specials. Jell-O and cottage cheese? A slice of melon and cottage cheese? How tempting. I couldn't wait.

All thoughts of a relaxing interlude in my life in the fast lane evaporated at the sight of Binky Watrous and Izzy Duhane lunching at my favorite table. When the gods were kind, they were very kind. When they were vindictive, they knew no mercy.

"Archy," Izzy waved. "I'm so glad to see you."

"I wish I could say the same," I rejoined cheerfully.

"Come sit with us," Izzy invited. "We're waiting for our burgers and fries."

"I don't want to intrude," I said, to no avail.

She was wearing a T-shirt that could fit a linebacker and a straw bonnet with ribbons down the back. Isadora Duhane was, if nothing else, an original. The new Binky was got up in one of those collarless shirts favored by the late Mao Tse-tung that I always thought was copied from ye olde one-piece union suit with a drop seat. I didn't know what these two fashion plates sported below the waist and considered it the only blessing of this most bothersome encounter.

Binky and I had yet to have a good man-to-man since I had met his benefactress and seen his new acquisitions. That those doe eyes still avoided my gaze told me he was not eager to hear what I had to say. As an ego booster, Izzy had a long way to go.

"We don't know who did it, Archy, but we think we know how it was done." Izzy spoke as I took my place at the table.

"Do you now?" I said.

"We do," Binky assured me, looking over my head. "Izzy visited the scene of the crime yesterday."

"So did I. Too bad you couldn't make it, Binky. Did you uncover anything of a forensic nature in the mail room in my absence?"

Izzy gave my shin a gentle nudge under the table as Priscilla ambled over to take my order, saving Binky from responding. God is on Binky's side.

"The usual?" Priscilla asked.

Not wanting to keep Al Rogoff waiting, I had only had a cup of coffee before leaving the house this morning, much to Ursi's disappointment. She wanted to hear all about the pool party, the mysterious doctor and, "Is it true the Talbot boy went in naked?" Maria Sanchez didn't miss a nuance and Ursi would have to entertain sensual thoughts until my return.

I ordered an egg-white omelet with low-fat Alpine Lace Swiss and rye toast, dry.

"Are you sick, Archy?" Binky inquired, with genuine concern.

"No," Izzy spoke for me. "The bathing trunks, remember?"

Gadzooks! She had told him about Lance wearing my trunks and probably written it up in her blasted notebook. I gave Binky a look that could curdle milk but he was busy examining the buttons on his union suit.

"Do you want to hear my theory?" Izzy persisted.

"Do I have a choice?"

"As a matter of fact, no," she said. "But you'll be happy you did." Leaning forward for effect, she stated, "The tunnel."

"What tunnel?"

"Archy, don't you see?" Binky cried. "The tunnel that leads from the beach to the MacNiff property. It's smack between the tennis courts and the pool."

I felt those icy fingers tickle my spine.

"I noticed it yesterday," Izzy picked up.

"The gate was locked. Was it open the day of the MacNiff benefit?"

I remembered that it was and could only nod in shame.

"Then the killer didn't have to be a guest. He could have been hiding in the tunnel, waiting for a chance to get Jeff Rodgers alone."

Finally looking me in the eye, Binky clamored, "What do you think, Archy?"

"I think I want to return my Dick Tracy decoder ring."

TWENTY-TWO

I pulled up behind a Chevy Impala that had seen better days. No doubt Joseph Gallo's, and the very car he used to escape Georgy girl in favor of Vivian Emerson. He had probably not gotten rid of it thinking one should never be without a getaway car.

It occurred to me that Georgy's landlady, the guardian of the driveway, must have recognized the Impala as belonging to her tenant's former roommate. Five minutes later, along comes the red Miata that belongs to her tenant's current, albeit part-time, roommate. Was she scandalized? One could only hope so. It would put a little zest into a life full of doilies and antimacassars.

Georgy and Joe Gallo were seated in the parlor, which was furnished in early IKEA. He was very much as I remembered him from our last meeting — tall, dark and handsome. If I were granted three wishes by a benevolent genie, my first directive would be to have Joe Gallo and Alejandro Gomez y Zapata meet at the Colony next

Thursday night and run off to Key West where they would open a B-and-B and live happily ever after. (Shame on me!)

Georgy was still in uniform, which I have always found more beguiling than her civvies. Sigmund would have something to say about that. Joe jumped up as I entered and, like a drowning man spotting a straw, I was pleased to observe that I was a shade taller than he.

"Mr. McNally," he said, sticking out his hand.

Mister? Was that a show of respect, or a reference to my age? "We meet again," I acknowledged.

Georgy was now up and moving towards me. She gave me a peck in sisterly fashion. "Thanks for coming, Archy. You two sit. I put up a pot of coffee and I think it's done. I'll get some cups and pour while Joe fills you in."

Gallo was in oatmeal-gray sweat shorts, sneakers and a rugby shirt. Were the shorts to show off the muscular legs that Georgy so admired? Was Archy being paranoid? A handicapper would give you twelve to seven odds on a likely yes.

"The place looks good," Gallo said, not returning to the couch he had occupied with Georgy when I entered, but taking the club chair. "Georgy told me you were into decorating."

"Just the odd piece here and there," I admitted. "I don't think it's changed much since . . ." Here came a significant pause.

"Since I left?" Gallo offered.

"No, no. Since I've been coming around."

"Would you two can it and get down to business," Lieutenant O'Hara barked from the kitchen. "You sound like characters in a coming-of-age novel."

"I think I came and went," Gallo called back, laughing.

Georgy also found it amusing. I didn't, but went along for the ride. It seemed to me Georgy and Connie got on much better than Alex and I, and now, Joe Gallo and I. Was this because women are more pragmatic than we men, or was it because they didn't mind sharing? Maybe Gallo's namesake Joseph Smith knew what he was talking about, but this is Worth Lake, not Salt Lake.

I sat on the couch. "I met you and Vivian Emerson at the MacNiff benefit, do you recall?"

"Sure I do," he told me. "Viv and I played a set with you just before the caterer's boy drowned in the pool. How could I forget it? I knew who you were because I had read your interview in the *Daily News*, but I never connected your Georgia with mine." That was met with silence, even from the kitchen. Gallo shook his head. "I didn't mean that the way it sounded."

Certain he didn't, I advocated, "Joe, we're here to see if we can find out what happened to Vivian Emerson, not to exchange sophomoric barbs about past and present relationships. It's uncomfortable, but we're here and Vivian Emerson is missing."

"Amen," cried Georgy, with all the fervor of a revival-meeting enthusiast.

Without preamble, Joe stated, "Viv went out Thursday evening, about six I think, and I haven't seen her since."

"Did she say where she was going?"

He ran a hand through his hair and gazed at the ceiling. "The truth?"

"It would help," I encouraged.

"I wasn't listening," he admitted. "I was at my PC, working on an idea I have for a column. I was a reporter for a small press but it folded."

Georgy did tell me Gallo had come to Florida after college when he was offered a position with a fledgling local daily.

"I want to get back in the business," he continued. "I heard Viv, but I didn't really listen to what she said, is what I mean."

Georgy, lugging a crowded tray, joined us.

"Why didn't you call the police?" I asked.

He explained that Vivian had a friend in Delray Beach she often visited. "Sometimes, when they had a few too many, she would spend the night. It was no big deal. It had happened before and I just assumed that's where she was."

Georgy had put the tray on the coffee table that fronted the couch. Now she poured and passed around the cups. Cream and sugar were on the tray along with a plate of chocolate-chip cookies. "Wouldn't she call to say she was staying?" Georgy spoke my next question.

Gallo shrugged as if he were unsure of the answer, but as an experienced interviewer I knew the gesture meant, "Don't ask." To save him the embarrassment, and to keep us all honest, I plunged in where her lover feared to tread. "She's a boozer, Joe, yes? And when she and her pal have those few too many the only thing she calls for is another drink."

With a tenuous nod, he said, "That's it,

Archy. I scrambled myself a few eggs, watched the tube and went to bed. Business as usual."

Georgy looked at him like a doting mother listening to her child's tale of woe. He didn't rate the sympathy. He was Vivian Emerson's fancy man and deserved whatever he got. I made a mental note to tell Binky what befalls men who trade their virility for riches. Armani suits, pearl cufflinks and Italian cars, that's what they get. I helped myself to a cookie.

Gallo started getting worried the following evening, when Emerson had been gone for twenty-four hours. He called the friend in Delray Beach and learned that Vivian had not been there the previous evening, or in several weeks. "I called around to a few more friends, but none of them had seen her. That's when I called Georgy."

As I knew she would, Georgy ran a missing persons check this morning and came up with nothing. "Hospitals, police blotters, accident reports, the works. Not a trace of her."

"I alerted Al Rogoff this morning, but not officially. We met on another matter," I said.

"Who's Al Rogoff?" Gallo asked.

"Sergeant Al Rogoff," Georgy answered for me. "He's with the Palm Beach force. He and Archy are working on a homicide. The kid that was drowned in the MacNiff pool."

"The police questioned us about that," Gallo said.

"What did you tell them?" I asked him.

"Nothing," he responded. "We didn't know the kid. We were as stunned as everyone else that day."

I was pleased that Georgy had reintroduced the subject of the MacNiff fete. I could query Joe Gallo on the subject of Holga von Brecht without giving away my hand too soon. "Was Ms. Emerson an annual contributor to Malcolm MacNiff's scholarship fund, Joe?"

He smiled. "No way. That crowd is out of Viv's league."

He related how one of Vivian Emerson's golf buddies, who was a regular invitee to the *Tennis Everyone!* benefit, had complained that she and her husband had purchased tickets as usual, but this year a business trip to Milan would keep her husband from attending, and she had decided to tag along at company expense. Vivian offered the woman twenty-five hundred dollars for the tickets, which was half their cost. The woman accepted, saying she wouldn't tell her husband, and would use the money to go boutiqueing while visiting our planet's boutique capital.

"So we got in on someone else's shirt-tails," was how Gallo finished the story.

"You didn't know anyone there?" I nudged.

"Not a soul. Like I said, I knew you by sight from the interview in the *Daily News*, and I knew who Dennis Darling was because everyone was whispering about him. I wanted to meet him but never got near him."

Zeroing in, I asked him, "Do you remember the woman who partnered with me opposite you and Ms. Emerson?"

He grinned. "Her? She really ticked Viv off."

Now we were getting to the nuts and bolts of this confrontation. "Why?"

When Vivian Emerson saw Holga von Brecht, she told Joe that she knew Olga from their undergrad days at Smith.

"Did you say Olga?" I cut in, carefully articulating the first vowel.

"Yeah. Olga something. I don't remember the family name. Viv went right up to her and Olga froze," he recalled.

"You mean she snubbed Ms. Emerson?"

"No," Joe said. "I mean she froze, pop-eyed, is the best I can describe it. Then she snubbed her. She told Viv she had mistaken her for someone else and walked away."

Needless to say, Vivian Emerson was furious. Being something of a gate-crasher, she thought it would boost her image if she was seen embracing an old friend who was there by invitation.

"Then came the discovery of the kid in the pool and after that, as you know, Archy, the party broke up."

"Helen MacNiff had to give the police a list of all the guests. How did she get your names, if the tickets belonged to someone else?"

"Easy," Joe said. "Viv's friend called the MacNiffs' secretary and told her we were coming in place of her and her husband. I mean it would be awkward if we weren't on the security checker's list and got bounced. That night, Viv told me about Olga — Norton, I think was her maiden name."

The girls had met at Smith and were acquaintances, if not the best of friends. Vivian had heard that Olga went to Europe shortly after graduation and had married someone in Switzerland, remaining there with her husband. Two years later, while on her own honeymoon, Vivian ran into Olga in Lucerne. "She said Olga had a son and seemed very happy."

I almost upset the cup of coffee I had balanced on my lap. "A son? Are you sure?"

"I think so. What difference does it make? Viv thought she was a perfect bitch. No, I think she called her a cow."

Holga, or Olga, von Brecht may be many things, but a cow wasn't one of them. I put my cup and saucer on the coffee table as Georgy, who was seated next to me, put a hand on my knee. "The von Brecht woman is the one you told me about, isn't she? The one who's here with Lance Talbot. Do you think Vivian's disappearance has something to do with the murder?"

"What?" Gallo shouted, leaping out of his chair. "What murder? The kid in the pool? Viv never knew him."

Taking charge, I told them both to simmer down and motioned Joe Gallo to resume his seat. Vivian Emerson knew Holga von Brecht. That seemed clear. But von Brecht wasn't happy to see her former school chum. That was even clearer.

Jeff Rodgers was connected to Lance Talbot, who was connected to Holga von

Brecht, who was connected to Vivian Emerson. And the hipbone's connected to the thighbone, and the thighbone's connected to . . .

"Yes, I now believe there may be a connection between Jeff Rodgers's murder and Vivian Emerson's disappearance." Raising my hand for silence as the two plied me with questions, I sought to extinguish the fuse I had inadvertently lit before it detonated the bomb in my noggin.

"There's no reason to jump to conclusions," I began, and that's as far as I got.

"We already have," Georgy said. "You told me . . ."

"Put a muzzle on it, Georgy. I confided in you because you wear that uniform. We've both said too much already."

"Meaning wait till little Joey leaves, and then throw it open for discussion. Well, I'm not leaving until I know what's going on," little Joey informed us. "I think I'm the guy who put you wise to whatever it is you won't tell me."

I looked at my watch. Mickey's arms were vertically bisecting the dial, with the little arm pointing down. In short, it was time for a liquid refreshment that would banish the taste of Georgy's instant coffee. The pot she claimed to have put up was

354

filled with water. When boiling she put in three teaspoons of the instant powder, and one for the pot. Oh, Georgy!

"I believe there's a bottle of a pretentious Chardonnay chilling in the fridge," I announced. "Let's clear the deck and fortify ourselves for the task ahead." I began clearing the coffee table. "Many hands make light work," I hinted.

I had them both bussing the table and, for the moment, off my back. I uncorked the wine as Georgy got out the glasses and Joe stacked the dishwasher. He was not unfamiliar with Georgy's kitchen, I noted. Filling the glasses, I informed them, " 'Tis said a glass of wine is nature's tranquilizer."

"Vivian said that, and look what happened to her," Georgy blurted. Joe and I paused in our labors. "Sorry," she recanted.

"What's going on, Archy?" Joe began as soon as he had tasted the wine.

"I don't think Vivian Emerson is in any way involved in Jeff Rodgers's murder, but I do think she unwittingly intruded upon a conspiracy and has made some people very nervous."

"Olga?" Joe guessed correctly.

This is just what I didn't want to

happen. Nonprofessionals knowing too much, blabbing and getting up the wind before the police had a chance to sort it all out. I had no proof that Vivian Emerson was abducted by the von Brechts, just as I had no proof that Lance Talbot was responsible for Jeff's murder. It was all circumstantial posturing. I needed something to hang my suspicions on and there was one chance in a zillion that Joe Gallo, of all people, might give me what I needed.

"Joe, does Vivian have caller ID on her phone?"

"Yeah," he said. "So does everyone in Palm Beach."

"What are you getting at, Archy?" Georgy asked.

"Does it keep a record of the incoming calls? I mean, can you check to see what calls came in in the last few days?"

"I think it has a memory bank," Joe stated.

"I know it does," Georgy cut in. "We have it at the barracks. It can store just so many numbers, so how many days back it goes depends on how many calls came in."

"Joe, this is very important. First, I want you to promise to keep your mouth shut about everything you heard here today. Can I count on you?"

"Is Vivian in danger?" he asked, and I think he was sincerely concerned. It went a long way in boosting my opinion of the guy.

"She may be. What I want you to do is go home and scan the caller ID screen. Write down all the numbers listed. After getting rid of the ones you know, call me here and give me the rest."

"What for?" Joe asked.

"Just do what Archy says," Georgy ordered. "After that, call the Palm Beach police and report Vivian's disappearance."

"But you already ran a check," Joe insisted.

"That was this morning," Georgy exclaimed, losing her composure. "You and Viv live in Palm Beach so you must notify the Palm Beach police. Just do it, Joey." When he reached for the Chardonnay for a refill, she ordered, "Now, Joey."

She followed him to the door where they spoke quietly. I saw Georgy pat his cheek before he left. Seeing my gaze, she said when she returned, "I asked him if he needed money."

"What did he say?"

"He told me to buzz off."

"Good. You deserve it." I consulted the little address book I always carry and picked up the kitchen wall phone. I dialed the MacNiff house and got Maria Sanchez. I held my breath. Mr. MacNiff was in. I asked him for Lance Talbot's phone number, which I had neglected to get from Lance when he hired me. Georgy slipped me a pad and pencil as Nifty gave me the info. Knowing Nifty was curious but too polite to ask the reason for my request, I volunteered the information, saying, "He walked off with my bathing suit and I want it back."

Georgy had taken the bottle of Chardonnay into the parlor and I followed her, and it, there.

"You think the von Brecht woman called Vivian and asked to meet with her?" she said.

Taking my place next to her on the couch, I nodded as I poured us seconds, then I kissed her.

"Before you get too comfortable, tell me what's going on, Archy."

"Where did I leave off last time I saw you?"

"From the beginning, please."

I took a deep breath and told her what I had shared with Al Rogoff this morning, adding the masked man in the tunnel theory, which I passed off as my own clever deduction. And why not?

She listened carefully and, like Al, said with what I had on Lance Talbot and the von Brechts, they could live a long and happy life in snowy Switzerland. "Even if von Brecht did call Vivian, all you know is that she called an old friend. That's what she would claim, showing the police photos of their days at Smith."

I didn't need Georgy girl to tell me that. What I was after was one more piece of circumstantial evidence to add to my collection, bolstering my resolve not to write off Lance Talbot & Co. and to enlist Al Rogoff in my cause.

When the phone rang I ran to the kitchen and picked it up along with the pad and pencil Georgy had supplied. Gallo read me a list of five numbers. One of them corresponded to the first number on the pad — the number Malcolm MacNiff had given me. I told Joe to call the Palm Beach police and to sit tight.

"Someone from the Talbot house called Vivian Emerson." I showed Georgy the pad. "And she went to meet that person."

Staring at it, she said, "This doesn't look good for Vivian."

"No, Georgy, it doesn't." I sat next to her and took her hand. "And there ain't tuppence we can do about it."

"Poor Joey," Georgy lamented.

"Poor Vivian Emerson," I corrected.

We sat in silence for what seemed like a long time. Me thinking about Vivian Emerson's encounter with her schoolmate in Switzerland, and my girl thinking about — what? Joe Gallo?

As it turned out our thoughts, like our hands, were intertwined. "You know," Georgy broke the reverie, "you used the word *conspiracy*. If this Talbot and Holga were in plain sight at the time of the murder, why couldn't Holga's husband have been in the tunnel?"

"Because he was in Switzerland," I told her.

"But you said he was at the pool party yesterday."

"He was. He flew in yesterday. Lance and Holga picked him up at the airport that morning and brought him to the party."

"Were you there?" she asked.

"At the party? Of course. I just told you all about it."

"No, silly. Were you at the airport? Did you see the guy get off the plane?"

I squeezed her pretty paw. First Izzy Duhane, and now Georgy girl, telling me my business. Maybe God created women for reasons other than the obvious.

"I'll ask Al Rogoff if he can check the incoming flights that day and their passenger rosters."

"You're welcome," she heckled. "Now I want to get out of this uniform and into a shower. How about taking me out to dinner, McNally, and calling Joey to join us."

"What?"

"Come on," Georgy pushed. "He's alone and worried, thanks to you."

Now I'm to blame. "I'll think about it," I said, more as a matter of form than fact. Little Joey would dine with us.

Putting my address book back into my pocket, I discovered the photo I had shown Al. I took it out and looked at it as if it contained the answer to all my questions. Funny thing was — it did.

"What's that?" Georgy asked.

"The prince and the pauper," I said, handing her the photo. "That's Lance Talbot on your right."

"He's a southpaw," was her only comment.

"A who?"

"A southpaw," she repeated. "The kid's glove is on his right hand, so he's a lefty."

I took the photo back and studied it. The Lance Talbot I played tennis with was not a southpaw.

TWENTY-THREE

Gens du monde, as the French call them. The fashionable people. Chauffeured limousines deposited them at Lady Cynthia Horowitz's front door before driving off to the mammoth parking area on her ten acres of surf and sand nestled between the Atlantic and Ocean Boulevard. Each time I approach the white-columned mansion, the theme from *Gone With the Wind* echoes in my mind and for a moment the limos become smart carriages drawn by braces of noble stallions.

It is said in Palm Beach that it never rains on Lady Cynthia's pageants, and tonight was no exception. The moon had risen to its height and beamed down on the ladies in their party finery and the gentlemen in their white dinner jackets. The patio was professionally lit with theatrical klieg lights in an array of flattering tones, cloaking the expanse in perpetual twilight. Who says money can't make time stand still?

A fountain erupted from the center of the pool, the sparkling water cascading in a rainbow of hues. Dozens of tables for four were covered in white linen and decorated with glass urns bursting with nosegays of yellow tea roses. Portable bars surrounded the area, the caterer's staff of comely youths passed around the finger food that included the bourgeois pigs in a blanket, and the palm trees swayed to the beat of a foxtrot emanating from a six-piece combo. Whoever said money can't buy happiness had no idea what they were talking about.

The hostess was in a shimmering knee-length red cocktail dress that showed off her remarkable figure and distracted the looker from a pedestrian, to put it kindly, face. She greeted me warmly with, "Who invited you, lad?"

"Not you or your emissary of printed trivia," I confessed. "I am Dennis Darling's date."

Looking me up and down, she concluded, "If that's his preference, he could have done better."

"Your kindness, Madame, is heartwarming."

A pretty young thing offered us a tray of miniature crab cakes pierced with toothpicks. I helped myself as Lady C petitioned me to exert my influence on Denny to give her and her party major coverage in his *Palm Beach Story* article.

"Only if they discover a body in your pool at the end of the evening," I said.

"Careful, lad, or it may be yours."

I had spent most of the weekend with Georgy and Joe Gallo. He went home after dinner on Saturday, but was back bright and early Sunday morning. There was still no word from Vivian Emerson, and the Palm Beach police had no more luck than Georgy in locating her. I talked Gallo into going home Sunday afternoon to man his phone in case the police or Vivian tried to contact him.

When I got back to my digs, I called Denny to see what he had been up to, which turned out to be nothing very much. He told me Lady C's party was this evening and asked if I were going.

"I wasn't invited."

"I was," he said. "Remember? And I was told to bring a guest. Consider yourself my date."

"I have nothing to wear," I moaned.

"Coming to sunny Florida, I packed a proper dinner jacket. Get into yours and come by at seven with the top down. We'll ride through town like two headwaiters with attitude."

A week in Palm Beach and he's talking like a native.

I picked him up at the hotel and as we drove to Lady Cynthia's I filled him in on Vivian's disappearance, giving him a précis on Vivian's encounter with Holga. I also told him that Lance Talbot was left-handed and expounded on the tunnel theory — taking credit for both. And why not?

"Someone at the Talbot house called this Vivian Emerson," he said thoughtfully. "Given the circumstances, I think there's a connection, but proving it is something else. If I were writing the story I wouldn't even hint that the call led to Emerson's disappearance because it would leave me wide open for a slander suit."

Down but not out, I said, "The Lance Talbot we know is a righty. Could he be ambidextrous?"

Denny thought it was possible, but, "People who are ambidextrous usually use their right hand for certain chores and the left for others. If they write with their right, for instance, they may play sports with their left."

"If it's consistent," I reasoned, "Lance used his left hand for sports as a kid, so he would do so as an adult. But he plays tennis with his right hand."

"His feet check out but his hands don't,"

Denny joked. "Unless he was born a lefty and switched later on."

"I doubt that's possible," I offered. "Wasn't the last King George, the Queen's father, a lefty they tried to turn into a righty?"

"I don't think it worked," Denny said.

Denny was impressed with Lady C's digs as well as her startling figure. She was so pleased when he kissed her hand, she didn't notice me until Denny wiggled out of her clutches and made for one of the bars. When she left me to chase after Denny, I took in the scene. Jackson Barnett, the von Brechts and Dennis Darling were the suns around which the party orbited. The doc paraded around like he was leading a brass band, and wore a red carnation in his white lapel. Holga was in a black strapless affair that went to her ankles but was strategically ventilated to show a lovely leg from ankle to thigh. Connie, no doubt out with her beau, was not present.

Lance was the center of a younger group who had congregated near the pool, where they were passing around a joint. Lance used his right hand to hold his drink and put it into his left to take and pass the offered cannabis. He was as ambidextrous as a one-armed paperhanger.

Lady Cynthia didn't allow smoking any-place on her turf, in- or outdoors, but was too crazed running between Jackson, the doc, and Denny to notice the kiddies. Before the night was over she had to get Jackson in bed, von Brecht to invite her to his clinic, and Denny to feature her on the cover of *Bare Facts*. Whoever coined the expression "idle rich" had never met our Lady Cynthia.

Did I mention that Barnett looked gorgeous? No? Sorry.

I got myself a bourbon on the rocks with a splash and met Lance Talbot at the oasis. "Are you here on business or pleasure, Archy?" he asked.

"A little bit of both. How did you get along with our police?"

"I told them my story and they told me not to leave town. Having no intentions of leaving before I have settled my claim, I promptly agreed. I think I am now their prime suspect and may have to call on your father sooner than I expected. If they dare harass me without valid cause, I'll sue them."

And wasn't that a mouthful. The guy was all P & V and hell-bent on election. Was it the funny cigarettes? I hardly think so. I had once called him feisty. I now upgraded Lance Talbot to an aggressive, pugnacious punk. There and then I knew he was as guilty of Jeff's murder as if he had shoved Jeff into that pool himself. I also knew I couldn't prove it. And who was he? As Denny had summed up, his right foot said he was Lance Talbot, but his right hand said he wasn't.

I moved off before I slugged the guy, lost a client and caused my father to serve me papers.

Lolly floated by, spotted me and stopped floating. "I don't remember inviting you," he warmly greeted me.

"I'm Dennis Darling's date."

"Well, if your dance card isn't filled, save the last waltz for me."

"You're on, Lol. Some party you and Madame put together in record time, even for this party town."

"Isn't it thrilling," he cooed. "The crème de la crème of Palm Beach society. Lady Cynthia has got a firm invitation from Dr. Claus to visit him in Switzerland. I'm going with her, naturally. I can't wait to get poked in the rear with . . . well, I won't spoil your appetite. And Jackson has just about decided to leave Meecham's yacht and move in here for the duration of his stay. He suffers from *mal de mer*, don't you know."

"Meecham's boat is docked," I said.

"Really? Promise not to tell anyone, dear heart. Ta-ta. And don't forget our waltz." With that he floated away.

"Amusing, isn't he?"

Startled, I turned to see Holga von Brecht. "He's a barrel of monkeys," I said. "Good evening, Mrs. von Brecht."

"So formal? The name is Holga."

"Or Olga, perhaps?"

The friendly smile turned into a frown. "I left Olga when I married Claus and made his country my home."

Clever, clever, clever. She knew I was wise to something, but not how wise. Rather than deny her true given name and get trapped in a lie, she quickly made up a perfectly natural reason for having altered it to suit her new environment. If Jeff Rodgers was matching wits with this group he was outclassed and outdistanced by a few light-years.

"I ran into Joe Gallo. He was the man who played opposite us with Vivian Emerson. Do you recall?"

"I recall that this is the second time you've questioned me regarding Vivian Emerson." The frown turned into a menacing glare.

"Gallo told me that Vivian remembered

you from your college days at Smith, but you didn't remember her."

The glare relaxed into a smile as ingratiating as an icy wind. "That tiresome woman," she said. "No, I didn't remember her immediately. She hasn't aged well, poor thing. I'm afraid I was rude, but I did find her name in the directory and called to apologize."

Clever? She was the Einstein of the instant retort. "Did you speak to her?"

"What is your interest, Mr. McNally?"

"Vivian Emerson is missing. She left her home Thursday night and has not been seen since."

"I know nothing of this. Yes, I spoke to her, briefly. She was still miffed by my rebuff and grudgingly accepted my apology."

"You made no date to meet her?" I asked.

"Meet who?" Dr. von Brecht suddenly joined in the conversation, having gotten away from Lady Cynthia, who was now clinging to Jackson Barnett's elbow and Denny's hand.

"That woman I was telling you about the other day," Holga brought her husband up to speed. "The one who knew me from Smith. It seems she's disappeared and Mr. McNally seems to think I might know where she's hiding."

"You are supposed to be working for Lance, Mr. McNally, but I get the distinct impression that it's us you are investigating, not the death of that waiter. I find it intrusive and ask you to desist."

His wife put out her arm to restrain him, as if he had threatened to belt me. "Really, Claus, there's no need to make a scene. Mr. McNally is merely doing his job, I'm sure. It seems Vivian Emerson is missing." To me she said, "No, I made no date to meet her, I don't know where she is and, quite frankly, couldn't care less."

I wondered if she gave Lance lessons in deportment.

"Lance has been to the police," Claus put in, "and explained that the waiter was blackmailing him. Lance also told them the reason why. It was most embarrassing for the boy. He is a victim being treated like the culprit. I find it outrageous."

What I found outrageous was the way he constantly referred to Jeff as the waiter, as if this somehow made Jeff inferior to the present company. I wanted to nab these poseurs so bad I could taste it.

Swallowing my pride, I said, "I'm sure the police appreciate Lance's honesty, and will keep what he told them in the strictest of confidence — unless it has a bearing on Jeff Rodgers's murder."

"Whose side are you on, Mr. McNally?" Dr. von Brecht inquired, as if he were offering me a choice between his patronage or his wrath. He was the most hubristic bastard I have ever had the misfortune to cross paths with.

"The side of justice, sir."

"That is ridiculous, sir. If you would render your statement, I will forward your check. You are no longer in my employ."

"I was never in your employ."

"Then don't submit your bill."

With a bow, he took his wife's arm and walked off to join the crowd.

Well!

"I think I'll throw in the towel and go back to New York."

"Take me with you."

Denny and I were sitting at the Four Seasons bar, getting sloshed. After being given the gate by Dr. and Frau von Brecht, I saw no reason to hang around and watch the rich folks having fun. When I told Denny I was going, he chose to leave with me. Lady Cynthia had Jackson Barnett sleeping over and an invitation from the miracle worker to check out his Alpine youth factory. She let Denny go without a whimper because two out of three isn't bad for a lady of her age.

"They're guilty as sin, Denny," I said, not for the first time since we left Lady C's gala. "And they're going to get away with it."

Denny twirled the ice cubes in his scotch and nodded. "The world is full of guilty people who will never be brought to justice. In my business I see it all the time. For every murderer, or con artist, or embezzler I expose, a hundred get away and a hundred more pop up to fill the gap. Don't take it personally, chum."

But I did take it personally. It wasn't so much losing, as having it shoved in my face by von Brecht. Three clients and the only one I had satisfied was Nifty, and now I wasn't even sure of that. Should I tell him that the foot checks out, but the hand doesn't? It was too ludicrous to even contemplate. The kid in the photograph could be wearing someone else's glove. Kids do things like that. Or Lance Talbot could be ambidextrous. People are.

"So before you got a chance to accuse Holga of calling the Emerson woman, she tells you she made the call, and why. I could use her in my business," Denny noted.

"And she'd have your job in six months. What do you think of the tunnel theory?"

He shrugged, uncaring. "There's a tunnel and anyone on the beach that day could have strolled onto the MacNiff property, chloroformed Jeff Rodgers and pushed him into the pool. Who and why is the question — and one that'll never be answered.

"You have a murder that's never going to be solved, Archy, and a woman that's never going to reappear. Do you know how many people vanish in this country every year and are never seen or heard of again? You would be astounded, believe me. There's nothing for me here."

Slumped over the bar in our white dinner jackets we must have looked like two also-rans who had lost their dates to better prospects. There was a group of Brits drinking not too far from us. We get a lot of visitors from England and Canada in season, seeking refuge from the harsh winter climate of their home base.

One of them was talking about a run-in he had with the clerk, pronounced *clark,* at his hotel. Funny how you could usually tell where people were from by the way they talked.

But how does a king talk? If he's an English king he says *clark* for *clerk* — and I sat bolt upright on my padded stool. I got it. Just like that, I got it. I didn't get the tunnel and I didn't get the southpaw, but I got how a king talks.

Fearing I would again fall off my bar stool in Denny's presence, I grabbed his shoulder for support and mumbled, "He stutters. He stutters."

"You okay, Archy?"

"King George," I exclaimed. "We talked about him on the way to the party. Old Mrs. Talbot was a young lady when he took the throne. He was a southpaw and they forced him to use his right hand because maybe royals aren't supposed to be left-handed."

"That's right," Denny said. "He was a stutterer and it was thought that forcing him to change hands caused it."

On a roll, I kept going. "The old lady said he doesn't talk like a king. Get it? He doesn't stutter. She knew her grandson was left-handed. Now she sees him using only his right hand. In her dotage, or medicated state, she must have thought they forced him to use his right hand in Europe but it didn't make him stutter. He didn't talk like the king.

"Malcolm MacNiff told me she often

slipped in and out of reality in the last days of her life. In a lucid moment she must have realized how foolish her reasoning was and knew if he was right-handed he wasn't her grandson."

"The king is dead," Denny said. "She meant her grandson, who was left-handed, like the King George of her youth."

"That's what Jeff had on the guy calling himself Lance Talbot," I elaborated. "Jeff knew his old teammate was a southpaw. When he saw Talbot was right-handed, he got to thinking. He must have started asking Talbot questions he couldn't answer. That's when Jeff was certain the guy was a phony."

"So who is he?"

"A von Brecht," I almost shouted, "that's who. He's their son. It figures. Jeff knew he wasn't Lance Talbot, and Vivian Emerson knew Olga had a son. That was your story, Denny old man. And what a whopper it is."

"You mean was, Archy."

"What?"

"Stuttering kings, southpaws and senile old ladies are not the gist of investigating reporting. I think you're right, Archy. In fact I'm sure you're right, but I need proof you can take into a courtroom before I can "publish, not clever speculation."

"Stick around a few more days, Denny."

"What do you have in mind?" he asked.

"I can't tell you."

He looked at me and laughed. "That's because you don't know."

"I don't, but the possibilities are endless."

Denny took out his wallet. "Am I paying for the drinks?"

"But of course. I'm your date."

The phone was ringing, the plop, plop, plop of raindrops were plopping into the brass bucket positioned beneath the leak in my roof, and I was hung over. Not a very propitious way to start a Monday morning. If late-night calls are harbingers of ill news, early-morning calls are cataclysmic.

I got out of bed in my half pajamas — I wear the tops — waited until the room stopped spinning like it was on its way to Munchkinland and picked up the bearer of bad tidings.

"Archy McNally here."

"Vivian Emerson is dead, Archy."

I kicked the chair away from my desk and sat before I fell. "When, Georgy? How?"

"The police called Joey a few minutes ago. He called me. They found her in her car in an isolated stretch of beach near Manalapan. She'd been there a few days, at least. It wasn't very pleasant."

"She was asphyxiated with chloroform," I stated.

"There wasn't a mark on her body according to what the police told Joey. They're treating it as a suspicious death until the autopsy."

"Chloroform," I repeated. "There've been more developments, Georgy. It would take too long to explain." I looked at the desk clock. It wasn't that early. I had missed breakfast with the McNallys — yet again.

"Archy? I told Joey to come and stay here. He's very broken up and he has to ID the body. I'm at work and can't go with him. Can you?"

"Sorry, Georgy girl, but I have to get to Al Rogoff before anyone else gets a whiff of that lethal perfume."

"Is it them, Archy? Lance and the von Brechts?"

"It is but I can't prove it."

"Yes, you can, McNally."

"Your lips to God's ear. And Georgy . . ."

"Yes?"

"You did right offering Gallo a port in a storm."

"Thanks, Archy."

TWENTY-FOUR

Dear Mr. McNally:

My deepest apologies for not responding sooner. I was in Berlin on business and only just arrived in Berne this day. I will relate to you as much as I know of the late Jessica Talbot, her son, Lance, and the Brechts. (You refer to them as the von Brechts, but to the best of my knowledge the aristocratic von is a new and unwarranted addition, perhaps to impress Americans, to Claus Brecht's name.)

To begin, sir. I have been Ms. Talbot's lawyer since her arrival here some ten years ago. Lance was a boy at that time. Our dealings were routine. Establishing of bank accounts and the transfer of monies from the United States to Switzerland. Nothing unusual. I learned Ms. Talbot was a very rich woman, and saw her intermittently over the years. Unlike a doctor, lawyers do not see their clients annually, but only when they are in need of legal counsel.

You asked when was the last time I saw her and her son. Researching my files I discover I had a business luncheon with Ms. Talbot just one year ago. Her son was not present. As he does not appear in my files I must trust to memory and say I last saw the boy when he was perhaps twelve or thirteen years.

I learned of the tragedy from newspaper accounts of the snow slide that killed many on the slopes that day and caused much damage to a small village. This was at Winterthur, on the German-Austrian border. Among the dead were listed the names of Jessica Talbot and Lance Talbot. I put in a call to the police in Winterthur, asking for details. The hotel that caters to the ski enthusiasts suffered some damage, but their records revealed that Ms. Talbot and her son were in residence and both had gone on the slopes after lunch. Not being among those few who returned unharmed, it was assumed that both mother and son had perished. I immediately called the senior Mrs. Talbot in Palm Beach, whom Jessica had designated as next of kin to be notified in case of emergency, and related the sad news, asking for instructions in handling her daughter's affairs.

To the best of my knowledge Ms. Talbot died intestate, or perhaps I should say I never drew up a will for her.

It was several days later, three days after the tragedy, that I received a call from Lance Talbot. He had not gone on the slopes with his mother that day, but parted with her after lunch to attend to personal business. In fact he had spent the day and evening with a young lady and was ignorant of the snow slide until the following morning when he put on the television for the early news. Not returning to the hotel that night, it was assumed he was among the missing, considered dead.

I again called the senior Mrs. Talbot who wired her grandson, using my address, to return to America. Lance called on me before he left Switzerland to secure funds from his mother's account, as Jessica Talbot's legatee.

Regarding Claus Brecht, it is not a pretty picture and I do not report gossip but only newspaper accounts of his history and what I know of him from his dealings with Ms. Talbot.

Having lost his license to practice medicine, he is the former Dr. Claus Brecht. He was a plastic surgeon who opened a clinic near Winterthur where it was said that he had come upon a remarkable formula for restoring a youthful appearance to aging skin without resorting to surgery. Unfortunately, Switzerland has long harbored practitioners of the science of rejuvenation, their secret being anything from sera derived from the semen of pubescent youths to the testicular fluids of monkeys.

Brecht's secret ingredient turned out to be amphetamine. In short, Mr. McNally, he was what you Americans call a Dr. Feelgood. His patients certainly felt younger under his care. Other, more potent drugs were also administered and available at Brecht's happy farm. When the police sent in a decoy to take the cure, the party was over for Claus Brecht.

I know that Ms. Talbot was involved with Brecht because she asked me to transfer a considerable amount of money to Brecht's account in

Winterthur. I believe, Mr. McNally, that Ms. Talbot financed the clinic. I trust you will understand that this is all I will say on the subject of the relationship between Brecht and Jessica Talbot.

Newspaper accounts of the raid and the subsequent closing of the clinic stated that Brecht was married to an American. They had a grown son whose name I believe is Hans, but am not certain.

You will note that I have faxed a copy of this correspondence to Mr. Malcolm MacNiff who is the executor of Mrs. Talbot's estate. If I can be of further service please do not hesitate to call upon me.

I remain your servant,
Gregory Hermann, Esq.

Father handed me the fax across his desk, shaking his head. "Not a very good show, Archy. Not very good at all."

"Hermann is insinuating that Jessica Talbot was an addict and Brecht her supplier. Naturally, he won't put it in writing, but we have it on reliable authority that Jessica Talbot was a drug addict. When she and Lance were killed the defrocked

Brecht saw a way to compensate for his loss of income by substituting his son for Lance and claiming the Talbot fortune.

"The boys were about the same age and both had blue eyes. I would assume they were also good friends, given Jessica's relationship with the Brechts. I think the Brecht boy's crew cut was a recent addition. I noticed the skin around his hairline had not been exposed to the sun for very long, so it must have been covered by hair before the close cut. The lawyer last saw Lance when he was a teenager and therefore could not possibly know that the person who called on him to tap Jessica Talbot's bank account was an imposter."

Father was tugging on his whiskers as I spoke and shaking his head so violently I knew what was coming. "It's all supposition, Archy. You're reading between the lines just as you've been doing since you started on this case. What you say is possible, even probable, but not factual. Suppose these von Brechts, or Brechts, are charged and they produce their son?"

"They have produced him, sir, in the form of Lance Talbot. The former doctor was a plastic surgeon. Being on such intimate terms with Jessica and Lance he must have known about the missing toe and he could easily have amputated his son's right toe for our benefit. A small toe in exchange for a half-billion bucks is a pretty good deal."

"Prove it," Father challenged.

"I could if we forced Hans to have a physician examine his foot and tell us just how long ago the toe was amputated."

"Archy, please. You can't force him to do such a thing just as you can't force the Brechts to send for their son for you to gaze upon. Jessica Talbot's body we know was recovered and subsequently cremated. Her son was not interred, probably because he was never recovered. That is very possible."

"How do we know that? How does Hermann know that? This is what the newly resurrected Lance told the lawyer. I think Claus Brecht took charge minutes after the tragedy. It was he, or his son, who reported that Jessica was cremated. They simply failed to report that poor Lance Talbot was also nuked with his mother."

"Really, Archy, your language."

"I'm sorry, sir, but I'm very disturbed by what this fax has to say."

"And you're not thinking clearly." Indicating the fax I still held, he said, "Have you talked to Malcolm about this?"

"I called him as soon as I read Hermann's reply."

"And," Father said, mentally predicting Nifty's response.

"He doesn't see how this makes any difference. Claus Brecht is a fallen doctor and con artist, but that doesn't make him a murderer. Nor does it make a liar of the guy calling himself Lance Talbot. Unquote."

"He's correct," Father pounced. "However, I think this fax has gone a long way in disrupting Malcolm's short-lived serenity. Just when he was certain Lance was the real article, you have him again wondering if he is doing right by Mrs. Talbot as her executor. I assume you didn't tell him to have a doctor look at Lance Talbot's foot."

He assumed wrong, but rather than verbalize I hung my head in shame. Holding up the fax, I said, "If we knew this earlier, both Jeff Rodgers and Vivian Emerson might be alive today."

"That's doubtful, at best, Archy, and you know it. Holga Brecht phoned Vivian Emerson. She admits it, and gives a valid reason for making that call. We know, as do the police, that Lance, or Hans, or whoever he is, did not push Jeff Rodgers into that pool." Father's tugging was growing dangerously rigorous. If he plucked himself clean I would never be forgiven.

"Claus Brecht was in the tunnel waiting for his chance to kill Jeff Rodgers," I persisted.

"Claus Brecht was not in Palm Beach at the time, Archy."

"I called Al Rogoff and set up a meeting with him and his superior, Lieutenant Eberhart. I want them to read this fax. I think there's enough here to at least have them check the rosters of the incoming flights from New York last Friday to see if Claus was on one of them. If he wasn't, I hope to enlist their help in exposing all three Brechts."

"What's your plan, Archy?"

"It's daring, but it's the only way to prove my case and stop these people from getting away with murder and the Talbot fortune."

When I laid out my game plan the Chairman of the Board vetoed the idea without even acknowledging its brilliance. "It's more than daring, Archy. It's dangerous, and I refuse to countenance such a move. Someone may be killed. Do you want that on your conscience?"

"No, sir. Nor do I want to live with the fact that I allowed these people to get away with murder because I, or the police, refused to stick our necks out to learn the truth."

"It's not your neck on the block, Archy."

Standing, I told him, "I'm doing this with or without your sanction, sir, but I hope I have your blessing."

He rose and extended his hand. "My blessing, Archy. Not my approval. They are two very different things."

I took his hand. It was warm and surprisingly firm. "That's all I ask, Father."

We met in the office of Lieutenant Oscar Eberhart, PBPD. The lieutenant and I were not strangers, having locked horns several times when he was called into cases that Al and I had already solved. Oscar was a social climber, and I think it irked him to know that his sergeant was a confidant of a private investigator who was a welcome guest in homes Oscar only got into if they were burgled or required police protection when they entertained visiting dignitaries.

I noticed the current issue of *Forbes* on his desk, the cover of which announced that inside was their seventeenth annual list of billionaires. Father subscribes, so I knew that our own John Kluge, the Metromedia guru, was numero seventeen with ten and a half billion in his kitty. Guys like John helped make Palm Beach the tenth richest community in the United States. Our neighbor, Jupiter Island, is number one. The Gold Coast is not a misnomer.

I had told Eberhart everything, from what I saw the day of Nifty's benefit, to Denny's dealings with Jeff Rodgers, the toe count, the left hand, Mrs. Talbot's dying words, and the phone call Holga had made to Vivian Emerson the day Vivian disappeared. I felt like a politician campaigning for votes.

After reading the fax, Eberhart commented, "Lance Talbot told us his mother was an addict and it was the reason Jeff Rodgers was blackmailing him. This only confirms Talbots' story."

"Jeff wasn't killed because he threatened to air the Talbots' dirty laundry, Lieutenant. He was killed because he knew this joker wasn't Lance Talbot. I'm not saying that Jeff Rodgers is blameless. He tried to use what he knew for personal gain but got in over his head." Remembering Jeff lying at the bottom of the MacNiff pool, I added, "Excuse the pun."

"But Lance didn't kill Jeff," Eberhart stated. "You know that."

"I now believe that Claus Brecht was in the tunnel waiting for his chance to get Jeff. I told you Lance was on his cell phone at the time. I think he was calling his father, Claus Brecht, to tell him that Jeff had gone to the pool for his break and was there alone.

"That's why I asked you to check the passenger rosters of all flights that came into Palm Beach from New York Friday morning. The guy who says he's Lance told me Brecht was flying in from Switzerland via New York."

"Look, Lieutenant," Al said, "we got two murders on our hands, both with the same modus operandi . . ."

"Chloroform," I got in, "a doctor's weapon."

"Before we have the press saying there's a serial killer loose in Palm Beach," Al continued, "which will go national by the evening news and ruin the tourist trade, I think we better check out Brecht and any other lead that comes our way. We can't afford not to."

Probably thinking of all those irate hotel and restaurant owners storming the castle, Oscar picked up his phone and talked to the desk sergeant. "If he wasn't on an incoming flight," Eberhart said, after instructing his subordinate, "all we'll have is more circumstantial evidence against these people."

"But we'll have enough circumstantial evidence to go to the D.A.," Al said.

Eberhart was a small guy with a barrel chest and a jaw that defied a razor. He ran a thumb over the stubble now and blasted Al, "You go to the D.A. and tell him to arrest a Talbot because he's not left-handed."

It was the Talbot name, more than anything else, that had the socially minded Oscar Eberhart worried. As the Los Angeles police are often intimidated by their movie stars, so the Palm Beach police are loath to badger their billionaires. Justice may be blind, but those doing her bidding are not.

It was like waiting for a jury to come back into the courtroom. We had all had our say and now there was nothing to do but wait for the verdict. If Brecht had flown in on Friday, I was out of business. If he hadn't, there was a chance Eberhart would go along with my plan, which I had yet to propose.

There was a perfunctory knock on the door before it opened and the officer's head appeared. "Claus von Brecht flew into Palm Beach on a flight from New York at about noon on Friday."

"That's it," Eberhart shouted, sounding relieved.

"But," the officer walked in, "he flew out of Palm Beach the night before."

I jumped out of my seat as Al Rogoff cried, "He what?"

"He flew out Thursday night and back in Friday morning," the man was reading from his notes. "Since the terror alert the airlines are recording anything of an unusual nature, no matter how harmless it may seem. This guy booked a round trip on Thursday night, returning in less than twenty-four hours — and he's a foreigner, so they reported it to the feds."

"You see," I said to Eberhart, "you see how clever they are. They announced that Claus was arriving from New York on Friday and, leaving nothing to chance, he flew out the night before just so he could fly in on Friday, in case someone checked, as we did. What they didn't count on was the efficiency of the carrier, which should make us all sleep better. He was in hiding all this time."

"Why?" Eberhart said. "So he could kill the boy and the woman without being suspected?"

"No," I sighed. "It's now all so clear. He was in hiding because he didn't want them to appear as a family. Mother, father and son. Holga and the imposter had all Palm Beach believing they were lovers, and that's just what they wanted, to dispel any thought that they might be mother and son. And it worked.

"When they told anyone who would listen that Claus was arriving, the gossips were agog with speculation regarding the strange trio, assuming all the most salacious possibilities, except incest. That would be just too much even for our scandalmongers. And it worked," I repeated, as if amazed at their audacity — which I was.

"They didn't know they would have to murder anyone," Al told his disappointed superior, "but when Rodgers and Emerson gummed up the works, they had to go. Brecht, the guy who wasn't here, could do the dirty work and get away with it."

"Even that played into their hands," I said.

"We still have nothing but circumstantial evidence," Eberhart reminded us.

"I have a plan, Lieutenant."

"Let's hear it, Archy."

His reaction was very much like father's,

only more vocal. "No way," Eberhart bellowed. "No [censored] way. It's theatrical, it's dangerous and it involves a decoy who is not a trained member of the force. We go by the book on this one."

"Claus Brecht wrote the book, Lieutenant." Remembering his social ambitions, I resorted to temptation. "Dennis Darling is in town, as I'm sure you're aware, Oscar. I'll bring him in on this and by next week your name will be a household word. I believe *Bare Facts* magazine also operates a television station. Think about it."

"If we do like Archy says, Lieutenant, we could make it airtight. The chance of anything going wrong is minimal, at best."

Gilding the lily, as I often do, I predicted, "You know those true police dramas they run on the cable networks, Oscar? You could star in one."

On the eve of stardom, Lieutenant Oscar Eberhart looked miserable.

TWENTY-FIVE

"You should have seen me, Mr. McNally. My first film role and I did it in one take."

"Tell me about it, Todd," I said, knowing he would whether I wanted to hear it or not.

I was once again in Todd's furnished apartment, having called, telling him only that I needed a favor.

"I went to the Meecham yacht and Max introduced me to the Hollywood crew. Then he got this great idea. He said I could be in the test."

"What part did you play?"

"A waiter," he laughed. "Typecasting, they call it. You see, the shot had Jackson Barnett and this real beautiful gal sort of meandering around the deck like they're on The Love Boat. Max thought the shot would look more authentic if a waiter came into the scene with a tray of drinks for the lovebirds, and I got my chance."

Todd had conveniently forgotten that Max Sterling had told him the screen test hoopla was pure Hollywood hype. I guess

when you're part of the hype it gains re-
spectability. But Todd was so thrilled, the
exhilaration was catching.

"I know it's just a test for their big star,
but I got my name on the clapboard. Rick
Brandt, in white chalk."

"You're no longer Todd?"

"Well," he hesitated. "I'm Edward at
home, Todd to the crowd, and Rick in
Hollywood. You see?"

No, I didn't see, but pretended I did.
One doesn't like to be thought dense. "Before you head west, Todd, I need a favor."

"Name it, Mr. McNally. I owe you my
life."

Bite your tongue, dear boy, bite your tongue.

"I want you to play a scene for me," was
how I phrased it.

"Is that all? I even sing and dance, Mr.
McNally." He cleared his throat and flexed
his knees, but I stopped him before he au-
ditioned.

"Sit down, Todd."

No fool, he quipped, "That bad, eh?"

When he was settled, I let him have it. "I
want you to call Lance Talbot. Tell him
you're a friend of Jeff's, the bartender at
the MacNiff party. He'll know who you
are. Trust me.

"Tell him you know Jeff was blackmailing him, and why. If he asks for specifics, just say the words *left hand*. He'll get it. Say you want ten thousand dollars or you'll go to the police and tell them he killed Jeff."

The movie star blanched. "Did he, Mr. McNally?"

Briefly, I let him in on what we now suspected. It was the least I could do.

"What do you think they'll do?" he asked.

"Try to kill you, I hope," I answered.

"That's what I thought. I'll go down in the *Guinness Book of Records* as the movie actor whose career spanned seventeen seconds."

"The police and I have given this a lot of thought," I assured him, "and we have all bases covered. I know the layout here and this is how it'll work."

The meeting would take place here, in Todd's apartment. Counting on Brecht to accompany his son, they would search the place to make sure it wasn't a trap. No fools they. The patio door was cut into the wall, leaving about six feet on either side of the frame. Two men, with their backs flat against the outside wall, could hide out there and not be seen from within.

"Is there a patio light?" I asked Todd.

He showed me the switch. "Even if they put on the light to check outside, they won't see us and I doubt if they'll take the time or trouble to come out."

"What if they do, Mr. McNally?"

"Then we're done for, but you'll be okay."

Denny and I would be on one side of the door, Al and Eberhart on the other. We would leave the door open a crack so we could hear what was going on. When they made their move, we would burst in, catching them in the act.

"Suppose they have a gun, or a knife," he wisely speculated. "You couldn't get in fast enough to stop them."

"It's not Brecht's choice of weapon. Chloroform is, and it takes time to work."

"I hope you're right, Mr. McNally."

So do I, son. So do I.

"You don't have to do this, Todd. I'll understand if you refuse."

He heaved a sigh. "For Jeff, Mr. McNally. I'll do it for Jeff."

"Todd, this phone call is going to show if you've got the makings of an actor," I said, to boost his enthusiasm for the plan. "You have to make them believe you're telling the truth and, at the same time, that you're stupid enough to leave yourself wide open for their retaliation. But not that stupid. That's why you insist they come here and not meet you in a dark alley or the Talbot mansion. You play the wise kid, not the wise guy."

Contemplating that, he said, "I'll play it like Willy Loman, Mr. McNally. Desperate. It's not his job going down the drain, it's his life. I'm stupid enough to do this because my mother needs an operation . . ."

"Cut!" the director cried. "Let's try it with less passion and more conviction, kid."

I knew Lance, or Hans, would fall for it because he had seen Todd at both the MacNiff parties and had asked me if Todd was a friend of Jeff's. Those who kill to silence an adversary will forever wonder who else knows their secret. Friends of Jeff were all suspects, because the young talk and it was well known that Jeff liked to boast about his achievements, true or false.

The Brechts would be relieved to hear from Todd. The guessing was over and their course clear.

Todd made the call and I silently nominated him for a Tony, an Academy Award and a Golden Globe.

"What should I wear, Mr. McNally?"

"A bulletproof vest."

TWENTY-SIX

I spent the rest of the day briefing Denny and Malcolm MacNiff. Denny was packing his bags but said, "I wouldn't miss it for a Pulitzer, chum."

Nifty was not as sanguine. "Can't we leave well enough alone, Archy?"

If two murders and a fortune to the perpetrators was well enough, what was Nifty's definition of a miscarriage of justice? Guccibaggers lunching at a gentleman's club, I suspect. I trust Mrs. MacNiff was telling her husband to get with it.

I picked up Denny at his hotel and we drove directly to the station house, where I had arranged to meet Al and the lieutenant at nine. Al was in uniform, Eberhart was not. The four of us were driven to Todd's house in an unmarked police vehicle, after which the driver left the scene. A second police vehicle unloaded three backup officers in civilian dress who were to remain outside and out of sight unless needed.

Todd had chosen to wear the PB uniform of the youth brigade: sneakers, jeans and white sweatshirt with sleeves pushed up above the elbows. "We who are about to die salute you," he welcomed us into his home. He was either calmer than any of us or a better actor than I suspected.

"You don't have to do this," Lieutenant Eberhart said. "It's not too late to back out, son. Say the word and we'll abort the mission."

"The show will go on, Lieutenant," Todd told him.

Denny was scribbling in shorthand on a minipad with a ballpoint. "It's B-R-A-N-D-T. Right, Todd?"

"Yes, Mr. Darling. But for the press it's Rick Brandt, Jackson Barnett's costar."

After that show of bravado we settled down to pacing and looking at our watches. The meeting was scheduled for ten. I asked where Monica was this evening.

"Working," Todd said. "She's staying with a friend tonight."

A few minutes before the appointed hour we went out to the patio and took our places. I turned for a final look at Todd and mouthed, "Break a leg, kid." He shrugged his broad shoulders and forced a smile. If Denny hadn't nudged me forward I would have turned back and fled, taking Todd with me.

Denny and I took the right wall, Al and Eberhart the left. As planned we left the sliding glass door open a crack.

The early-morning rain had given way to a light drizzle in the afternoon and partial clearing later on. Now it changed its mind and began to pour as we stood, rigid, our backs to the wall. In minutes we were drenched, but I doubt any of us noticed. The rain muffled any sounds coming from within but in a matter of minutes we heard voices raised in anger. There were two of them. Claus and his son, surely. Then the sound of doors opening and banging shut as one of them searched the apartment.

Water ran down the back of my neck and over my face. I held my breath as the patio light came on. A second later it went out. I heard the sliding door close and the un-mistakable click of the lock falling into place. I was paralyzed with fear. We were locked out and Todd was in there with two killers. There was a flash of lightning and the distant sound of thunder bringing with it my father's warning, *A man who would chloroform a boy and shove him into a pool to drown is deranged . . .*

I made a dash for the sliding door when I heard the first shot. What had I done?

Oh, God, what had I done? I stumbled, and Denny collided into my back. A second shot. A third. When I gained my footing and wiped the water out of my eyes I saw Al Rogoff firing at the lock. In seconds he had the door open and was in the room, followed by Eberhart. The men stationed outside entered from the opposite direction.

Al was pulling Claus Brecht off Todd, who was reeling from the pad Brecht had pressed against Todd's mouth. Eberhart went for Hans who was kneeling, his arms in a brace around Todd's struggling legs.

"Get an ambulance for the kid," one of the men shouted.

Denny and I were beside Todd, holding him steady. He looked at me, panting, and gasped, "My performance made you cry, Mr. McNally."

"It's the rain, you conceited ham. It's the rain."

There was a crack of light coming from under the door of my father's den. I tapped lightly and looked in. Father was seated behind his desk and I was even more surprised to see Mother in her nightgown and robe, her hair in a long braid, nodding in a chair.

"Archy?" Father called when he saw me.

"It's me, sir."

"Was it a good show, Archy?"

"It was a splendid show, sir."

Mother opened her eyes. "Oh, Archy," she said. "Your father was so late coming to bed, I came down to see what he was up to and I must have fallen asleep in my chair. How silly of me."

"Yes," Father said, "we were both a bit silly, it seems, staying up till all hours."

A simple thank-you seemed so inadequate; anything more, unnecessary.

"Now let's all go to bed," Mother said. "And if we get up late enough, we can have breakfast with Archy."

TWENTY-SEVEN

Brecht was indicted on two counts of murder one. Holga, née Olga, and Hans were charged with aiding and abetting, and the boy was also charged with carrying a counterfeit passport with intent to commit fraud. Being Swiss citizens, there were complications, but nothing insurmountable in giving the three their due.

Talbot and Reynolds relations, however distant, are lining up to petition for their share of Mrs. Talbot's fortune. I'm keeping my distance from the beleaguered executor. Iago is with child and Othello is suspected. More reason to keep clear of the MacNiff abode.

Since bringing the Brechts to justice, Izzy Duhane has lost interest in Skip McGuire and, I fear, Binky Watrous. She spends more time at her mother's apartment in The Breakers and less in her trailer love nest. The mousse has gone from Binky's locks but his brush with a Kalamazoo Battle has left him a tad haughty. Like a spirited colt, he will have to be broken.

Joe Gallo is back caddying at the club where he met the late Vivian Emerson, and living in a motel until he can find affordable digs. He's in line for Izzy's trailer should she give it up. Al Rogoff is not thrilled.

Denny called from New York to ask permission to use "The King Is Dead" as the title for his story, which will be *Bare Facts'* lead next month, with a photo of Lieutenant Eberhart and Edward Todd Rick Brandt on the cover. Eberhart has taken to applying a cream called Erase to the stubble on his chin and Edward Todd Rick received rave reviews for his portrayal of Biff in *Death of a Salesman.*

Joe hangs around Georgy girl a lot and I feel that we've acquired a child. Or at least, I have. Is the honeymoon over? Connie finds it all very amusing. We took Joe, at Georgy's insistence, to the Pelican and ended up at a table for five with Connie and Alex. My dream of mating Joe with Alex and leaving Archy in charge of the harem came to naught as the two charming young men took an instant dislike to each other. God got me for that one.

I look over this final entry in my journal, enjoying my first, and last, English Oval of the day before retiring. As I close the book on "The King Is Dead," the phone rings. It is midnight. I could crawl into bed, pull the covers over my head and pretend I never heard it, or . . .

"Archy McNally here."